A DAUGHTER'S PROMISE

by

Christine Clemetson

*To Anne,
I am so happy to
share this story
with you. Fondly,
Christine
Clemetson*

A Daughter's Promise

Cover Art by *Rae Monet*

The Wild Rose Press
PO Box 706
Adams Basin, NY 14410-0706
Visit us at www.thewildrosepress.com

Publishing History
First Vintage Rose Edition, 2008
Print ISBN 1-60154-340-9

Published in the United States of America

Serene's heart pounded as she peered around the silent restaurant, alive hours earlier but now masked with an eerie paleness.

This room and her life would never again be the same. She whisked off the wetness around her eyes, sucked in a daunted breath, and remembered her purpose.

"Are you all right?" She hoped her English was still understandable.

No response from the American.

Leaning a little closer, she gently placed her hand beneath his, finding it warm and moist with life. "Can you hear me?"

Still nothing.

"If you can hear me, squeeze my hand."

Serene checked behind her. She unbuttoned his coat, soaked in warm blood, and slid her hand inside, relieved to feel at least a slight rise and fall to his chest.

"I want to help you, but not now. I have to go, but I'll be back. Can you hear me? I'll be back."

"*Halten Sie!*" Boots clicked toward her on the stone floor.

As she let go of the American's hand, the slightest pressure passed her fingertips.

He had heard her.

Dedication

For Mike,
who takes my breath away with his support.
And for Jake and Chase,
my greatest inspirations.

Prologue
Rome 1939

They all took turns saying goodbye. First Margot. Then Harry. And finally the eldest, Serene. She bent down and grasped the thin hand that hung limply from the window of the rear car seat. It was her mother's hand.

"I love you, Mama." Serene gulped, her green eyes wide. She held the cool hand to her cheek.

"I...know." Maria Moneto struggled to say something else, but her thin lips stilled. Her eyes searched Serene's face.

"What, Mama?" Serene stood by the car, riveted. She bit the inside of her cheek and forced her trembling legs to bring her body closer. "What did you say?"

"Box...in top drawer," Maria whispered, "for you."

Serene's heart raced, pumping fear into her stomach. "I don't need anything, Mama." Tears ebbed at the surface of her eyes. *I just need you.*

"Take...it." Maria gasped, her dark eyes ablaze and unmoving.

Serene nodded, remembering that day nearly three years earlier, the week of her twelfth birthday. The doctor had spoken those fateful words that still resounded in her head. The disease would eventually overtake her mother, he had explained to her family. She remembered her father yelling that it was 1936 in Rome, for God's sake. There had to be something better, some new cancer treatment. He would pay anything. But the doctor just shook his head and

1

said he was sorry. How beautiful her mother looked that day, sitting in the leather chair and cradling baby Harry in her arms. Serene knew she could never get sick enough to leave them. Leave *her*.

She reached through the car window and adjusted the silk scarf around her mama's head. Tired gray strands peeked out from beneath the scarf, revealing none of the golden color that used to shimmer in the sun like honey drizzling from a jar.

Bringing her face closer, almost touching her cheek, Serene filled her senses with the clean scent. She smoothed her fingers over the ashen skin, trying desperately to memorize every detail, every line.

Maria smiled, her hollow eyes softening with tears.

With a quivering smile, Serene promised herself that she would never, ever forget the way her mother's nose crinkled when she smiled. "I will never forget you, Mama." Their eyes locked on each other. Her young voice wavered. "Never."

From behind, Serene heard her father's quick steps down the stone walkway. Anthony Moneto carried only the necessities, his wife's dress, neatly wrapped in white tissue, and their family's Bible. He paused next to Anna Salvetta, their housemaid, and handed her a list of scribbled errands before he laid the dress in the trunk, slammed the door shut, and walked around to the other side.

"How long will you be, Papa?" Margot asked matter-of-factly.

Anthony bent down and kissed the top of her curly head. "Soon." He approached the driver's side and paused by the door. "Serene," he commanded, "take your sister and brother into the house. Anna will help you."

Harry jumped in front of Serene and pushed her back away from the car. Even standing on his toes, his small hands barely gripped the door ledge.

"Where you goin', Mama?"

Hoisting Harry on her hip, Serene held him steady. "Remember, Harry? Mama is going away…"

Maria beckoned Harry to come closer. He pulled himself away from Serene and reached through the car window, wrapping both arms tightly around his mother's neck. He giggled and planted a wet kiss on Maria's cheek. "Bye-bye, Mama."

"Grow…strong," she said, grazing her hand across his forehead and down his cheek.

Serene pulled him back and held him to her side. Margot stood to the other side, her hands clasped. Serene watched her younger sister, knowing she didn't understand, couldn't understand something so important.

"Take care…of Papa," Maria said, gazing up at Serene.

Serene nodded quickly, then put Harry down. Her bottom lip quivered.

As the car started to pull away, Maria turned and waved to her three children through the rear window.

Ignoring Anna's pleas to go into the house, Serene stood motionless for only a moment, watching the car drive away, before she began to run as fast as she could, reaching to touch her mother's hand one last time. With a stumble, she fell to the ground, her bare knees hitting the road with finality, her hand still grasping the empty air.

"Wait," she screamed. *Wait.* She dropped her head, unable to swallow back the sobs any longer.

Chapter One
Anzio, Italy 1944

No one was left alive.

Digging his fingernails into the dirt, Miles Coulson leaned up on his elbows and vomited. He gritted his teeth and leaned up a little more, staring at the swollen sky, trying to figure out what the hell to do. His buddies were strewn across the rocky mounds of Anzio like common debris.

The firing stopped abruptly and another gush of terror flooded his stomach.

Miles gripped the gun and tried to steady it upright, wanting so badly to just cut his leg away. Below his knee, his pant leg hung in shreds, most of the skin blown away. It hurt like the hottest hell he ever could have imagined. He gulped the foul air as he clutched at his thigh and yanked away the rest of the stringy pant material from his skin.

Shivering, he lay back down and heard a whizzing sound high above his head, followed by a black stream of smoke that zipped through the moonlight, heading toward the north shores. *No more*, he wanted to scream. *No more.*

"Stars?"

"Stripes," Miles whispered back, immediately acknowledging the American countersign.

From the darkness came Clay Forrester, a soldier from the south, Tennessee or somewhere, and the damnedest shot the army ever had.

Clay knelt, put his index finger to Miles' neck and quickly yanked off his pack. "You're gonna be okay, Coulson. No one else alive here but you and me."

Miles had stopped listening. The pain in his leg subsided as warmth spread across his face. Boy, he thought, it sure felt like the same smoldering sun that stretched lazily across Pop's land in the late afternoons. He filled his nostrils with the sweet smell of fresh, knee-high corn.

"Stay with me, Miles."

Miles rolled his head to get a better look at the thickness of the crops. "I better go harvest—"

"Harvest, m'ass," Clay muttered, taking out the canteen hooked to his belt. "You're stayin' put and not givin' up, you son-of-a-bitch." Holding the water to Miles' mouth, he used the nozzle to prod his lips open. "Go ahead, man, drink."

"I don't want it." Miles coughed out the water.

"Keep drinkin'." After unhooking the first aid pouch from his waist belt, Clay slid out the sulfa powder and sprinkled it on the entire wound. "We gotta stop the bleeding." Not having a bandage long enough, he tore off some of his own pant leg and wrapped it tightly just above Miles' knee. "That'll hold for now."

They both froze at the sound of boots crunching on debris, not more than a few yards away. Miles pointed his index finger away from Clay and then let it drop to the ground. "Get out of here—"

"You crazy, man? We're both gettin' outta here alive."

Miles swallowed back the grit in his throat. "God dammit, go. "You have children—"

"Shut up, man. Lay still."

"Kommen Sie hier!" The ugly-sounding words were followed by a shrill whistle.

Miles recognized the German call for backup, and tried to sit up a little. "Go," he whispered to Clay.

"Oh, sweet Jesus." Clay grabbed his gun and

dove to the ground. He yanked a grenade off his pack, his hand cemented to the pin.

Miles spread his arms out over his head, closed his eyes, and started reciting the Hail Mary silently and as quickly as he could remember it.

The air quieted again, but Miles knew the Germans had closed the gap. He could hear them rustling, kicking up the rock. Checking. Checking again. Making sure the dead were dead.

He waited. *Holy Mary, Mother of God...*

A boot kicked the bottom of his foot. Someone whispered. The familiar sound of a chamber broke the dark air.

Chapter Two
Rome, Italy

Restless with uncertainty, Serene Moneto excused herself from the buzz of conversation in the main dining room of Cucina Moneto and slipped into the kitchen. The scent of roasting lamb wafted past her nose, almost relieving the panic lodged in her throat. She propped herself against the icebox and inhaled deeply.

She couldn't marry him.

With a platter of dirty dishes hoisted on her shoulder, Veronica Giulian barreled into the kitchen behind her. "What are you doing in here, Serene? Your father is asking for you."

Serene gathered her shoulder-length hair with one hand and used a kitchen rag in the other to dab her neck and chest, wishing she hadn't chosen a sweater. "I'm keeping Luigi company."

"You don't cook for your own party," Luigi said, pointing a wooden spoon in Serene's direction. Luigi had been a chef at their restaurant for years, and it was under his elbows that Serene had learned the art of blending foods.

"He's right," Veronica said, raising her eyebrows at Serene. "It's your engagement dinner, and you shouldn't be in here. I've worked for your father long enough to know he'll be looking for you."

"I'm just taking a breath, if you really must know."

"From what, may I ask? Your skin is white as cotton."

Serene made sure Luigi wasn't in hearing range

before whispering, "It's all so new to me. Marcus. The marriage. It's so soon for all this to be happening."

After taking the dirty plates from the platter, Veronica paused. "You've known him for years."

"Uncle Jack and Papa have been friends for as long as I can remember, but that doesn't mean Marcus *knows* me, or that I know him."

"Don't you worry, my sweet. You'll be perfect for him. He's a handsome one, that Marcus. I've heard he's wonderful with the la-a-a-a-dies."

"Veronica, stop. It's not that."

"Then what is it?"

The truth choked Serene's throat. Without an ounce of discussion or forethought, and without her knowledge, her father had promised to give her hand away. *Honor to your family lives and breathes in your soul. It's like your blood—it stays with you through your time on this earth. Without honor, you are better off dead.* Those exact words had come from his mouth only an hour earlier. She vowed never to admit that to anyone, including her friend.

"Well?" Veronica asked, "What's got you all shaky?"

With a shuddered inhale, Serene steadied her reply. "We don't have anything in common and, well, doesn't that mean anything?"

The question went unanswered as Luigi handed Veronica the silver platter of baby lamb, roasted in spices. He put his first three fingers to his lips and bowed, as if to kiss it away in a grand gesture. *"Buon Appetito."*

Lifting her brow in approval, Veronica rested the platter on the counter, and returned her attention to her friend. "You're the only girl I know who doesn't want Marcus Sturini."

Serene twisted the string of pearls clutching her neck. "I'm not ready to be a wife."

"Look around, my dear. With all of your father's restaurants and his father's money from all that spaghetti he makes, I wish I had the kind of luck you have. I'm just the lowly servant."

"You're more than that, and you know it, Roni."

"Love will come." Veronica winked. "As sure as daylight."

"You know that as truth?" How Serene admired her friend's confidence and ease with men, but she didn't want the same thing as Veronica. She had seen the pain her father went through at the death of her mother, and she didn't want that kind of love from Marcus or anyone.

"Of course." Veronica chuckled and pretended to whisk her away with a towel. "Now you better get out there so you don't lose him."

"Would that be so terrible?" Serene murmured, her thoughts retreating to her conversation with her father. With parts of Rome still volatile from the bombings, and the meager pickings at the piazza, her father still had insisted upon the dinner.

She stared at the thick, wooden door leading to the main dining room. Touching the polished grain with her fingertips, she knew her life could never feel as smooth and right. In the course of one evening, Papa had drawn a life for her that she would never willingly accept.

With the softness of a feather, Serene sucked in her fledgling courage and pushed the door open.

****

"The Allies must push through Cassino," Anthony Moneto announced, his voice rising. "If they don't make it to Rome, our city may as well be forgotten."

Jack Sturini shook his head in disagreement. "Hitler's army is much stronger. The *Americani* only got through Sicily by the grace of God."

"The Germans must be forced from here!"

Anthony's fist hit the table, his face reddened. "Only then will we be able to walk freely in our own country."

Taking the cue from Margot's pleading eyes, Serene approached her father, kissing him on both cheeks. "I thought we were only to talk about pleasant things."

"Ahhh, Serry, where have you been? Come. Come sit down." Anthony sat at the head of the table with Harry and Margot on either side.

"You're right, my dear. A promise is a promise. No more unpleasant talk, Jack. My daughter says so."

Serene shook her head at her father's mischievous wink at Uncle Jack. They both knew full well he had set that rule before they'd even sat down for the evening. "Even if the bombs tear through the ceiling," he had yelled, "there will be no talk of war during my daughter's dinner."

She caught Marcus' dark gaze watching her as he pulled out the chair. The satin patch hugging his left eye held down a portion of the wavy black hair that surrounded his temples.

"Where have you been?" he asked.

"In the kitchen with Veronica. I can't stay out of it, sometimes," she said, hoping her voice would not reveal the churning in her stomach.

"You look divine, Serene," Jack Sturini interrupted. "Doesn't she, Genna?"

Unsmiling, Genna Sturini seemed to take stock of Serene. "Perfect. Or as close as any girl should be, to marry my son."

Uncle Jack frowned at his wife and then drew his attention back to Serene. "You are perfect, my darling."

With the warmest smile she could muster, Serene reached her hand across the table and touched his arm. How Uncle Jack could be with a woman so mean-spirited was hard to understand.

Marcus leaned closer to her ear. "My father's right," he whispered in a husky tone, his warm breath fluttering down her neck. "You look beautiful."

"*Grazie.*" From the bottom of her toes to the top of her shoulders, Serene felt coldness creep into her limbs. Taking a sip of grappa, she wouldn't let her gaze meet his.

"Margot looks nice, too," Harry piped in, teasing. As the only other male Moneto, Harry felt his responsibility was to take care of both sisters.

His comment went unnoticed as the latest blast echoed from the restaurant walls. They all waited as the last of the dust and small debris snowed down in the quiet aftermath.

"Papa," Margot's voice wavered. "They're getting closer."

Anthony set his glass on the table. "Although I, myself, have broken the rule already, we agreed the war would stay outside for this one night."

"We're fortunate to have food on our table and family to share it," Jack said, raising a fist. "We are only celebrating the love we have for our children."

Anthony waved his finger in the air. "The one thing Mussolini couldn't take."

Harry left his chair and darted around to his father's side. "My friend at school said they *can* take our restaurants and use them to make guns, just like they did to Uncle Jack's factory. But I told him we won't let them. Right, Papa?"

"With Mussolini gone, they can't anymore," Serene said matter-of-factly.

"The fascists are still living off our resources," Marcus said. "We need to get back to making spaghetti rather than bombs. It'll take months, if not years, to recover once the war ends."

Anthony cleared his throat and stood up, picking

up the carafe of grappa. "Everyone, please, get a glass. Come, Veronica, join us." He shouted toward the kitchen, "And Luigi, you, too."

Veronica set down the platter of lamb and held out a glass for Anthony to fill. Luigi wiped his hands on his apron and followed suit.

"To Serene." Anthony's voice boomed above the gathering, his eyes resting on his eldest daughter. "And to Marcus Sturini, her future husband. I have handpicked the best man." He raised his glass higher. "Your mother would have been as proud as I am."

"I know, Papa." Serene's eyes stung. Her hand gripped the glass, her fingers aching.

"It seems like only yesterday," Anthony continued, focusing on Serene, "when Serene and Maria used to..."

Serene gave Margot a fleeting glance and approached her father, wrapping her arms around his broad shoulders. "Mama is here with us."

Marcus joined them. "I'll take the finest care of your daughter, sir."

"I know, son. I know."

"Come, let's eat," Genna said, impatiently. "The lamb will be cold." She signaled to Veronica to finish putting out the plates.

"*Va bene.*" Anthony took Serene's moist hand and put it into Marcus' palm, squeezing them together. "She's a good girl, Marcus. You take care of each other and you'll live a long, prosperous life. You know what I'm preaching here? Take care of her."

"I'll make you more proud than you are today, sir."

Serene kissed both of Anthony's cheeks. "With all the fighting going on right outside, Papa, you gave us this beautiful dinner, right here, in the first restaurant you built from the soil of Italy."

"This marriage is meant to be," Marcus said,

lifting his glass high in the air. He gulped the remaining grappa in his glass. "She'll be by my side until death takes us apart."

Watching her father, Serene took a hesitant breath. His worn, dark eyes lit up like polished stones. Even through the pain of having an arranged marriage, she could never turn her back on him. He had taken her and Mama in when they had no one, and he had given them a family name when otherwise shame would have overcome her family. Feeling the warmth in her eyes, Serene realized it was pride that had kept her father from admitting that all these years.

"A beautiful bride my Serry will make," Anthony said, raising his glass again.

"And she'll be a mother, of course," Genna Sturini added. "Our family has always been blessed with children. She'll be no different."

"Aaahh, grandchildren!" Anthony smiled. "Once this war has ended." He gestured to the first of the vegetables and sweet rolls Veronica put on the table. "*Mangi, mangi.*"

"I don't like babies," Harry announced.

Taking a sip of wine, Serene glanced casually at Marcus from above her gold-rimmed glass.

Marcus put down his glass. "Does that scare you?"

"Children? I'm not ready for that, are you?" she asked.

"No, not children. Afraid of having children with *me*?" He held his fork in mid-air as he glanced up from the big hunk of lamb.

Serene coughed, then swallowed a gulp of water. Seeing him smirk, she wondered what it was about him that rattled her nerves. Other than doing business with each other, once or twice a year the two families joined together for a meal, but even then she had always kept her distance. Now, at twenty-two, just two years older than herself, Marcus seemed much older and wiser and seemed to know much more about the ways of the world.

Marcus wiped a napkin slowly across his mouth and surveyed her dead-on. "I guess you've already heard I'm the wild Marcus Sturini? Is that why you're acting like a scared cat?"

The gasp that came from Serene's mouth quieted the room. She waited until the others returned to their conversations before giving him an answer. "I don't know what you're talking about."

"A late night here and there?" he continued. "What if it all were true? A reason not to want to spend your life with me? This marriage has a lot at stake, no?"

Serene stopped cutting her lamb. "What do you mean?"

"You can't be naïve with me."

Staring at him, she didn't know whether to ask another question or try to figure out what he was referring to. Either way, his jaw was set in a way that told her to avoid it—for the moment.

"Marcus, what happened to your eye?" Harry's question saved Serene from having to answer, although her curiosity was piqued.

A wave of silence washed across the table quicker than a glass of spilled water.

"You don't ask things like that." Anthony scolded him. "I'm sorry, Marcus. My son is old enough to know better."

Seeing Marcus' jaw stiffen, Serene waited, holding her breath. It wasn't the right time or place, but little Harry didn't know that.

"American grenade just outside Sicily."

"Can you ever see again?"

"Never, and they won't let me go back and fight. How can a man make things right when they won't let me go and fight?"

"That's terrible for you," Serene heard herself saying.

Marcus leaned over and rubbed his finger over her bottom lip, his good eye resembling the blackness of coal. "Never feel sorry for me."

Whether it was that darkness or the tilt of his chin, something in his gaze repulsed her. As if he knew her thinking, he slowly sat back, as if waiting for her to challenge him. "When you're my wife, you won't pull away at my touch."

Before Serene had a second to digest her surprise, the restaurant walls began to vibrate. Two of the gold sconces on the dining room walls smashed to the floor.

They heard Veronica's scream come from the kitchen. "The Sturinis' factory has been bombed!"

With a firm grip, Marcus held onto Serene's arm and pulled her outside with the others.

"There. Over there!" Serene pointed in the direction of the factory.

For a long second, they stood captivated by the dire bursts of flame spraying little specks of gold into the black night. The spiraling thick smoke spewed from one side of the huge factory building like the discharge from a fighter plane.

Chapter Three

In horror, Serene watched the scene unfold. Men ran toward the factory, screaming against the howling of flames. She pressed her lips together and wished it away so badly that her jaw hurt.

The rims of her eyes burned against the penetrating smoke, the smell mixed with the hint of Marcus' cologne still lingering in the air.

Marcus Sturini.

She'd wondered about him for a lifetime, the man her father would choose as her soulmate. But always she'd found comfort in the idea that it would never happen. Or if it did happen, that her father would make an arrangement with someone she had chosen herself. Or that things would change by the time she was old enough to marry.

But none of that had happened. She was obliged to marry a stranger who now had a name. A perfect match in every visible way. He was strong and independent. She had to admit that it was probably that dark, dangerous look of his that gave him the advantage with other women. But that same darkness sat like a cold stone in her belly.

She was his officially, sealed with an engagement party amidst a world war. Ironic, she thought, barely containing the sad chuckle that bubbled in her throat. Like a spider web, the threads of her life had been woven since she was young, but she had no part in the loom's process. Her eyes stung with old tears that somehow always managed to find their way out of her heart, no matter how many times she tried to swallow them back.

When her mother died, she remembered, her father had knelt beside the bed with glass rosary beads dangling from his hands as he sobbed to the Blessed Mary, night after night. Even as a girl she'd understood the desperation in his voice as he bellowed to God, demanding a reason why his wife had been taken from him. Long ago she had vowed to herself that she would never experience the pain of loving anyone. In an odd way, marrying Marcus would save her from hurting in the same way as her father.

With a shiver, she tried to exhale it all away.

She could never love Marcus. She might grow to respect him, and maybe even cherish him as a friend, but never love.

And—she couldn't marry him. Could she? With a spot of panic, she turned away from the heat of the explosion to let the cool air wash away the smoke. If she didn't marry him, where would that leave her father's decision? A girl didn't just defy her father or her family's wishes. With a silent sob, she pushed the decision further into her chest.

"Come. We need to go back inside," Anthony commanded. "It's not safe out here."

Coughing away the thickening smoke, Serene whisked away a single tear that had trickled to the bottom of her chin. For the first time in her life since her mother had died, she was truly afraid.

****

Hours later, shopkeepers sat in vigil, praying their shops would meet the morning sunrise unharmed. Blast after blast, they waited, and Anthony Moneto was no exception. He knew how dangerous it was to stay in such a volatile place, but like the others he had grown his business from the ground and would do anything not to lose it. But it would only take one bomb and all that he had worked for would be gone. He knew it as much as

17

the others, but still he sat at the window night after night and prayed.

He stared at the inside of the restaurant as if he hadn't already memorized every detail. Each of his three restaurants had its own unique style, designed according to each of the Moneto children's favorite colors. Olive green in Sicily was for Harry, and a royal, rich blue for the one in Naples was to complement Margot's personality. But Serene had liked this restaurant the most because it was in Travestere, her favorite quarter in Rome, just west of the Vatican. And his daughter's favorite color was maroon.

Sighing, Anthony stood and peered out the front window. The cobblestone street was quiet. He eyed two German soldiers patrolling, glancing his way.

As he stepped away from the window, his heart broke for the Sturinis. Ever since their business had been taken over for weapons, the Sturinis had hoped to get it back once the war ended. Now, nothing could be done to save the part of the factory that had been bombed; that would have to be rebuilt. Luckily, the factory was one of the biggest in Rome, so half of it could be salvageable.

Anthony did the sign of the cross and said a small prayer. It had been more than two hours since his children left, and he knew they would be getting anxious about him, especially Serene. He had known deep down it wasn't a good idea to have the engagement dinner, but he'd wanted his daughter to be able to get on with her own life despite the war. She had worried over him since the day Maria died, and he thought it was time.

He untied the cord from the brocade drape and pulled it across the window. As he did each evening, he stopped at the painting of Maria where it hung next to the fireplace. He kissed his index finger and then pressed it to the canvas. The first time he had seen her, standing in that field holding Serene on her hip, he had decided to marry her. Watching her golden hair swinging carelessly in the wind, he vowed in the eyes of God that he would take care of both of them and be Serene's father, unlike the coward who had left Maria pregnant and unmarried. After their wedding, Maria's family welcomed him, pretending to love him as a son, but Anthony knew he was viewed only as the proper husband, needed to mend the shameful bridge back to society for the Attilio family. Happiness came second to money in Maria's family, if it came at all. But Anthony fooled them. He loved her first, and everything else came second.

And now, through the arrangement with Marcus, he would fulfill his obligation to his wife and provide their daughter with the same kind of stability, a secure life with room for happiness, God willing.

He picked up the sack of garbage Veronica had left and opened the back screen door. Cool night air filled his nostrils, and he realized most of the smoke from the bombing had evaporated high into the clouds. Dropping the garbage next to the cement stoop, he gazed up to see the moon almost visible through the high, billowy smoke. "It's a good sign," he said, heading back in.

"*Signore?*"

Anthony froze. Even his heart seemed to stop momentarily. He didn't turn, nor did he proceed back into the restaurant. He stopped his breath, unsure whether he'd actually heard something. When no more sounds came, he shook his head in disgust at his old ears playing tricks, and opened the screen door wider.

"Please, *signore*. We need help."

He stopped the door in mid-swing. There was no mistaking the voice of an American. With the

German rampage going on, Anthony couldn't imagine how any of them could have made it so far into Rome.

"Please." The voice was urgent. "My buddy's leg is hurt. Can you help us? Do you speak English?"

Anthony still didn't move. In his head, he turned over the consequences. For that brief second, he thought only of his children before holding the door open from behind. "Come inside, quickly," he said in impeccable English.

Clay nodded and flung Miles over his shoulder, and they staggered to the stoop.

In silence Anthony led them through the dark kitchen and into the dining room, where Clay steadied Miles on one of the high-backed chairs. After Anthony lit a small candle, Clay removed the gun from its leather sling, held it up to the height of his shoulder and then placed it on the table.

Anthony ignored the gesture. "Were you followed?"

"We kept off the main streets. Hidin' in the olive groves made it easier."

"Unfortunately, that doesn't mean that you weren't followed." Disappearing behind the large kitchen door, Anthony returned quickly to the table, carrying a large basin filled with water and strips of material that could be used as a tourniquet and bandages. "Where have you come from?"

"We made it into Anzio early last night." Clay shook his head. "It was real bad on the beach."

Anthony dragged another chair to the table and pulled Miles' leg so it rested sideways on his own thigh. "All the roads are blocked. How did you get through?"

"A local from a small town outside Anzio took us. He knew a way to bypass Cassino. The Germans were buzzing around that abbey—"

"I know the route." Anthony dipped the rag in

the warm water and wrung it out. "He's been in and out of consciousness?"

Clay nodded.

"You got the bleeding to stop. That's good, very good." Wiping the excess blood from around the outside of the wound, Anthony avoided any direct contact with the inner part of Miles' calf. "A lot of skin is gone, but I can't see any bullets here," he said, half talking to himself. "Maybe they went in farther than I can see." To Clay, he asked, "Can you help turn his leg a little so I can see better?"

When Clay moved Miles' leg no more than a hair, Miles' eyes flew open and he let out a silent scream, gripping his upper thigh with both hands.

"Go to the cabinet at the end of the hall," Anthony ordered Clay, "and get the tall black bottle and one of the small glasses beneath. Your friend needs something for the pain."

Surveying the shrapnel surrounding the wound, Anthony reached for a strip of cloth. "You're a lucky man that you made it this far," he said, eyeing Miles over the top of his gold-rimmed glasses.

"How bad is it?" Miles asked.

"More than I can help you with. We have to go now, while it's still dark," Anthony said, wrapping the strip around the upper part of Miles' shin.

Clay returned with a bottle and filled a small glass. "Take it for the pain."

Miles gulped the whiskey like water, causing a fireball of pain to erupt in his throat. Flinching, he held up the glass for more. "Can we make it out of here?"

"The Germans are patrolling," Anthony announced, securing another bandage. "If they see Americans, they'll kill them."

"Can't we bring a doctor back here?" Clay asked.

"It's too dangerous."

"Just tell us where to go," Miles prompted. "You

can't risk anything else for us."

"Hush," Anthony said, disappearing into the kitchen to throw the dirty towels into a basin before returning. "I know a way."

Trembling, Miles wiped his blood-soaked hand on his shirt and offered it to him. Anthony took it quickly and squeezed.

"You'll be fine, my boy. But we must go." Just as he reached to blow out the candle, two German soldiers burst through the front door. With guns aimed, the soldiers charged toward the men, pushing through chairs and tables.

The first soldier shot Clay in the middle of his chest, spit, and then aimed his gun at Anthony, shaking his head back and forth slowly. "*Verrator.*"

Anthony stopped pleading and backed away, slowly.

"*Verrator,*" the soldier repeated.

"What is he saying?" Miles yelled, wedging himself off the chair and onto the ground.

"Traitor."

Quicker than it takes a heart to beat, Miles grabbed onto the bottom of Anthony's shirt and yanked him down. The last thing he heard was the echo of a bullet casing hitting the floor.

****

"Papa?" Serene tried to run through the two German soldiers blocking the entrance to Cucina Moneto. One of the men caught her by the elbow.

"It's my father," she hissed in Italian, keeping her focus on the jagged scar that ran across his chin.

The Monetos' house servant Anna came from behind Serene, staring at the soldier closest to the door. "Her *padre.* You understand, no?"

The soldier tipped his gun closer to Serene, his lips curling up in an evil grin as he twirled the ends of her hair. She bit the inside of her lip, wanting to spit in his face but knowing she'd probably be dead before his face dried. At the command of the other soldier, he grudgingly let her by.

Pushing through the maze of chairs and tables, Serene's knees threatened to buckle at the sight of her father. He lay crumpled on his back, like a discarded sack of potatoes, his eyeglasses resting just a few feet away. An American solder lay sprawled across his legs, face up, and another sat slumped against the back wall, a thick red line smeared down the surface behind him.

Nausea thickened in Serene's throat as she went closer and fell to her knees, ripping open the bottom of her knee-length coat. Swallowing hard, she held her breath and used all her force to roll the American off her father's legs.

"Papa?" Leaning closer, she brushed the gray strands of hair from his forehead. "I'm here, Papa. It's me, Serry."

Relief soared through her limbs when Anthony lifted his head momentarily and then eased it back down. His eyes fluttered open for a few seconds.

"Papa," Serene whispered. She caressed the side of his face, his being, the soul that had given her love like a blood father. He was the only papa she knew, or would ever want to know. At his ear, she whispered, "I will never forget that you took me when I was so small, and gave me and Mama the world."

His eyes opened wider. "I'm—sorry I—didn't tell you—that night."

That fateful night when Mama died. Serene remembered it like it had been the previous day. Standing at the doorway in her nightgown, Serene had watched the metal box he was holding crash to the floor, sending the contents sailing across the floor. Together, they'd listened to her mother's wedding ring bounce and roll before finally resting in the corner of the room. When Serene scrambled to pick up the papers, she caught a glimpse of her adoption certificate. Later, she had begged the truth out of poor Anna but then was sworn to secrecy.

Now, watching another of her family perish, she was sorrier for that promise more than anything.

"What matters is how much you have been there for me," she whispered. "Just stay with me, Papa. Please stay."

Tears trickled down the side of his cheek. "You must—save him."

"Who?" Serene followed her father's motion toward the man lying beside him. "He's dead," she whispered.

Slowly, Anthony shook his head back and forth. "No."

"Did he do this to you?"

With the sound of a tired moan from his chest, Anthony's gaze slid away. Serene grabbed onto both of his shoulders and rubbed her cheek on his shirt. "Don't leave me, Papa!" Heat enveloped her body. "Please don't leave."

Anna touched Serene's shoulder. "He's gone."

"No!" Serene lunged from Anna and started toward the Germans, who now sat at the tables.

Franci Petrione, the shopkeeper from next door, darted from the shadows and grabbed her arms before she got more than two steps. "Stop and think about what you're doing," he whispered between his clenched teeth. "They will kill you, too. And probably the rest of us."

Serene struggled to pull free. Like uninvited guests, the soldiers had already helped themselves to her engagement dinner. Large chunks of the half-eaten lamb and empty whiskey bottles lay strewn on the tables and floor. In Franci's tight grip, she could do nothing but bend over and wait for the next wave of nausea to pass. "How could they?"

"I know how hard this is, but you must protect

your own life now."

"I don't want to live without him." Her eyes ached with the pressure of new tears. "It's too soon for him to leave."

"Don't you understand? It's your life at stake, and ours."

"I don't care." She wiped one cheek with the back of her hand.

His grip tightened. "At least care about the rest of us."

Serene stopped struggling, and Franci let her go. She sat down beside her father's body and pushed the loose hair away from her face. "Do you know what happened?"

"I heard shots while I was in my own store. I came and found this. From what I heard them say, and my German's no good, the Americans broke in here to get some food and shot your father. The Germans then killed them." Frank pointed toward the two American bodies.

"They did this? Why would they come to kill us when they've been trying to free Rome?"

Franci half nodded, as if he didn't think it probable, either. "We must leave now before—"

The Germans pushed back their chairs and strolled to the front stoop, outside the restaurant.

"How can we give him a proper burial?" Serene wailed quietly, feeling the warmth of life leaving him.

"There is no time." Franci glanced furtively to the front of the restaurant, his eyes darkening. "Once they're done with the cigarettes—"

"Can't we take him?"

"They would kill the Pope if they thought a good reason existed. Please don't do this, Serene. I'll help you and Anna get home."

"This is my Papa." With a shaky hand, she smoothed wrinkles from Anthony's white shirt, now stained in deep pink.

"You must listen to him," Anna said, behind her. "They'll kill you."

Serene whipped around and faced them both. "I'm not leaving without him." Scowling at Franci, she said, "Talk to them."

"There is no time," Franci hissed. "We must go now."

"Then I'll ask them." Serene jumped up. "I won't leave Papa with them."

"Wait." Franci fumbled to block her, perspiration breaking through his shirt. "You wait here. I'll see what I can do."

With a nod, Serene pulled her coat closer to her body and sank down next to her father. "I can't. I just can't leave him like that." Shoving her hand in her pocket to pull out a handkerchief, something rubbed against the bottom of her coat. The American soldier's fingertips rested within an inch of her coat hem.

She waited, not letting a drop of air leave her lungs.

The American's hand moved again. This time, it brushed her knee.

Serene held her mouth, daring herself not to scream. The pounding in her chest had moved to her ears.

Franci came through the front door. "We must hurry. They didn't understand—I'm sure they wouldn't hesitate to—"

"What happens to them?" Serene bolted from the ground, pointing to the two Americans.

"Let's leave now." Anna whispered, grasping Serene's forearm.

Serene hurled back an icy stare. "Please tell me, Franci."

"I'll take care of it later."

"What will you do with the—the bodies?"

Franci raised his eyebrows and seemingly brushed aside her question as craziness. "It doesn't matter. Come, get a cloth to wrap him, and we'll get your father in the truck."

Her thoughts raced to her father's request about saving the man next to her. Poised to broach the subject, she thought better of it and retrieved a tablecloth, richly embroidered with roses and vines. She shook it open and draped it over her father's body, pausing as it reached his face. With a sob aching to come out, she touched her fingertips to her lips and then closed his eyes.

Between the three of them, they brought his body to the pickup truck parked in front of the restaurant. Anna got into the passenger seat and waited while, with a fleeting glance at Franci, Serene closed the back of the truck and stepped up into the driver's seat.

Gripping the metal steering wheel with both hands, she stared through the windshield, knowing exactly what she had to do. Slowly, she inserted the key in the ignition and took a frantic breath. "I lost my hat!" she wailed. She hopped out and started up the restaurant steps.

Both Germans lifted their guns to block her entrance, but she patted the top of her head to indicate her purpose. The German with the ugly scar laughed viciously and moved aside, motioning her through with his gun.

****

Serene's heart pounded as she peered around the silent restaurant, alive hours earlier but now masked with an eerie paleness. This room and her life would never again be the same. She whisked off the wetness around her eyes, sucked in a daunted breath, and remembered her purpose.

"Are you all right?" She hoped her English was still understandable.

No response from the American.

Leaning a little closer, she gently placed her hand beneath his, finding it warm and moist with life. "Can you hear me?"

Still nothing.

"If you can hear me, squeeze my hand."

Serene checked behind her. She unbuttoned his coat, soaked in warm blood, and slid her hand inside, relieved to feel at least a slight rise and fall to his chest.

"I want to help you, but not now. I have to go, but I'll be back. Can you hear me? I'll be back."

"*Halten Sie!*" Boots clicked toward her on the stone floor.

As she let go of the American's hand, the slightest pressure passed her fingertips.

He had heard her.

With a jump backwards, she snatched the light brown knit hat from her pocket and spun around on her platform shoes. Smiling through quivering lips, she waved the hat in the air and started to walk past the German. As she reached him, he blocked her with his arm, and slid the tip of the gun inside her blouse, resting it at the center of her breasts. Slowly, he moved it downward and the buttons popped rhythmically, one by one dropping to the floor like pebbles.

His steel gray eyes probed every inch of her.

When Serene tried to scream, he slammed his hand over her mouth and pushed her flat against a wall, pressing his thighs against her. Her body recoiled in horror as the reek of whiskey sent quakes of fear running up her spine. With heated eyes, he dared her not to move as he fumbled for his trouser zipper, using his other arm to hold her.

As he began to peel away her flesh-colored stockings, a shot startled the restaurant walls. The German tensed, and his eyelids flickered for a moment before he fell, knocking her to the ground and drawing a smeary line of thick blood down the length of her beige coat. Serene shuddered, gasping for air, and struggled to free herself from beneath his body.

The sound of another pair of boots clicked toward them.

A second blast. The other German dropped to the ground. Serene cupped her ears against the sound, turning her head toward the source of the shots. She met the American's eyes, clear, blue, determined, as if they hadn't seen her at all. He dropped back down, smoke still smoldering from his pistol.

"Serene!" Anna ran through the front door, followed closely by Franci.

"Help me get him...off me."

Franci rolled the heavy body partway off Serene and helped pull her legs free. She immediately crawled to the soldier, her shredded stockings dragging behind.

With his eyes closed, his hand still clutched the gun. She rubbed the side of his face, doing nothing to stop the sobs of gratefulness for this stranger. "We have to take him with us," she said, half to herself and half to the others.

Anna shook her head in denial. "We must go before more come."

Serene's gaze darted to the soldier, and then back to Anna. Fear and determination together lodged in her belly, threatening to kill every ounce of logic she was holding onto. "Then you have to go alone."

Chapter Four

Serene let the truck coast down the long driveway to the house, her body shaking with relief—or fear, she couldn't tell which. The heavy American sat slumped against her shoulder, sandwiched between her and Anna. Avoiding the main roads had made the trip nearly a half hour longer.

She turned off the motor and stared blankly at the massive two-story estate. The early morning light cast a grayness on the tall white pillars that outlined the ends of the terracotta-colored villa. A large white stone emblem hung above the front oak door: *Moneto,* in gold print. The day the sign was hung, her father had swung them around, one by one, Mama too. Even at five years old, Serene had understood the importance of her family name.

She slammed her hand on the steering wheel. All for nothing! Her father had built it all himself, and now she would never have the chance to tell him how much it meant to her. Never! She cried out in the cold, silent truck, her whole being absorbed with heartache as she buried her face in her cupped hands. All the years Papa had given her and Mama. His name, his fortune. But in the end, human vengeance took him, forever took something from all of them.

"Go." Anna stretched her hand in front of the soldier and caressed Serene's cheek. "Tell them."

Walking up the speckled path to the side entrance, she pulled at her hat, angry that she hadn't forced her father to come home with them after the party. Since the beginning of the war, he had insisted on protecting the Rome restaurant and hiring men to watch over the other two restaurants. And each night, Serene and Anna pleaded with him not to go, warned him of the danger. But night after night, God spared him and he would return safely, late in the night.

Serene threw her hat on the foyer table and hastily slid her arms out of her wool coat, now caked in dark crimson. She hid it behind the others on the coat hook and tore up the steps to the second floor.

"Margot?" Serene shook her sister. "Margot!"

"Hmm?" Margot turned over and pulled the quilt over her dark curly head.

"I need your help."

"With what?" Margot mumbled.

"There's been an accident. Get Harry and come downstairs."

Ripping the quilt from her face, Margot jolted to a sitting position. Large curls cascaded haphazardly around her face. "Where's Papa? What happened to you?"

Serene followed her sister's gaze to the missing buttons in the front of her own blouse. She quickly folded her arms in front. "Let's go downstairs, and I'll tell you."

Within seconds everyone had rushed into the parlor. As she related the night's disaster to them, Harry sat on Serene's lap with his eyes half closed.

Her words hung in the disbelieving air.

"How can we help that American?" Margot began to cry. "He killed Papa."

"No. No, he didn't." Serene placed Harry beside her on the velvet settee and stood up. She toyed with the ceramic music box on the table before throwing her hands up in exasperation. "We don't know."

"How can you be sure?"

Serene took in a long breath and softened her

voice. "I don't know what happened, but before Papa died, he was trying to tell me something." Scowling at the story she barely believed herself, she shook her head in irritation. "I think he wanted me to help that American."

Anna gasped. "I went along with it at the restaurant and brought that man here because you're stubborn. You put us in danger. If the Germans find out that—"

"No," Serene said evenly. "I know in my heart that Papa wanted us to help that man." Inside she was breaking, unsure of anything except she had a dead father, and she had a man in the truck that the Germans wanted.

"I want to help." Margot stood up, arms folded.

"Me, too," Harry piped in.

Anna stared, her eyes troubled. "Your family has been good to me for a long time, *Signorina* Serene. You took me in when I had no one. Especially Anthony. He was a good man. But now you ask something like this of me?"

Serene knelt in front of her. Her father had humored away her stubbornness many times, encouraging her independence and regarding her as equal in all senses. This time, Serene wasn't giving in, not when a man's soul hung between life and death. "I'm sorry to scare you, but all of us are scared. I'm doing my best to avoid the danger, but sometimes there isn't a way around it."

"You must try and find a way, *Signorina*, or we all will die in this house."

"We'll die?" Harry yelled.

"No." Serene snapped. "But we need to get him from the truck. Harry, can you get some blankets from the other room and turn out all the lights except for the back room?"

"Don't we need a doctor?" Margot asked.

"We need someone, but it has to be a secret."

Serene bit her lip. "Do you understand, Harry?"

Harry nodded.

Margot's eyes widened. "What about Samuel?"

Serene had already thought of Samuel McCarthy, who had just completed his second year of residency at the university medical school. He had fancied Margot for close to a year. "You think he'll help us?"

"Of course," Margot retorted.

"I know you care for him deeply," Serene said evenly, gripping the back of the chair with both hands, "but can we trust him?"

"Yes, of course. How can you ask a question like that?"

Looking past her sister to the others, Serene felt the weight of a rock being lowered onto her shoulders, forcing her to choose between this stranger's life or the safety of her family. "I mean, really trust him? It could mean our lives, Margot. We have to be sure."

"Yes. I think so." Margot's dark eyes bore into Serene's. "Yes."

****

Serene cradled her knees against her chest and gazed out the window. No clouds or smoke, just a glorious blue overhead. Since they had pulled the soldier from the truck and brought him upstairs to their mother's room, Anna had not spoken a word. Samuel had arrived less than an hour later, and Margot swore she would help him to the best of her nursing ability. Thinking it better that one of them stay downstairs, Serene agreed, resigning herself to a long wait at the kitchen table as the soldier struggled for his life directly above her head.

How Serene wished Anna would talk with her as they waited for Samuel to come down and let them know of the man's condition. Instead, across the kitchen, Anna twisted and maneuvered the soft buttery dough on the block of wood, her fingers like those to a violin, fluid and with purpose.

As she watched the flour puff from beneath the dough each time Anna flipped and pummeled it, she thought back to Samuel's first raw estimate of the man's condition. Despite the deep cuts on the soldier's forehead and chest, saving the leg became the mission. Taking him to the local hospital posed too much danger to all of them. The fascists had not disappeared, by any means, and they still wanted the Americans and British dead. Samuel's matter-of-fact explanation had made her feel sick to her stomach.

Stretching out her legs, Serene's thoughts drifted back to her father and seeing his quiet body lying alone in his bedroom. "People will start coming tomorrow," she murmured.

Anna finished and wiped her hands on her apron. "Of course they will. But with that man upstairs in the same house, you will want other people here? How long can you keep it a secret?"

"I don't know what will happen now, but I'll do my best to protect you and the others."

"You shouldn't have brought him here."

"Papa was gone and I couldn't help him anymore. As much as I wanted to bring him back, I couldn't. Can't you understand? The man upstairs is alive and needs our help. You need to trust me. I'm begging you, please, to trust me."

With a raised eyebrow, Anna went about her cooking. "I've already prepared the room for the viewing. Your papa, bless his soul, has been waiting long enough."

Fresh tears filled Serene's eyes. Even amongst the turbulence of regular bombings, civilian deaths were followed by a vigil. Whether the next hour or the next day, family and friends would come together to celebrate the soul. It was no different for the Moneto family, and Serene knew that if her family did not accept visitors soon, it would draw unwanted attention.

"We'll start accepting mourners tomorrow."

"Not today?"

"It's only a few more hours. Things need to be settled here." *I need to be settled.*

"How do I answer the questions? When I go to the piazza for the morning fruit, there will be all kinds of questions."

With a throb at the base of her head, Serene didn't have the strength to continue the argument. Anna wanted him out and she would do anything to make it known. "I'm asking you to do your best."

"How about a cup of your coffee, Anna?" Samuel's voice boomed as he came into the kitchen.

Serene jumped up. "How is he?"

"In and out of consciousness, but I gave him morphine to help him sleep."

Anna handed him a steamy cup and walked back to the stove.

"What about his leg?"

"The bullets chewed up part of the bone, I'm afraid." He picked up the delicate saucer and took a sip. "I took them out and cleaned him up a bit. Someone put a fine makeshift tourniquet on it, and I think that saved his leg."

"And his chest? "

"Besides a large nick, he was a lucky man to survive at all. In a few hours, we'll see if he needs more attention."

"He'll never make it somewhere else, not with the Nazis patrolling everywhere. You said so yourself."

Samuel ran a hand through his short carrot-colored hair. "He seems like a strong bloke. We'll see, when and if the time comes."

Serene hated asking so much of him. Treating

the enemy was a severe offense for Italians, but as an Irish student he more than likely faced the consequence of death if he were caught. Knowing the relationship between him and Margot was fairly serious, she had hated to ask for his help, yet that was her only assurance that he would also keep silence. "Did you talk with him?"

With a nod, Samuel took his lips from the cup. "He talked about your father and mentioned something about the scuffle. I couldn't quite understand. He fell asleep quickly after I administered the medicine. Margot is sitting with him, but it may be several more hours before he becomes conscious."

Anna turned from the stove. "When can he leave, *Signore* Samuel?"

"As soon as he is well enough, I assume." Samuel's voice trailed toward Serene. "If he does improve quickly, we want him up and moving around as soon as possible. It helps the healing process up here," he said, tapping his index finger to his temple.

"I don't like this," Anna said. "Those Germans may know where we live. If they ever found out—"

Serene drew her sweater more tightly around herself and gazed half-heartedly in Samuel's direction, hoping for some kind of encouragement. From the moment her father had passed, her immediate responsibilities as the eldest left her no room to doubt her own decisions. Being second-guessed by Anna wore on her patience.

"The Americans want their soldiers back," Samuel said, "but it'll be dangerous trying to get him back to his unit. Mussolini surrendered, but it doesn't mean the Germans are finished with us."

"*Signore* Anthony would not have liked this," Anna said, shaking her head.

Samuel glanced her way. "We can't make this

any more difficult than it has to be."

"He's right," Serene said. "It would be better for us to keep him here for now. Just trying to contact someone to take him makes it more dangerous. They intercept everything."

"I'm not afraid just for myself, but for all of you," Anna cried as she ran from the kitchen.

"I suppose you would rather have him die?" Samuel called after her.

"Don't." Serene put her palms to her forehead. "She's scared. I'm scared, too. We all are."

"What's going on?" Margot came into the kitchen with her sweater sleeves pushed to her elbows and her long curls pulled tightly into a tail at the nape of her neck. "I could hear you all the way upstairs."

"Nothing," Samuel said quickly. "I should go, and all of you should get some rest."

"Anna's right about the danger, isn't she?" Serene whispered.

"And so are you." Samuel buttoned his overcoat. His straightforward tone did nothing to allay her fears. "That man would have died if you hadn't brought him here." Hesitating, he closed up his bag. "Anna is only a servant here, not the one who should be judging."

"To *you* she is only a servant," Serene snapped. "Maybe in Ireland you think of the hired hands as just help, but here we treat them as family. For years, she's lived here, breathed here, slept here. She may not be part of this family by blood, but she has every right to her own feelings. I can understand her fear because I feel the same way. I think we all do."

"Please, both of you, stop this," Margot interrupted.

Samuel eyed Serene grimly. "You shouldn't let a servant question your decisions, Serene. Part of the role you have to take on now is the decision-making.

Your decision-making. As the eldest, you have to show—"

"We've all been through something terrible," Margot said. "We, not Serene alone, have made the decisions together so far. With or without Anna's consent, we stand by what we chose."

With a sigh, Samuel picked up his bag. "Be careful of her—that's all I'm saying."

From the worry lines creasing his forehead, Serene caught his real intention. "Surely you don't think she would turn us in?"

"War does crazy things to people." He headed toward the door and turned back as if to say something else but instead planted an effortless kiss on Margot's forehead and then tipped his hat to Serene. "I left pain pills by the bed, and I'll check in later today. Any changes before that, have Margot come get me."

Fully understanding the weight of her responsibility, Serene watched him leave. She hugged her arms across her middle, wanting to call to him. To tell him to come back. To say she was scared, torn between protecting her family and honoring her father's wishes at the last moments of his life.

Most importantly, she wanted to thank him for making her decision feel more right. Sam had reinforced her position as head of the household. By standing against Anna's doubts and fears, even though Serene herself had fears, he had given her the strength to follow through with the course she was taking.

Serene needed that strength if she was to live through the next twenty-four hours.

****

Serene climbed the main staircase to the top floor of the villa. Two guest rooms, one on either end of the hall took up the entire floor, with a narrow, spiral staircase at the opposite end that led up from the back of the kitchen. Everyone except Serene's father and, of course, Anna had been forbidden to visit that floor without permission during her mother's illness. But Serene had used the back stairs endless times to sneak visits, most of the time without being caught. The delight in her mother's face was worth every trip. They would talk until the wee hours of the morning, and when her mother wanted to rest, Serene would watch her sleep.

Turning the door handle of her mother's room, she heard the familiar creak that made her stomach flutter. She eyed the grand mahogany bed, her breath quickening. The soldier lay on his back in the center, covered by only a sheet and a thin blanket. In the soft reflection from the fireplace, she could see his eyes were closed.

Watching him sleep, she resisted the urge to check his breathing. Instead, she paced to the other side of the room. Her gaze settled on the dulled glint of a crucifix, attached to a silver chain, where it lay on a knitted doily on the chest of drawers, exactly as her mother had left it. On a whim, she touched the chain to her lips and put it around her neck. She undid the top button of her sweater to see it more clearly in the oval mirror. Looking at the dusty glass, she wondered about her own fate, as she had so many times since her mother's death. After thinking for a moment, she glanced back at the still soldier and then slid open the top drawer.

Under a pair of stockings, the sleek, long black box still sat in the spot where she had first found it the night her mother died. Slowly she lowered herself to the floral chaise and ran her fingertips across the name, *Mercurios*, scripted in raised gold letters across the front of the box. Opening the lid, she found her mother's elbow length white gloves, just as she remembered, and smoothed her hand over the creamy material. She stuck her hand in one of the gloves and slipped out the folded piece of paper still tucked deep within it.

To my Serene. As she read her mother's handwriting on the front, the words blurred and slid off the paper. She bit her lip and didn't dare unfold the note she had memorized those years ago. Holding the gloves closer to her chest, she gazed at the oil canvas above the bed. Painted in a happier time, her mother smiled warmly back at her. Barely fifteen when her mother passed away, Serene had known her days of being a child were gone. She had become an adult, caring for the younger children, helping Anna prepare meals, and working with her father at the restaurants. And now she was ready to fulfill her mother's request in the letter and participate in an arranged marriage to a man her father chose. Ignoring the hot tears, she stuffed the letter and gloves back in the box, holding them on her lap for a few minutes before returning them.

Just as she pushed the drawer closed, the soldier began thrashing, yelling and throwing his arms over his head as if to protect himself.

Serene scrambled to the bed. "What is it?"

With a quick flick of her hand across his forehead, she felt the heat of a growing fever. A sheen of sweat formed quickly on his face.

The soldier kicked his good leg and threw his arms back and forth, mumbling things Serene couldn't understand. Struggling to control his movements, she used the weight of her upper body to hold his arms down. "Shh. You're safe. It's only a bad dream."

When his body stilled, she released his shoulders and whispered close to his ear, "Go back to sleep. You're safe with me."

She sat beside him and placed her hand on his chest until his breathing reached a slow, rhythmic hum. Something about him pulled at her. He had saved her life and now she was going to save his.

Deep down, she knew Franci's version of what happened had to be wrong. The Americans didn't harm innocent people, especially a restaurant owner who probably offered them food.

She took the cloth from the basin, wrung it, and wiped the perspiration from the man's forehead. His eyes shot open and he grabbed her wrist. His stare mimicked the iciest winter sky. "Don't touch me."

"I'm sorry," Serene gasped, the pain of his gripping fingers ran up her arm. "Please, let go, you're safe here."

The man's eyes flickered and then shut, releasing her wrist at the same time. When he opened them again, he focused on her for a moment, and then sank back into sleep.

"It's a nightmare. You've been having a lot of them," Serene whispered. As she dabbed the cloth down his neck, he grabbed her hand again and held it against the mattress.

"I need to get out of here," he murmured, squeezing her arm tighter. Creases pinched the outer corners of his eyes and he tossed back the covers. "Don't go in there. The Jerries are waiting."

Serene struggled to wriggle her arm free, watching the desperation cross his face like a storm. "Don't go where?"

He moaned and turned to one side. "Go home to your family. They're coming. We need to get out of here."

"No one's here. It's me, Serene. Shh. It's a nightmare—"

The American bolted upright. "What are they saying? No! He's not a traitor."

"Who?" she breathed. Kneeling on the bed, she struggled to ease him back in a resting position. Then it came to her like the first crack of morning thunder.

"Not him, you sons of bitches!" He cried out into the dim air, his eyes unfocused. "Not him. Take me—take *me*, you bastards."

Serene wrapped her arms around him and rocked him as if he were a child. "Was that my Papa?" she sobbed close to his face. "Is that who you were trying to protect?"

"I wanna die," he moaned, "God, please let me go."

"It's only a dream," she said, holding him tighter. *If only it weren't a real dream.*

With quivering hands, she held him tighter and kissed his forehead, holding him until he drifted back into sleep.

Chapter Five

Serene awoke from a catnap in the chaise, her legs swung over the side with a black loafer dangling from her big toe. The emerging sunlight streamed in through the windows, casting dull panes of architecture against the tapestry rug.

She studied the man lying on her mother's bed. It had been nearly four hours since his nightmare, and he hadn't awakened or spoken again. Sam had returned to check on him and then had gone downstairs to talk with Margot. Serene hoped the American would become alert enough to talk, or at least open his eyes for longer than a flutter of eyelashes. Even through the cuts around his face and neck she could tell he wasn't much older than herself. Maybe twenty-two or twenty-three, at the most. Little sprigs of hair, the color of newly cut oak, popped out through the pieces of bandage wrapped around the top of his head. The color matched the shadow on his chin.

Serene took a deep breath, rolled up the sleeves of her sweater, and wrung out a cloth. Wiping his face between the bandages, she hesitated on the sliver of a scar that ran through the center of his left eyebrow. From its smoothness, she guessed it must have been the result of a childhood accident. She dipped the cloth again in the water, squeezed it, and paused for the merest of a second before adjusting the blanket to be even with his waist, not daring to move it further down. At the sight of his taut muscles crossing his midline, her face warmed. She smoothed the cloth over the swollen skin of his upper arms and neck, dabbing between the bandages on his chest, her hand gliding under the metal tag that hung from his neck. It read *Coulson Miles M.* She scanned the few lines to learn his home was Hazel Run, Minnesota, USA. Just as she wondered about the meaning of his name, she heard footsteps bounding up the stairs.

Margot burst through the door. "The Americans are on their way!"

"Sshh." Serene dropped the cloth beside the bed and met her sister halfway across the room. "What happened?"

"Old Alberto from next door told me more American troops landed and are trying to get past the Germans." Margot clapped. "They're on their way and the war will end!"

Serene covered her hand over her mouth, muffling her scream. "Rome will be saved."

They both began to cry and laugh and hug, spinning each other around and around.

When they collapsed, falling out of each other's arms, Serene glanced over toward the bed to see the soldier's eyes open, staring straight at them. Not taking her gaze from him, Serene gestured for Margot to get Samuel. She approached the bed and poured some water from the pitcher. "How are you feeling?"

****

Miles turned toward the sound of the water. Where was he? He rubbed his head and found a thick bandage wound around his forehead. A dull pain throbbed at the side of his head and he had to blink several times to relieve the burning in his eyes.

"Here. Have some of this." Serene lifted his head and leaned the glass against his mouth.

Miles couldn't stop his lips from shaking, but he managed to take a small sip. He caught a faint smell of lilacs, just like the ones he remembered at home.

44

"Where am I?"

"Rome."

Miles squirmed, trying to sit up. "Where?"

"After the accident—at the restaurant—we took you to our home, in the outskirts of Rome." She leaned to give him another sip of the water. "Our friend Samuel took care of your wounds and your leg."

Miles reached for the lower part of his leg and stopped, wincing.

"It's still there," Serene said, adjusting the blankets around him. "And it will stay there if you will stop moving and let your body recover."

He fell back onto the pillows, his whole body burning in places he hadn't even known existed. It seemed as though only a second earlier he had been fighting out in a field, then leaning over the remains of his buddy Walter. But now this beautiful girl, smelling so nice, sat beside him with a glass of the best water he'd ever tasted. He wondered how he could've ever got hitched up in her house. Taking another sip, he tried to remember. And then her name hit him like a bullet. "Serry? Is that it? Your name, I mean?"

"Yes. How do you know—did my father tell you? He was there at the restaurant," she stammered. "I think he might have even helped you somehow."

"Who is your father?" She talked so fast in broken English, Miles had a hard time keeping up with her. Her voice was so familiar. He closed his eyes and probed his memory for any kind of recollection.

"You're lucky you're alive, m'friend." Samuel came through the door, with Margot peering over his shoulder. "If it wasn't for Serene here, the Germans would have finished you off."

Miles jerked his eyes toward her, remembering her kneeling beside him, saying something in a soft voice, and—"That was your father?"

Serene nodded, her face coloring to a deep shade of cherry.

"Did he live?"

She shook her head, her jaw lowering.

He hated the memories that now came flooding back and he hated even more that she began crying. "I tried," he said.

Covering her eyes with both hands, she didn't meet his stare.

Buttons. He remembered her buttons falling to the floor. He lifted himself from the pillow. "Did he hurt you—that German—?" he managed to ask in an audible fashion, but the rest stuck in his throat like mud.

Samuel opened his bag. "There's time for all the questions later. Now, let's have a look at you."

Miles fixed his gaze on Serene, around Samuel, pushing away the stethoscope, his heart pumping in realization. The thought of that bastard Jerry ripping open her blouse made his temples throb harder. "Did he?" He saw her hesitate. "Wait. Don't go." He kicked off the blanket with his good leg and used his arms to leverage himself off the bed.

"Whoa. You're not going anywhere," Samuel ordered.

Miles steadied himself against the dizziness and tried again. "I need to tell her." He grunted and tried to resist Samuel's restraint, but finally slumped back on the bed and cradled his head in both hands. Pain seared up through the back of his neck. Hours or days earlier, he didn't know, she had held him with comforting arms while he cried like a baby. Talking to him in that soft, tiny voice, she had soothed away the nightmares that had overwhelmed his sleep. He didn't care much about his leg or the pain, but the pain in her face haunted him. He had to try to explain what had happened to her father and hope to God she believed him.

****

The room was cool when Miles awoke. As his eyes adjusted to the dim light, he felt life returning to his body slowly. He equated the feeling to stepping out of the house after a long winter to see the first signs of spring. Despite the pain in his lower half, his mind felt more clear, more ready to tackle the enormity of his situation.

As he attempted to piece together his memories, he looked around the bedroom. The flowery curtains and fancy stuff reminded him of his grandma's house. Even the quietness seemed similar, despite the sound of snoring coming from across the room. He spied a girl with lots of curly hair sprawled out on the chaise. He would've chuckled if his face hadn't been so bandaged and stiff.

When another woman came in the bedroom door, Miles recognized her immediately as the shopkeeper's daughter, Serry. He watched her set aside a small bowl, then throw a few new logs onto the dying fire before poking at them with a metal rod.

As Miles heard the beginnings of the warm crackle, she turned and found him staring. His face grew hot, like a boy being caught peeking in the girls' bathroom. *Jesus.* He couldn't think of a single thing to say.

She returned the rod to the metal bin. "You're awake, *Signore*," she whispered in English. "Did you sleep well?"

The sound of her voice, familiar and warm, took away any intelligent answer Miles could give. At that very moment, he swore, his tongue became glued to the roof of his mouth. So he simply nodded.

When she didn't continue the conversation, Miles glanced toward the curly head on the chaise and mumbled the first comment he could get out.

"She likes to snore."

"Margot wants desperately to be a nurse, but falling asleep isn't good, is it?"

"Guess not," Miles said, rubbing the back of his neck.

"Is the pain getting worse?"

"I think the medicine is wearing off."

"Here," She handed him two pills from the bottle on the table. "Samuel left some here. He did wonders with your leg, and these will help, too."

Miles watched her reach for a glass of water. Even in the darkened room, her skin resembled fresh cream against her exotic dark hair. They sure didn't make intoxicating girls like that in the Midwest. He pulled his eyes away from her and gulped down the water. "I'm glad you came back. You need to know what happened with your father."

"I think I know some of it."

"How could you?"

"You told stories in your dreams last night."

"I tried so hard, dammit. Your father tried to protect me from them. The krauts—Germans, I mean. They came busting in and I tried—" He stopped, feeling useless.

"Do you remember anything else?"

"It was my fault, dammit. Your father was a good man and didn't deserve to die like that."

"You weren't to know what the Germans would do."

"Still, he took me and Clay in, and tried to help, and I couldn't return the favor."

"To have yourself killed is returning a favor?"

"For three years, I have tried to save my friends. I tried, Serry, to save him, too. Don't you see? I would have taken that bullet if I'd been quicker."

Serene sat at the edge of the bed. "Why him? Why did they have to shoot him?"

"They probably followed us," he answered,

wanting to take away her torment. "Or they could have just been hungry, and we were there."

"I knew inside," she touched her chest with her fingertips, "that you helped him. That last minute of his life, Papa was so desperate to help you. I didn't understand, then. I only understood his loyalty. I trusted that. But Anna, she didn't want to take you here—"

"Maybe she was right. It was our fault. Your father took us in, fixed up my leg, and was about to get us more help. They called him a traitor for it." Miles watched Serene grimace and slammed his fist against the mattress. He knew it hurt her for him to talk about it, but it had to be said. For him to leave her in peace, it had to be acknowledged between them. "That's why they killed him. He was a decent man, and they killed him for it."

"I just knew my papa wanted to help you."

Miles reached over and wiped her cheek with the back of his hand, finding himself commiserating with a woman he didn't know yet cared about with such force. He never would understand why the Germans had shot her father but he himself had survived. But if he could help her to accept it...

"I can see why your father had so much faith in you," he said. "I can't say I would have helped someone like me, risking your family the way you have. You're putting yourself in a load of danger having me here."

"That's something you don't need to worry about right now."

"It's your practice to take in a foreigner?"

Her eyes grew to the size of olives. "No, *Signore*."

"Miss—uh—Serry, I was only making a joke," Miles said. "Back from where I come from, we laugh when things get heavy. But you did what a lot of other people would have been scared to do." His eyes narrowed. "You risked everything to bring me here. Your family. Even your own life. Lying here got me thinking about the danger you're in and how grateful I am. I can't even imagine what it must have been like for you."

"You needed help that night, and for now we're safe. You just need to get well. Anyone else would have done the same."

"I don't think they would have. I'm sorry about your father," he said. "About what happened. He was a good man to us—to me and Clay."

Serene touched his hand. "Clay was your friend?"

Miles nodded, searching her face. Her green eyes were so clear and honest. They held the kind of strength and determination that could comfort the world without actually saying a word.

When he realized he had been staring, she had already started to get up. "I brought some soup, and then you need to sleep."

"Some people are going be wondering where I am. My C.O. is dead. I don't want to put you in more danger, but is there any way to contact the U.S. Army for me and let them know I'm alive? Maybe medics? They can pick me up."

"They will not make it to the villa. Germans are hiding all over in the niches of Rome, and the outskirts of the city, closer to the coastline. Just taking a bus across town risks them asking for papers, questioning. I'm afraid if we—"

"We can wait a few days, then."

"At least until you're able to move around some."

"Before, when your sister yelled about the Americans landing, trying to get past the Germans, in army terms, it's called the Gustav Line, at Monte Cassino, an old abbey about 50 miles from here."

"I know it well."

"The Germans held the line for months. That

was part of my mission, along with the thousands of men who tried before us to break through it." He glanced away. "Our troops were buried in all kinds of caves. I hope some of my buddies made it out alive."

"I hope so, too," she said. "We'll get you home soon, *Signore* Coulson." She held out the bowl and a spoon. "In the meantime, eat the soup to gather your strength. I'm sorry it may be a little cold."

He took the bowl and tried to meet her gaze. "I'm so very sorry about your father. He was a good man." Aggravated that his words felt inadequate, he vowed to tell her sometime about her father's bravery. He wanted to take the pain from her, and put it on his own back.

On her way out, Serene crouched down beside Margot's chair. "Wake up, Margot. I'll help you to your room." Her sister moaned and sat up, at first disoriented but then slowly standing and shuffling to the door.

Turning back to the soldier, Serene asked, "Can I get you anything else?"

"I want to send a note to my girl back home. You know, let her know I'm alive. Did you find my pack anywhere? I have a pencil and paper in there."

"*Si*," she whispered. After a hesitation, she asked, "Is she, how do you say it in America, your wife?"

"Not yet, but I hope someday."

Serene nodded. "I'll be back in the morning. Anna will check on you before she goes to bed."

****

To Serene, the twenty-four hours since her father's death had passed with the speed of two lifetimes. That morning she hung a gathering of the customary three white roses on their front door, and mourners began to arrive immediately. She wandered into her father's bedroom and stared at the bed, his body covered in a sheet to his chin. The curtains were drawn, and the only light came from candles placed on the chest of drawers and a nearby table. Since her childhood, vigils had frightened her.

Unable to bring herself closer to his body, she stood rigid. Without his soul, he didn't resemble the same man she had known as her father.

Instead, she turned her gaze to the table in the front of the room, covered with a white crocheted cloth and her father's most precious belongings, including his favorite pocket watch.

She rubbed the bone at the top of her spine and arched her neck, recounting the story in her head of her father's death. *He died as part of a random ambush.* It sounded so cold and final, but the explanation would defray the questions and hopefully guarantee their safety from a Nazi storming. She budged the thought away and fingered Anthony's rosary beads, hanging off the corner of the family portrait.

"Am I doing the right thing?" she whispered to the picture. "Is it right to put our family in danger?" She already knew his answer. Her papa was a man of pride. If a person needed help, he would help and expect her to do the same. The offer never hinged on who asked or where they came from.

Lifting her black face veil to wipe away some tears, she wondered if the void her father had left would ever be filled. With her mother, the pain had dulled to an ache, but it never truly went away.

"Your Papa was a fine man." Her father's attorney, Everto Cucitto, touched her shoulder.

Dragged from her thoughts, Serene turned and held Everto's hands. "You were so good to him."

He tilted his head up to see her behind the eyeglasses perched on the tip of his nose. "As he was to me."

Harry, clad in his school uniform, tugged on

Serene's dress sleeve.

"My, you're getting to be such a young man." Everto commented, bending to see him hiding behind Serene. "You look more and more like your Papa."

With a nod, Harry stood out from behind his sister.

In a lower voice, Everto questioned Serene, "If you have time, can you come to my office tomorrow?"

"Is anything wrong?"

"Just some legal matters I was taking care of for your father."

"Your eyes are worried. I can see it."

"Get through today first." He patted her hand. "We can discuss it tomorrow."

"You're scaring me, Everto."

"It's nothing we can't get through. Be with your family now, and we'll talk tomorrow." He sipped the last drop of his coffee and lifted the empty cup upwards. "May I?"

"Please," Serene said, "help yourself." She gestured toward the silver coffeepot on the kitchen table, still wondering if his evasiveness meant something more.

Veronica came slowly into the room, her eyes glassy. "Sweetie, how could they have taken your Papa? Everyone was so happy at your dinner."

The two hugged, and Serene fought to keep herself steady. "Papa always loved you being at the restaurant, Roni."

"He gave me a chance, and I'll appreciate that for my whole life."

"When we re-open, you'll be the first to come back, no?"

"All of our lives changed because of this war. I'll help you make things right again. I know how much you love Cucina Moneto."

Another knock at the front entry quickly

interrupted their conversation. Jack and Genna Sturini stood at the door. Jack hugged Serene tightly and then stood back and held her hands; his mocha-colored eyes were puffy and lined in pink. Without any words between them, Serene could feel her own eyes become moist.

"We all loved him." Genna kissed her delicately on each cheek. Dressed in a fashionable black knit suit that fit snugly around her waistline, Genna's eyes showed barely a flicker of concern.

"It was good of you to come. How is the factory? Was the damage extensive?"

"Not as bad as we thought," Jack explained. "It will take some time, but the important thing is that, with a lot of hands, it's fixable."

Genna scowled at her husband. "Tell her the truth. It's awful. No roof, and most of the equipment has been destroyed."

"Now is not the time," Jack said, touching Serene's arm.

Genna breezed by them. "She asked, and she deserves a truthful answer. My son should be here soon. He's been working at the factory every waking hour since the bombing, right, Jack? He's a hard worker, my Marcus."

Serene nodded, motioning them into the front room, to the two empty velvet chairs. Her insides rattled at Genna's coolness. If it weren't for Jack's gentle manners, there would be nothing to smooth his wife's hard edges.

Not even a minute had passed before she heard the door again. *Marcus.* Uneasiness swept through her as he approached. He removed his hat and pulled up her veil, cupping her face in his hands. As he kissed her roughly on both cheeks, she breathed in his musky scent. Her skin stung from the soft burn of his shadowed chin.

"How did this happen? I will kill whoever did

this."

"After we left, Papa stayed, as he normally does. It was the Germans who came in. There is nothing else we can do."

"You know I will be the one to take care of things for you now?"

"Being here is enough."

"Of course I would come. No factory is worth missing this with you."

Serene managed to smile, but overwhelming dizziness forced her to steady herself against his arm. She squeezed her eyes shut and waited for it to pass. They mustn't find out about the American upstairs.

"Come," Marcus said, wrapping his hand around her waist. "Sit." He motioned to Anna to bring water and a glass of wine for himself.

"You must not be eating enough," Genna said. "You're too thin. This whole ordeal is awful. No wonder you're not eating."

"I'm eating fine," Serene said.

"Anyway, it must have been awful, dear. Such a shame. There were Americans there, too?"

"*Si*, but they were all killed. It was random," Serene retorted, her face heating at the lie.

Anna returned with a silver tray of drinks, and Serene prayed Genna's questions would end and the conversation be diverted. Marcus handed her a cup and set his glass on the table next to the sofa.

Ignoring the interruption, Genna continued. "Are you sure? That shopkeeper, what's his name, Franci? He said there were two Germans and two Americans, besides your father, of course, but when Jack went to help clean up the restaurant, there was only one American. That tag on his neck said his name was Clay something or other. Neither of them could figure out what happened to the other one. Isn't that right, Jack?"

"*Si, si,* but not now, Genna." He cast Serene an apologetic gaze.

With all that had happened, Serene couldn't remember if Franci had seen them take the American to the truck.

Genna shrugged. "The other one probably got away."

"Ran away," Marcus said and gulped the last of his wine. "They're all cowards."

Serene gazed in his direction, her pulse rushing. "How can you pass such harsh judgment without knowing the truth?"

"You talk like you know."

"I only know my father's dead. I'm willing to accept it and mourn for him. Please understand. I don't want his vigil to be marked with darkness."

"The girl is right." Jack stood. "I'm going to help prepare Anthony for the burial."

Genna didn't acknowledge Jack. "What I can't understand is why the Germans would murder an innocent restaurant owner? An *Italiano,* no less." Genna sipped her coffee. "Or maybe it was that Clay fellow, or his friend. You know how vicious those Americans can be, right?"

"No, no, I don't," Serene blurted. That vicious American tried to save my father, saved me from another man taking advantage, and he's sleeping just above your head.

"They took my son's eye with a grenade. I define that as vicious. Wouldn't you, Serene?"

"I don't know any personally," she managed to choke out, "but I do know they are trying to help free us from Hitler's hold."

"Nonsense." Genna waved her hand as if to brush away Serene's comment. "The allied forces want to take it all for themselves, and it needs to stop."

"They will save Rome." Serene ran her moist

palms across her skirt.

"You sound like your father. But your hopes are too high."

"I would rather have hope than die with no hope." During the conversation, her fear of their finding out had slowly turned to anger, then defiance. They had no right to expect her to mourn her father and defend the world's actions. "I apologize, but I need to excuse myself. Please stay and enjoy the good food people have brought. Papa would have been grateful for your kindness."

"Stay," Marcus whispered.

"I have to prepare Papa for the burial, and I need to be alone."

Marcus leaned his cheek against hers, putting his lips against her ear. "You will never be alone anymore. You are my responsibility now."

Serene tensed. *Responsibility*? She pulled from him. They would join hands in marriage, but she would never be a *responsibility*. "I need to get him ready."

Marcus held her shoulder, but she tugged it back. "Please understand." Not waiting for any further arguments, she walked out onto the porch just in time to see the black funeral carriage pull up with the empty coffin.

Chapter Six

Following the church ceremony, guests had returned to the villa. It was approaching midnight and Serene had poured as many cups of tea, coffee, and grappa as she could bear. She leaned on the stove, trying to summon the energy to bid their final guests goodbye, despite her weary body and soul. Somehow, even with her mental exhaustion, she was surviving.

She had managed to avoid Marcus and his mother but still hadn't had the opportunity to escape upstairs. They had decided that Margot would slip out of the service early, feigning sickness, and stay with the soldier until they returned.

Serene scanned the parlor to find Marcus deep in conversation with his father. Good. It seemed like a safe time, so she slipped quickly to the back of the villa and up to the third floor.

"He's asleep," Margot whispered.

"I'll sit for a while," Serene said, patting her shoulder. "Please tell whoever asks that I went to bed. I think Samuel arrived a few minutes ago." She took a deep breath, sank into the chair and closed her eyes, rubbing her temples.

"Serry? Is that you?" Miles asked in a slurred voice.

At the sound of her nickname, Serene smiled to herself and leaned closer to the bed. "*Si.*" She pulled her veil up and away from her face.

"Why am I so God-awful tired. I can't even—"

"It's the medicine. Let yourself sleep."

"What if I don't wake up?"

She tucked the cover closer to his body. "You will."

At the steady in and out of his breath, she sat back, her thoughts lingering on him. He had mentioned a girl from his own country, but his ring finger was bare. Craziness, she thought, even considering it. The man should have his privacy, regardless of her endless curiosity. Two things she knew for sure: Minnesota was his home, and his voice made her insides melt. The sooner she realized he was only a stranger who needed medical attention, the sooner she could get over this nonsense.

Marcus should have been first in her thoughts, but instead of becoming closer he was becoming an intrusion. She both liked him and feared him. Maybe the fear outweighed the like, but he deserved to have a chance. He meant well, too, but his determination to control everything got in the way. Putting all of that aside, along with Genna's inquisitions and snide remarks, his family had done so much for them through the last two days, especially Uncle Jack helping Franci to clean up the restaurant.

Right at that moment, they were downstairs, probably worried about her. Avoiding them only made her guilt worse.

Now the time had come to face them one last time before ending the night. She remembered her mother saying that strength came from deep within, from a place discovered only when times seem unbearable.

Serene realized she had found that place.

****

From the shadows in the far corner of the porch, Marcus watched Serene go to the railing and stare into the sky. His first inclination was to say her name, but instead he leaned a shoulder against the wall of the house, and studied the entire line of her body. It moved and curved in places like none of the others he had taken to his bed. That black dress hugged her rear like the fuzz on a smooth, ripe peach. She arched her neck slowly, took off her hat and veil, letting her hair drop against her shoulders and move freely in the breeze. As she leaned over and rested her palms on the iron railing, he focused on the way her slender legs dipped into those black heels. He wanted to take her right there on the cold concrete.

The arrangement had been about making a secure deal for both families, but somewhere along the course of their engagement he had become outright tantalized by her. She was as appealing as a kitten, and what a sweet conquest their wedding night would be, with him being the first man to hear her purr. Just the thought made his loins go hot.

"That's Cassiopeia," he said, moving from the rear of the porch, and pointing to the puzzle of stars.

Serene stood up straight. "I didn't know anyone was out here."

"Everyone else left an hour ago, but I knew you had to appear sometime."

"I was upstairs—resting. It's been a hard few days."

"So you said before." He paused, and then, pointing again to the sky, he traced along the string of stars making up the letter W. "Do you know the story of it?"

"Cassiopeia thought herself more beautiful than most women."

Marcus dropped his hand. "She challenged Poseidon, and to teach her humility, she was banished to the sky."

"She proved him wrong, I guess. Her cluster is the most beautiful one up there."

"Poetic," Marcus drawled. He flipped a silver lighter open, cupped the flame with his hand, and took a drag of his cigarette. He turned and leaned against the railing, facing her. "She shouldn't have defied him. It's as simple as that."

With a pensive gaze, she asked, "Even with your eye injury, if you had a choice to fight any more, would you?"

"I would, but now we are forced to recover from making weapons at my father's factory. Or what's left of his factory."

"You think it's salvageable?"

"It's not up to me. My father has the control." He opened his mouth and let out a ring of smoke that dissolved quickly into the cool air.

"You'll help, no?"

"It's not whether I want to help. He doesn't trust people when it comes to his empire."

"But you're his son."

"Of course I am, but my father needs to learn that he should be giving me more of the responsibility. For reasons I don't understand, he doesn't trust me." Marcus laughed sarcastically and wandered closer to her, motioning to the villa and land. "What are you going to do with all of this?"

"Stay. Keep it as our home." Serene folded her arms in front of her. "Margot and Harry still need to be here."

"And our arrangement? Where does that fall into the plans?"

"Arrangement?"

"The dinner we had. We're supposed to give our hands to each other soon," he said sarcastically. "Don't you remember?"

"Of course," she retorted. "I mean—with my Papa gone, is it still something we should do now?"

Marcus stamped out the cigarette slowly with the tip of his boot and moved closer to her. "It's an agreement, Serene. Your father signed a contract." He touched his hand to his chest, in half-salute fashion. "I am indebted to that contract."

"It was between our fathers. Mine is no longer here to keep up his end of it."

From the lightning in her eyes, he didn't want to agitate her any further. The details would have to come later. "It's between us now. We have the choice."

"Of course we do," Serene said, and paced to the edge of the porch, where a thickness of bare trees grew close. She whipped back around, facing him. "My father didn't sign me away without my say."

"And you said yes."

"That was before." She pushed her finger along a dipped curve in the railing's intricate pattern.

"Your father died, but that doesn't mean his wishes changed."

Serene dropped her finger, and stared at him. "As the eldest, I have bigger responsibilities now with my family. Does that matter to you?"

"To me," he said, his finger to his chest, "it is an agreement between old friends. But now that your father is gone, it may be even more beneficial to you and your family to keep it."

"As beneficial as it is to you to get a good dowry." She raised her eyebrows. "I knew my father well, and I do know you must be getting a good one."

He eyed her, surprised at her courage and the obvious challenge. She couldn't possibly know what was truly at stake. Enough money to let him be free of his father's control. Once they were married, she would need a lot of straddling, but at the moment he needed to calm his temper. He had the good sense to know that her father's vigil wasn't the place to argue, especially with her in such a state of mind. "I meant what I said in there. I'll be the one responsible for all of your needs. That is the agreement your father signed."

"Is that the agreement *you* signed?"

Marcus put his arms around her small waist and pulled her to him. "Just become my wife and stop the questions and concerns. I'll take care of everything you'll ever want or need. Our fathers brought us together, and now it's our turn to make a life with each other. Isn't that what you want?"

"I wonder if it's still the best decision. A lot has happened in two days, and my thoughts are scrambled. I need to think through all of this."

"Through what?" he asked, tightening his grip. "I'm the best for you. You have to do this for your family."

"It's not about you," she wailed and pulled her arms free. "It's about death and life, and the way we choose to act out our days in between. For my father, his life was cut too early and it left a hole right here in my heart. I want to cry and yell and moan about the unfairness of losing him so unexpectedly. But others, especially Margot and Harry, need me so desperately to keep this family knitted together, and the only mending device I can think of is time." She stopped and took a deep breath. "Please give me at least that."

Time? Marcus watched her walk down the steps toward the back of the estate and he fought the urge to follow her, knowing if they talked again he wouldn't be able to control his anger at her indecisiveness. He had plans that she wasn't going to ruin. This once, he would give her the time she asked for.

****

The inner muscles of Serene's throat squeezed away any remains of fresh air, and attempting to breathe easily proved hopeless. All she could do was walk faster. Overcome with pounding in her chest, she finally stopped at the edge of the rear yard. She kicked up each foot behind her and slipped off her platforms. Massaging her left ankle, she moaned, scanning the woods beyond the yard, and then tiptoed down the cool brick path in her stockings.

A few yards into the woods, darkness covered the old playhouse, nestled beneath the tall oak tree. She smoothed her hand over the tree's bark, sighing as her fingers extended around to the spot that boasted her carved initials. How proud she had felt when her father used his good knife to put them there. He had picked the enormous tree so Margot and Serene would have a special spot to breathe and think, whenever they needed it. And once in a while they would bring Harry along. They were only children then; her father could never have foreseen that she would run to the house as an adult.

In the moonlight, the little yellow house gleamed, despite faded wood planks and a weary steeped roof. White window boxes hung beneath the two front windows. Serene leaned closer to the boxes and took a deep breath of the January air, hoping to rekindle the scent of marigolds planted there so many springtimes before.

She swatted at some branches that blocked part of the door and then stifled a cry as she drew back her hand and plucked a thorn from the center of her middle finger. Sticking the finger in her mouth, she used her other hand to pull on the thin metal door handle. The door creaked and loosened only at the bottom. Serene stood back, put her hands on her hips, and then dropped to her knees and stuck her hand inside one of the window boxes. Pulling out the cool brass ring, she smiled and touched it to her lips.

She unlocked the door and tugged it open, just enough for her to straddle the remaining thicket. Stooping down to go in, she didn't need to squint through the darkness—her heart held every inch of it in memory. Near the door was a child-sized wooden table and two chairs. Red-checked curtains adorned the two small windows. The back part of the room was just big enough for a makeshift doll bed. She held back a laugh, remembering her anger when Margot had bounced her little red ball incessantly while Serene tried to put her doll Ginny to bed. Poor Ginny. She couldn't remember what had happened to her.

Serene sat in the corner and hugged her knees to her chest. How she wished she could be that child again and live through a child's eyes. To be able still to dream about helping her Papa run the business and someday having a family of her own.

The image of Marcus' brooding, dark face, questioning her on the porch, made her stomach hurt. She closed her eyes, wishing the picture away, but his words stayed close, still stinging with a truth she had been avoiding. Ultimately, her promise to her father would force her to marry him, not Marcus' assurance of security, of a solid future. The realization made her body quake harder.

She draped a dusty doll blanket across her legs and wept. For the first time since her father's death, she wept for herself.

****

Miles awoke in the morning to soft laughter. Margot, whom he'd figured out was Serry's sister, stood to the left of the bed, and Samuel on the other side. He couldn't understand a word of their conversation, but the girl was swinging her hair around and he swore one of those curls might strangle someone, including herself. She was flirting with the doc like a son-of-a-gun.

"You're awake." Samuel told the girl something in Italian, and she glanced at Miles before quickly leaving the side of the bed. "Show me where the pain is."

Miles pointed to the outer side of his shin. The throbbing came in spurts and rolled up and down his leg with the weight of a rolling pin.

65

Samuel got closer, palpating the skin along the edges of the uncovered wound. "We'll watch it. The infection has traveled some since yesterday. The good news is that the healing process has started. We'll need to change the dressing every few hours." He motioned to Margot. "She can help with the dressings." He took a vial from his pack and sucked the morphine out with a syringe. "She doesn't know English but we can improvise a little."

"Is she your girl?"

Ignoring the question, Samuel rolled Miles on his side, swabbed a spot with alcohol, and stabbed an injection into Miles' left buttock.

"Ouch. I guess that means yes?"

Samuel half-smiled and said something to Margot in Italian. She left and returned with a basin.

"I guess you're not going to let me in on it?" Miles asked dryly, wishing the throbbing in his head would subside.

"We're almost done, I want to re-bandage a few of these smaller cuts on your chest, and then we'll do your leg."

As he finished, Serene came in the room.

"Ah. Just in time," Samuel said. "I want to show both you girls how to change the bandages."

"*Buongiorno, Signore* Coulson," Serene said. "Are you feeling better?"

Miles watched her approach the bed. Her accent, thick and husky, had started to sound familiar. "A little. With all this swell care, a guy can't ask for much more than that."

Samuel unraveled the dressings from the lower part of Miles' leg and tossed them in the basin. "Here, Serene, take this." He handed her an arm's length of cloth. "Wrap around the lower part in a circular motion. Use only slight pressure, not too tight. We want to promote healing, not suffocate the

66

wound."

Rubbing her hands together quickly, she sat at the edge of the bed. As she lifted his foot to her lap, the new bandage slipped to the ground and, trying to grasp it, the back of her hand tapped against the raw wound.

Miles fought the scream as the searing pain went straight up his leg into his upper body.

"I'm so sorry! Please, Sam, you do it."

"You're doing fine." Miles clenched his teeth. "I can handle it."

Serene frowned and re-started the first wrap, fumbling with it at each turn. "Am I hurting you?"

"No." *It hurt like hell.* But her eyes, green like grass, forced him to keep his manners in check.

"Here, let me show you." Samuel said, heaving a sigh of irritation and pulled the wrap from Serene's hands.

Serene's face reddened, and she moved aside, clasping her hands in front of her nervously.

"Like this, see?" He corrected the position of the cloth and secured the next wrap.

"She was easier on me." With his nails sunk into his palms, Miles could see that his new friend Samuel had to learn some tact when it came to women.

"I can do it." Serene elbowed him out of the way and sat back down, glancing at Miles. "Let me know if I hurt you."

Wetness ran down his back, but in a million years Miles wouldn't have told that gorgeous face if anything hurt. Instead, he grabbed fistfuls of sheet and squeezed. *Holy Joe.*

Samuel cut in. "That should be the last one."

When Serene secured it and finished, she pulled the sheet over his leg, her hand grazing his knee. "Next time it will be better, I promise."

Laughing, Samuel handed Margot the full basin.

"That's why your sister is going to be the nurse."

"Easy there, doc. It wasn't that awful." Miles stretched out the stiffness in his knuckles, winking at Serene.

Her face brightened against the deep walnut color of her hair. She didn't have the wild hair like her sister. It was calmer and shiny, twisted in a fancy hairdo in the back.

"I'll be back tomorrow," Samuel said. "I'll bring a wheelchair to get you up and out of this room. Not too far, but at least to get you moving."

"I'll do anything to get me out of this bed, but no wheelchair. My muscles are getting used to this relaxation, but I'm not. I want to walk out of this room."

"Your leg won't be ready for that kind of pressure for at least longer than you want to be in this room."

"I'm going outta here on my own."

"There really is no question here. The chair will simply help you get around until you're able."

Miles held his jaw firm.

"How about a wager?" Samuel asked. "If you're no better in a few days, you can go back to the bed."

Both of them knew going back to the bed was not a probability, and Miles wanted out of the bed as much as he didn't want to be put in the chair. "Fine."

"And Serene can get you a shave, too."

Miles ran his hand over his chin, finding a thick, new growth. "I can do it myself."

With a laugh, Serene raised her eyebrows. "I've never shaved a man before, but I can become an expert with anything these days, no?"

"No." He tried not to laugh. "If you would just give me a straightedge, I'll take care of this scruff myself."

"Not with those shaky hands, you're not," Samuel said. "Let Serene do it. We don't need you losing any more skin."

"*Non capisco*," Margot moaned irritably.

"I know. We need to get you English lessons, m'love."

Margot quipped something back at him and hurried out of the room.

Serene listened to their banter, feeling that familiar envy creep up her spine. When Margot and Sam were together, their strong wills certainly clashed at times, but Serene guessed it was the reason they were so attracted to each other.

"If you don't mind me asking, what's eating her? How come she doesn't speak English and you all do?" Miles asked.

"She had the chance to study English, but she didn't take it. Maybe because the sun wasn't shining that day."

When he raised his eyebrows at the description, Serene chuckled. "There was no real reason. She didn't want to learn the language. Papa encouraged her, but she had no interest."

"I'll tell you why." Samuel said. "Pure stubbornness. It's a Moneto trait."

Serene swatted him playfully on the back. "I'm not stubborn. You can't name any one time."

"Is that a challenge?" Samuel retorted artfully.

"Absolutely not. Come, give me the rest of the dressings, and then you can get back to the hospital."

"Go ahead, Sam." Miles prompted him. "Answer that. I'd like to know." He put his hands behind his head and waited.

"Stop, Samuel," Serene said, feeling her face grow hot. "This is silly. This man doesn't want to hear. It's, well, it's embarrassing."

"How about just one little story, Dr. Sam? A fella that just got shot up needs sleep, but I think I have time for one story."

Samuel put his hands together in a prayer position and put them up to his mouth, walking the length of the room. "Let me see. Ah, ha. The luck of the Irish is with me. I do know one."

"Not the sauce story. Please..." Serene moaned.

"A woman came into the Cucina Moneto, in Rome, for a meal, and I caught some of her conversation with Serene. The woman's husband had complained that her sauce had lost its zing, so the woman left him without giving him dinner. This exhausted woman sat there for an hour gibbering to Serene about how she had slaved over the sauce and couldn't quite get it right. Then, much later, the woman's husband came to the restaurant and demanded his wife come home with him. Well, our girl Serene wouldn't let her."

"Stop, Samuel, it wasn't like that!"

"Like the fightin' Irish, Serene wouldn't let the husband take his wife home until she, herself, showed *him* how to make red sauce on his own."

"That's the story?" Miles asked. "There's no cat's meow about making sauce. Hell, give me a pot and a tomato, and even I can make it."

Serene burst out laughing.

"Well then, I'll be on my way." Samuel said, feigning an insult. "And see what else is *eating* Margot, as you said it so elegantly, Coulson. But the minute you're up to it, I'll be expecting a big pot of your famous Minnesota sauce. For now, I'll be back tomorrow."

"I should leave you to your rest, too," Serene said, fixing his blankets.

"How did you ever meet a doctor from Ireland?"

"Samuel planned to finish out his internship at the local hospital and then go back to Ireland. Then the war started and all traveling outside the country ceased. He stopped at the restaurant one day, and Margot felt sorry for him and gave him a free meal.

From then, they became inseparable, and Margot declared she was becoming a nurse."

"Am I her first patient?"

Serene nodded. "Samuel insisted that she should start practicing her schoolwork at home, and what better way—"

"Is it serious between them?"

"Sam seems to understand her, really understand her dramatic ways, far more than most people. Now, you really need your rest, *Signore* Coulson."

"Would you please call me Miles?"

"Yes, uh, Miles," Serene stuttered, keenly aware that she had not used his first name before. Feeling her cheeks grow warm, she quickly changed the subject. "I brought the paper and pencil from your pack. You still want to write a letter, *no*?"

"To my girl back home. Let her know I'm still alive."

"They black out information they don't want leaving the country. We'll put a phony name and address on it, and you mustn't sign your name." She stopped and took a breath, realizing she was spinning words quicker than wool on a wheel.

"I'll write it in secret code then." Miles grinned.

Serene ignored his attempt to add humor. "If they find out I'm harboring a soldier, they will storm in here, and we'll disappear. I've seen it happen to neighbors, not just for holding a person, but for practically any action that defies them."

"I didn't mean to fool around about it. I just wanted to make you feel better."

"It's become such a horrible way to live. Going to bed at night and hoping, praying that everyone will still be in their beds when morning comes."

"But I thought you were safe if you supported the fascists."

"Not us. Our history plagues us, especially with

my father's ways. He hated Mussolini and his men because they broke down true Italian principles, and it sat above us like a dark cloud. With old Italian ways, and celebrating our own principles, we're the kind of people the fascists want to destroy." Her eyes swelled with tears.

"Mussolini is dead. His people can't touch you now."

Serene sat at the edge of the bed. "You're wrong. Until the day all of his men die, they will still go after the resistance. There are bugs all over the city." She lowered her voice. "They even put them in people's homes."

"Here?"

"Not here. Papa had the house checked not too long ago. But I don't want to scare you, and we can keep you here for as long as you like. Even though we have an armistice with your country, we are not even close to being safe. I don't know what safe is anymore."

"Forget about the letter. I don't want to risk anything."

Serene disregarded his statement with the swoosh of her hand. "I know the workings of my country. I like to say I know who to trust, but really, it's a feeling in my stomach. The person I know performs miracles when it comes to getting correspondence across the seas. He's from the underground movement at the Vatican. A brother to one of my friends."

"You sure?"

She nodded quickly, determined to take in a steady breath. In truth, worrying about keeping him there kept her awake at nights. But, despite the danger, she liked having him near.

"The last thing I want to do is put you in more jeopardy." He rested his hand on the lower part of her arm.

The warmth of his fingers spread over her body, and she desperately tried to ignore the overwhelming feeling of compassion that overtook her senses. She forced her lips into a steady smile. "God gives me only what I can handle."

"Much more than most," he said.

Serene didn't move or breathe, overtly aware of his hand kneading her arm. She wrestled with the urge to use her other hand to cover his. Her heart pounded recklessly, and she wanted to jump and dance and fret at the same time.

He continued talking, seemingly unaware of her quandary. "I can't wait to move around on my own and get this bum leg working again, so I can get back out there."

"You just need to get well, and I'll take care of the rest." Ever so casually, unable to resist the temptation, she gently placed her hand over his. "And trust me."

"If I didn't trust you and your family, I wouldn't still be here. You must know that, Serry."

"I do," she whispered. "I'll be back a little later for the letter."

Chapter Seven

"I'm sorry, Serene, but that's all there is." Everto Cucitto removed his gold eyeglasses from the lower half of his nose and folded his hands on the stack of financial papers sitting on the desk in front of him.

Serene sat across from him in one of the two maroon leather wing chairs, clutching her handbag with both gloved hands. "Even Cucina Moneto in Rome has a debt against it?" she asked, her lips shaking.

Everto nodded. "It's a shock, I know."

"That one has been in the Moneto family since the beginning." Her eyes brimmed with fresh tears. "How can that be?"

"Things happen when you own a business." Everto stood and pushed the chair away from the desk, tugging his tweed vest down over his stomach. "Your father needed help managing things."

Serene jumped up, dropping her handbag on the chair behind her. "Managing what?" She knew him well enough to prod him for the truth. "Please, Everto," she said, leaning forward, her palms resting on the desk. "Tell me why there is so much debt?"

Everto strolled to one of the long, thin windows, overlooking the street. His protruding belly rested against the glass.

Serene went closer. "If my father stood in this spot, you would tell him what he wanted to know. He trusted you with our family."

"Come, Serene, sit down." He touched her elbow and ushered her to the sofa.

The meeting had become much more than a

review of the family assets, and it scared Serene. She pulled off her gloves and waited as he unplugged the top from the crystal decanter and poured himself a drink.

When he offered her one, she shook her head with impatience.

"After your mother became ill, your father lost control of the restaurants, at least the business end. I did a lot of the paperwork for him, but he handled most of the financial parts, like the employee payment and ordering supplies. But it was hard for him, running from restaurant to restaurant and taking care of your mother..."

"And trying to taking care of us."

Everto loosened his tie. "You children had Anna, which helped tremendously, but the day-to-day activities the business needed, those he couldn't do by himself. So, he hired Georgie. You remember him, no?"

"Of course. He managed the restaurants for a long time. I loved him as a brother."

Everto gulped the last of the drink and grimaced. "Yes, but I didn't know about him until much, much later."

"Georgie used to play with us sometimes, at the restaurant in Naples," Serene explained. "When Papa was busy, that is. He used to crawl underneath the tables and pretend to be a lion. How Margot would scream. And Harry would try to protect her." Serene clasped her hands around her knees and chuckled sadly. "Harry was only a baby then."

The glass trembled in Everto's hands. "Harry was four years old, to be exact."

Serene raised her eyebrows and gently took the glass from him. The smell of the brandy shocked her nostrils and cleared away any remaining wetness around her eyes. "You're scaring me."

"You must believe me, Serene. I didn't know any

of it." He took a white handkerchief from his pocket and wiped it across his forehead.

"What, Everto? You didn't know any of what? What does Georgie have to do with this? He left to go live with an aunt in America."

"No," Everto said, "if only that were the case. The day after your mother passed away, he called your father and told him if he didn't pay him a ransom, your family would never see Harry again."

"What?" Serene's eyes opened in horror. "Did he take Harry?"

"Yes. Georgie took him from his bed that morning. You girls were with your Aunt Lucia, preparing food for your mother's vigil. Anna didn't notice until she checked on him an hour later. They were long gone by then."

"How could we have not known about it? Or why don't I remember it?" The days surrounding her mother's death were so clear, like an ageless picture, especially the day of which Everto spoke.

"Your father did everything in his power to protect you, and to protect his family from the scandal and shame it would bring. If he didn't, you children would never have a future. Putting aside all the scandal, he still tried to get through the death of his wife. People take advantage of others in your father's situation."

Anger shot through her. "Papa gave Georgie the money?"

"Georgie dropped Harry at St. Peter's Square, took the money, and your father never heard from him again."

"You didn't try to stop him?"

"It was only a few years ago that your father told me." Everto got up and reached for the decanter, then dropped his hand. "He had to tell me. Frankly, I think it was killing him. He gave Georgie everything he had. Eventually he had to take loans to keep the restaurants. For a long time he had been running his business like that, taking loans and trying to repay them. Anthony did it all without ever saying a word to me. He did the best he could, but he could barely meet the bills month after month."

Serene twisted a short tendril of hair that escaped from beneath her small brimmed hat. "How can I salvage all of the three restaurants and take care of my family at the same time? How, Everto?"

"There's more." He cleared his throat.

Barely digesting all that he had told her, Serene took a deep breath and couldn't imagine the worst had not come. "*Si?*"

"Another reason he couldn't meet the bills was your marriage arrangement."

"Papa told me about the arrangement just the night of the engagement dinner. How long has he been committed to the Sturinis?"

"The day he adopted you officially, he arranged it with Jack Sturini. Marcus was just a baby himself."

"No..." She held onto the words with disbelief. "And he never told me?" She fought to understand all he was telling her. "He'd risk his business for a dowry?"

Everto readjusted his vest and returned to the desk to put his glasses on. He picked up a paper, crumpled it, and threw it across the desk. "He wanted so much for you to have a comfortable life, Serene, so much that he committed himself to paying me a set amount each month. All of this so he could give you a decent dowry. Please believe that I didn't know until much later about the other debts, or I would never have let this happen. He could have used that money elsewhere."

"Why would he—"

"He knew there would be shame if there ever came a day that he didn't have the money to give you, and you would end up like—"

"My mother?" Serene's eyes stung with venomous tears.

Everto didn't answer.

"What happened wasn't my mother's fault. Anna explained the entire story to me. The boy left her. It wasn't her choice. Everyone knew that, especially my father."

"Even still, he made a vow to your mother that he would protect you from the threat of being alone and make sure you had a good husband, one that would provide for you. A good dowry would give you all that. With your mother so sick, he wanted it all the more."

Serene couldn't bear to hear any more. "I can use the dowry money, then, to pay off the loans and restart the business."

"Only when the marriage is made to Marcus Sturini, and no one else, will the dowry money reach your hands."

"The money will be his?"

"Your father couldn't foresee his untimely death, Serene. He would never have left you like this if it were otherwise. After your marriage, you will be able to pay off those loans and move on with your life. You must believe me, you won't have any worries."

Serene's patience hung on a spider web. She ran her finger over the porcelain Madonna statue sitting in the center of the fireplace mantel. "Our marriage isn't planned for months. Can I do anything to pay the bills on my own?"

Everto exhaled slowly. "I spoke with the officer from *Banca di Roma.*" He shuffled the papers around and pulled out two. To pay off the two largest loans, you must sell at least the restaurants in Sicily and Naples, which will probably cover the majority of the debt. You can hold onto the one in Rome for now."

"No one will buy during a war. I couldn't sell."

Everto's graying brows came together. "Serene, listen to me. The bank won't wait. Your father was well respected, but there isn't an option for a debt of this magnitude, and we're in wartime."

"I won't sell," she said in a fierce whisper.

"If you decide to sell," he said evenly, "you can do it once this war has ended. The rumor is that it will end soon. I know you can't count on that, but the little that is left will get you through until it is over."

Until it is over? Serene studied the ground from the third-story window. German soldiers patrolled the outside of the building, resembling a cluster of ants searching for a hole to get warm. None of it will ever be over, she thought bitterly.

"Marry Marcus like you had already planned, but sooner. Make it easy for yourself, and you'll be able to keep all three restaurants and lead a comfortable life. Margot and Harry will not need to worry, either. Your father suffered much to save this money for you. You should do what is right, Serene. Otherwise, you risk losing it all."

Serene crossed her arms. "How much will Marcus get?"

Everto dropped the paper on the desk and put a hand to the side of his jaw. "Enough to buy you four villas in the finest area outside Vatican City."

"What? How could my father have possibly saved that much? No wonder the business was suffering." Suddenly, the assurances Marcus had made to her the night before popped into her head. She backed against a wall and tossed them over in her mind a few times until her eyes widened in realization. "Marcus knows, doesn't he?"

"Jack knew. Not how much it would be, but he knew his son would receive a considerable sum. Whether he divulged it to his son, I don't know. You have to believe I didn't know about the money Georgie took."

"It's the money. He wants it," she blurted.

"He's following through with your father's wishes."

Serene shook her head. "There's more to it than that. I can feel it."

"It's tiredness you're feeling. Go home and rest. Think about this, and we'll talk again."

"When we marry, how can I be sure Marcus will give me the money to rebuild and pay the loans?"

"He's a good man. You have to trust in what your father planned for you. But I know how hard this is for you, and I'll help you as much as I can."

"How could my father have made this so difficult for me?" Her voice didn't waver, and without waiting for an answer she continued, "I can't sell any of the restaurants. No matter what my father did to get us into this mess, I can't sell off my family's heritage. Those restaurants were his life." She put her hand over her heart. "And they were my life, too. Those are the last memories of my whole family together. It would be like selling our memories, our lives together. And our future."

Everto walked around the desk and held her shoulders. "You were his life. He only wanted you to be happy and secure. Marry Marcus and be happy. You need that security. Not just for you, but for your family. That's all your father wanted."

****

Serene stepped from Everto's building and pressed her back against the stone wall, gulping the cold air. She took in the molten sky, seeing neither beginning nor end to the weary clouds.

Walking through the soldiers to reach the bus stop, she kept her head up and her eyes forward. The next bus came within a few minutes. Plopping into the first vacant seat, she sucked in a weighted breath and leaned her head against one of the small, dirty windows, welcoming the ride home.

Everto's words strummed at her heart as she watched the bell tower, with a huge crucifix sculpted on the top, pass by in a slow, agonizing motion. The noon chime hadn't sung in nearly three years.

She opened her purse and took out a leather fold where she kept her identification papers. From the main pocket, she slipped out a small picture of her parents and rubbed her fingertip across her father's broad smile as the bus pulled aside to let a German tank pass, the bus windows shaking like paper.

Serene stifled a sob. She needed the dowry money to take care of her family; she couldn't put off marrying Marcus. Besides providing for her family, it was the only way of realizing her dream to restore the restaurants, a purpose she couldn't ignore. With old customers and good cooking skills, she could lead a happy life. Marcus could have his life, and she could have hers, too.

A thread of hope crept into her heart as she watched the first drips of rain trickle down the windows. For years her father had paid on the secret debt to protect his family. It must have been a worrisome, wrenching way to live. She chewed her lip and pushed the picture back into her purse, twisting the clasp shut.

One principle her father had taught her about drawing up a successful business relationship was to formulate a solid understanding between the two partners. Her relationship with Marcus would be no different. In her gut, she pushed aside the feeling that Marcus was in it for the money. Maybe he would back out if she accused him of that. No, it was too lucrative an agreement for him to back away. He needed her. And, sadly, now she needed him, too.

His claims of wanting to take care of her and support her were just a ploy to gain her affection.

But one question prickled at her the most: Why did he want her money, when his father had made his own fortune?

She could never refuse to honor her father's request that she marry Marcus, but now the impending relationship had become much more than she imagined. It became about money, hers and his, and how she was going to access enough of it to support her family and rebuild the restaurants. Marrying him was the only way. An arrangement. A deal. A lucrative plan she would propose to him. That's all it would be. No feelings. Certainly no love.

Serene traced a raindrop scurrying toward the bottom of the window. First, she would tell him the marriage was on, and she would marry him. Any other plans between those two actions she would still need to figure out. Sealing the agreement meant never looking back, and never, ever wondering about truly loving a man.

She clutched her purse tighter. Such a simple plan. It stung.

****

"I prayed when you left that Everto wouldn't tell you something bad." Anna didn't take her eyes from the large pot of minestrone soup she was stirring.

"Nothing too bad." Serene unwound the scarf from around her neck and leaned over the pot, sniffing. She waved her hand in front of her nose, feeling her eyes water.

"Lots of onion is good for the soul." Anna stopped stirring and turned to Serene. "Everything from your Papa was in order?"

"*Si*." If she told another lie, Serene knew a wart would grow on her chin.

"Was it something bad?"

Serene hung her coat on the hook. It hurt to even think about what she had just learned; she wasn't ready to talk about it with anyone, including

Anna. "It's raining out there. Doesn't everyone appear disheveled when it rains?"

Anna stopped stirring the soup. "Sit. I'll make you some coffee."

Serene smiled at her compassion. One minute she mimicked a nervous old woman and the next she presented the softness of an indulgent grandmother. Of course Serene preferred the latter, a mother who was looking only for their best interests. Still, Samuel's concern about Anna's loyalty cropped up in the back of Serene's thoughts.

"Anna, I've wanted to ask you—well, about things going on here."

"Will I be leaving once you marry *Signore* Marcus?"

"Why would you ask that?"

Anna handed her a cup. "You probably won't need me, once the house is—filled."

"We'll always need you here. Nothing about that will change, no matter who is in this house."

"Of course, *Signorina.*"

"Who else could I fight with about cooking?"

From the side, Serene could see Anna's mouth curl in a small smile. As far back as she could remember, Serene had always wanted to cook at home. But their kitchen was technically Anna's territory, and she didn't give up her spoons and pans easily. Many times Serene had resigned herself to watching Anna with the eyes of a hawk, learning how to season fish and knead dough. It was in Cucina Moneto's kitchen that she had learned how to blend simple ingredients, like chocolate sauce or fruit plates, and then only when the dining room had few patrons.

"Anna?"

"Hmm?"

"How about I prepare our afternoon meal tomorrow? Maybe polenta, or ravioli?"

Anna raised her eyebrows. "Then what will my job be?"

"Take a day to do something for yourself. It's been a long time."

"My job is here. I'll take care of the meals. You take care of that man and get him well."

"Do you feel better about things here? About him being here, I mean? The vigil went fine, and no one seemed to question anything."

Her only answer was the sound of the spoon clinking against the inside of the pot, playing rhythmically with the rain spattering the windows.

Serene went to her. "I wish you could understand and not hold your fear in. You must know that you're truly a part of this family and not just a servant. We care about your feelings, too."

"*Signore* Miles is getting better, and once he is well, you said he would leave." Anna turned her head slightly, giving Serene a cool stare. "That was the promise you made."

"Yes." Serene crossed her arms in front. "But he is certainly not yet well enough to leave, and it's not fair to make him feel unwanted."

"Did he tell you that?"

"We should make him feel as if he belongs here, too, if only for a short while."

Anna mumbled that the soup was burning and dragged the pot off the stove. "Death comes to those who hide things."

"That may be for others," Serene said, trying to control the exasperation in her voice, "but I believe we made the right decision about this. As I've said before, I'm not forcing you to stay."

"I have no choice." The spoon slipped from Anna's hand and landed at the bottom of the pot of soup with a thud. "There is nowhere else to go."

"Because you belong here."

"I'm scared, but I'm forcing myself to follow the

Lord's mission for me. *Signore* Miles is a nice man, but I worry if they find him here."

"They won't!" Serene declared it as forcefully as she could. "Once the Americans come into Rome, we'll all be saved."

"They couldn't save your father."

Serene froze, hearing the venom in her voice. "If you decide, Anna, I'll understand if you need to go be with Eluina."

"My sister? Sweet mother of the blessed Virgin! Naples is under attack, too. I pray day and night for them." Anna lifted the cross from the chain around her neck and kissed it lightly. "I can't go there now."

The sorrow in Anna's eyes deepened Serene's worries. Holding her by the shoulders, Serene turned her squarely to face her. "The risk you are taking for us is admirable. It means the world to all of us, especially me. You realize that, *no?*"

"If I don't get back to it, this soup won't cook by itself. And *Signore* Miles needs the food. He's too thin."

Serene stared at her for a second, decided the argument wasn't going to get either of them anywhere, and helped her fish the spoon from the bottom of the pot.

To Anna, food filled the void between the sun and stars. If she made you one of her specialties, it meant she liked you. In this case, she might not like Miles or the idea of having him there, but she had made the minestrone soup for him. In her mind, if you ate good, you felt good. Giving Miles something as minor as soup was a good start toward getting him out of the house.

Serene touched her arm. "Isn't there anything else I can do to make you feel better?"

"Nothing. Just get the man well."

Getting Miles Coulson well had already become a mission that Serene wanted desperately to finish.

Chapter Eight

When Serene came into her mother's room carrying a pitcher of water, Miles was sitting upright in bed, leaning toward the window.

"You got a lot of property here. That barn is huge, bigger than ours back home. You must have tons of animals. What do you raise?"

Serene put the pitcher on the table. "We used to have many cows, chickens, but now we only have one horse left, Margetta—" She stopped herself in mid-sentence, transfixed by him, by the difference in his face. The growth that covered his chin and neck had disappeared, leaving his face fresh and new and young; even the gray color in his skin was replaced by a healthy pink.

Miles inspected himself. "Oh, the shirt. Anna brought it to me. She doesn't speak English well, and she kept saying 'Anthony,' so I figured it must have been your father's. If you want me to take it off, I will."

"It's fine," she said briskly, her face growing warm. Her feeling had nothing do with the shirt being her father's. Just seeing the new life in his face, in his spirit, made her insides jelly. This broken-down soldier was now ready to take on the world.

"I hope you don't mind."

Serene struggled to pull her gaze from him. "Of course not. Would you rather sit by the window? I can help you into the chaise."

"The window won't show me the inside. Will you give me a tour when I'm up and about? A fancy barn like that deserves better than a glance."

"Fancy?"

"Meaning it's a swell barn."

She laughed. In all the years they'd had the cows, she had hardly even noticed the inside of the barn.

"Why are you laughing?"

"In all of Rome, and all the sites I can show you, you pick the barn?"

"I didn't realize you would be interested in taking me on tours. You're on. I'll go anywhere you think is good. But the first stop is the barn."

"Does your head feel better?" The bandage that had covered his entire head had been replaced by a smaller, square one. Without the bulkiness around his forehead, his eyes stood out on their own, narrowing inward toward the bridge of his nose. Their color reminded her of a bluebird.

"Samuel removed the bandage last night. I did the shave myself, after all." He smoothed his hand over his chin. "Feels good, and no cuts."

"And your leg?"

"Much, much better." He laughed. "Sam said I could keep it. And soon I'll be on my way."

"It seems so soon for you to leave."

"As soon as Doc Sam says I'm fine, I'm going back to the front, or home, or wherever I can make it." He raked his fingers through his hair. "Anna wants me gone in the worst way."

"You think that's what we all want? Anna has been against this from the beginning. There is no talk in the piazza, and people think both Americans died that night at our restaurant. We're all afraid—she's afraid too, but she just doesn't understand the reasons why I brought you here." She sat on the bed beside him, somehow closer than she'd intended. "She doesn't understand what my Papa wanted—"

"He was a brave man. And he would be very

proud of you, too."

Serene shook her head, feeling the warmth of his palm on the skin of her forearm. An overwhelming sense of attraction overcame her, enough that she could sense her face reddening. "Do you have that letter you wanted to send? I'll see what I can do about sending it."

He took an envelope from under his pillow and handed it to her. "Josie must be going nuts with worry. I wrote to her almost every single day before this."

"I'll try my best. I know how hard it is to be away from those people you love so much."

"Yeah." His voice was dulled. Miles studied her for a second. "I met her in high school, and she considered us the marrying type."

"And you didn't?"

"Not then. I didn't want to be tied down unless I had to be. I had enough of that at home with my father."

"I'm sure he must not have liked you leaving. No parent likes to see his child go to war."

"It's more than that. My mom left us when I was a baby, and he was left holding the bag. Dad had to take care of me all those years by himself. He wanted the best for me, but it turned out not the way he expected, with me volunteering for the draft. It made him mad. For me to settle down with Josie was something he wanted more than I did. Now, hitching up doesn't seem like such a bad idea anymore—"

"Shouldn't you at least let him know you're all right?"

"He up and died a few months after I enlisted."

"Oh, I'm so sorry." After a pause, she asked, "Did you get to tell him how much you cared for him before you left?"

"No. I wish I had, though. I'll feel sorry about

that until the day I die."

"Cherish the time you had with him. I didn't have my Mama long enough at all," she blurted, then realized she was probably telling him too much.

"I want to hear about her."

"Sometime. Right now, I think you should rest. And I apologize for how Anna has been acting toward you. I talked with her, and she'll try to be nicer."

"I have a feeling Anna does what she wants."

Serene laughed. "You're only here a short time and you've figured her out. Smart man."

"Beautiful girl."

With a twinge in her abdomen, her eyes leapt to his and she came closer, as if it were a natural thing between the two of them.

Breaking the moment, Miles took her hand. "You didn't know me from any other Joe. Your father died, and you didn't even know if I was the one who put the bullet in him. You took me in like a stray dog and saved my life. No matter how long I live, I'll never be able to repay your selflessness. It kills me to see how much Anna hates what you did. She huffs and puffs around here as if I'm going to hurt her. Because of the threat it means to you, I'll leave as soon as I can."

"You don't need to worry about me."

"You're not a girl that a guy can easily stop worrying about, you know that? For now, if you will have me for just a few more days, I'm just an MIA. Samuel said when I'm ready I can make the necessary arrangements through him."

****

Serene stood at the outside of the room, breathless, holding the letter. She closed her eyes and fanned her face with it, trying to regain her composure. Talking with Miles comforted her in an odd sort of way that played havoc with her insides.

Not a bad havoc, but one that made her lose her breath and tremble like a scared rabbit.

Taking a deep breath, she scanned the outside of the cream-colored envelope. It was yellowed and dirty in spots, but the name on the front was written clearly in black ink: Josie Jefferson. A Minnesota address. No return address. With shaky fingers, she turned the envelope over and rubbed her thumb across smooth paper. She put it close to her eyes, almost relieved to find no gaps in the seal. Would she really have dared to read it? In an ordinary situation, probably not, she surmised, tapping the envelope a few times. But this was no ordinary situation.

The contents of the letter tempted her innermost curiosity. She could only imagine the words, words that would say how much Miles missed Josie, how much he desired to be back in her arms. A little pang jabbed her stomach. Jealousy? She had never known jealousy, except the tinge of envy when Margot first met Samuel.

Miles had a commitment to someone else, and so did she. But still, when she talked with him, she had these feelings she couldn't put aside. Maybe she knew how much he needed to be taken care of. Her father had needed that for so long, it almost was a natural reaction for her. She laughed, thinking it positively hideous that it took less than a minute to explain away her attraction to him. It wasn't an attraction, she decided. It more resembled a girl liking a boy. Margot had had hundreds of such likings, and they became the topic of humor with her family. Never with Serene. She had never met anyone who made her lose her words and all five of her senses.

Turning the letter back over, she tried hard to swallow back the smile that sat at the edge of her lips, begging to come out.

She tapped her index finger on the envelope. In a matter of days, he would be gone. And it would be better for her if he left sooner rather than later. It would be ridiculous to make him leave before he was ready. But then she could stop tormenting herself with thoughts of him. Thoughts of his dusty blond hair and those eyes that bore deep into her soul.

He had to go back. But back where? To the States, a million miles away, or back to the streets of Rome, where the Germans were waiting? She bit her lip and said a silent prayer that his recovery would take just a little longer, and then she promised to send him away.

****

In the center of the Vatican, Serene met the underground coordinator in front of the statue of the Virgin Mary. Like a tourist, she made the sign of the cross, kissed the tips of her fingers and pretended to drop her purse, then placed the letter at Mary's feet. A few yards away, she glanced casually back just in time to see Veronica's brother Davido slip the letter into his coat pocket. Feigning the letter was for a friend of a friend, she had cleared the delivery with Veronica the previous day.

Another ten-minute bus ride brought her to the Sturini factory, where guilt swept through her as she wondered how big the bomb had been that hit the factory and realized that, even after her words with Marcus on the night of her father's vigil, not once had she gone there to see the damage. She stepped out of the bus and examined the massive two-story building. The front section of the top floor was shaved off, so that it resembled an open dollhouse. From the street you could see each room and crevice.

Serene maneuvered her way through the onlookers and up the steps. After pushing through the front doors, she entered the large reception area, where sunshine streamed in through the small windows, creating ribbons of light in the dust and debris.

A petite woman with waist-length dark hair brushed soot from the desk. "We're not open, as you can see," she said in a silky voice, keeping her head down.

"I'm looking for Marcus Sturini."

"And you are?"

"Serene Moneto."

The woman surveyed her. "Let me check. He's a busy man." She disappeared through the double doors behind her.

While waiting, Serene tiptoed between pieces of rubble to examine the standing gray walls that still outlined the reception area. The missing pieces from the stone wall made it resemble a jigsaw puzzle. The few pictures that had survived the blast were of the Sturini family.

Her eyes drifted to the largest, the center-most, a photograph of Jack Sturini with Mussolini. Resembling old friends, *Il Duce* was smiling as Jack held up a sign that read "Italy's Finest Spaghetti." Serene was surprised, since Jack had always sided with her father in detesting the fascists. She assumed the picture must have been taken before Mussolini forced the Sturini factory to make weapons.

In another photo, Jack held up a handful of spaghetti with his arm around his wife, Genna. Marcus, not more than four or five years old, stood just in front of them in a salute. His mouth and eyes were wide open as if ordering a command. Serene laughed and cupped her hand over her mouth. It must have been taken the first few years the Sturinis were in business.

"Which one do you find funny?" a voice said stiffly from behind her.

Serene spun around, feeling her throat tighten. "I came to see what they did to your factory," she said, her smile fading as quickly as it had come. "And I thought we should talk."

Marcus glanced at the secretary, then took her arm. "Come into the factory. You can see for yourself."

The entire first floor was covered with scattered roof debris. Men on makeshift scaffolding were stretching a heavy, course material across the top.

"Please be careful. My men tried to create a path to make the cleanup effort easier. And we need to protect what is left. For now at least." When he put his hand on her waist to guide her through the maze back to his private office, her instinct was to push it away.

Inside the small office were a desk and two chairs, with an adjoining small room off the back.

Marcus pulled the chair out for her, and she sat, not removing her coat. All the while, she fought the urge to cough away the filthy air. "Have you made any more progress on the rebuild?"

"There isn't much left. Fifty percent of the equipment is gone." He sat in a chair on the other side of the desk.

"I'm sorry I haven't come by sooner. I didn't know it was so bad."

"Neither did I," he said, his good eye piercing her like a sword.

Serene was fully aware he wasn't referring to the bomb damage but rather to her apprehension of their engagement. "I didn't mean to offend you the other night. With my father's death so unexpected, I'm not sure of a lot of things and this wedding was one of them."

"You made it quite clear," he said. A smirk slid across his lips, and she wanted to tell him about her meeting with Everto and how she wouldn't let her family lose their heritage simply because she didn't want to marry him.

Instead, she focused on her goal. "I think you need this marriage as much as I do," she stated evenly, before losing her courage.

Marcus' jaw seemed to tighten. "You have no idea what I need. All of us have been faced with decisions we don't like, but our families made a commitment to each other. I have honored that from the beginning."

"That's the reason I came." With a long breath in, she surveyed the smugness on his face. Without a doubt, he had learned about the money. "I'll accept this marriage with one condition."

"You're not making sense." His face hardened. "I don't play games like that."

Serene had prepared herself for his candor and rehearsed the answer in her head relentlessly the night before. Standing up, she leaned against the door, already feeling perspiration as it began to soak the back of her neck. Centering her eyes on him, she gripped her hands tightly together to brace herself.

"I want to propose a deal."

Chapter Nine

"A deal?" Marcus moved closer to the desk and put his elbows on it, clasping his hands together. "And what would that be?"

"A lot of money is at stake for this marriage. You know it, and now, fortunately, I know it."

It's getting better, Marcus thought sarcastically. The silly girl was thinking too much for her own good. "It has nothing to do with the money, regardless of how much it is."

Serene raised her eyebrows. "Enough to support us for a long, long time, probably our entire lives. Isn't that a lot for a dowry?"

"Your father's generosity isn't the issue here."

"Would you say it was enough to rebuild this factory on your own? Possibly open your own factory?"

Marcus clasped his hands behind his head, his curiosity piqued. "My father has his own money. I have my own money. What is this leading to, Serene? You're not making any sense."

"Once we're married, we split the money in half. You get to do what you want with your half only."

The sheer momentum of her words put them in a bubble, away from the hum of noise outside the office.

"From what you are saying, I must assume you would give your blessing to the marriage. But you wanted out of it so badly, why not just break the agreement and keep the money for yourself? I'm sure you can find things to do with it."

"Don't pretend with me, Marcus. You must know

the money is ours only when you marry me. I won't get any of it unless I marry you and only you. This deal makes the money ours—yours and mine."

"I see you've done some research. Whether you choose to believe me or not, it's you I want to marry, not some deceased man's money." It had been Anthony Moneto himself who had confided to Marcus that the money was for him once he married Serene, something his own father had known for years and never divulged to him. And now Serene was in on the secret. It complicated matters, but he still had the control.

"We don't love each other, and this is the way for both of us to win," she proposed.

Marcus decided to bite at her challenge. "I'm not looking to win anything. I just want you as a wife."

"All we'd be sharing is the money."

"And the rest? What about love, children—you know, the happily-ever-after?" He tried hard not to smile. "What purpose do you have for this? I'm curious."

"We both get what we need. You get your money to do with as you wish, and I get the other half to rebuild my father's restaurant business. In truth, without the money, I won't be able to keep the restaurants or the villa or even properly take care of my family."

Marcus tapped his fingers on the desk. Of course he would never let her lose the villa. Once the marriage took place, all of her possessions became his, including the villa, which was worth more *lire* than he made in a year's time. Re-opening those restaurants, however, wasn't a particularly attractive option for him. Yes, the success of Cucina Moneto might pay him in the long run. But more appealing was the satisfaction of building his own factory without his father's questioning. His gaze wandered the length of her. Beautiful and naïve.

Still, he could practically taste the money. "You've thought this through, I see."

"How could I not? You deserved an answer, one way or another. I just added another option."

Marcus knew how to change women's minds. She was no different. He would play her way for a while, but with a little maneuvering she would come around and see things from his side, as all women tended to do. Keeping her happy for a bit longer wouldn't complicate his plan too much.

Slowly, he made his way around the desk, close enough to smell her perfume. His eyes followed the curve of her neck. "My, Serene, you've grown into a real woman."

"Do we or don't we have a deal?"

Leaning on the desk, Marcus came eye level with her. "If a man doesn't get milk from his own cow, he's forced to visit other farms." He lifted her chin. "I'll give you half the money, but you will be a wife to me. In every sense of the word."

****

"What did the wealthy bitch want this time?" Ava Stallone asked, nuzzling Marcus' neck and twiddling a curl of his dark chest hair. "I almost wouldn't let her back to see you."

"She wants to marry me more than ever."

The two lay together, coverless, on the bed in her flat in the center of Rome.

"I'll bet," Ava drawled. "Like the rest of us." She crawled on top of him like a lion mounting its prey.

Marcus playfully slapped her naked bottom. "Jealous?"

"Why should I be? I get to play your secretary every day, no?"

Marcus entwined some of her long black hair between his fingers and feathered it across his mouth. "Don't fret, *caro.* I'll still have room for you."

"You'd better," she growled and dove her head

down low on him.

****

Samuel snapped open his medical bag and pushed the chair closer to Miles. He lifted the lower part of Miles' bad leg and released the bandages. Pain shot up through the middle of Miles' calf.

"That hurt, m'friend?" Samuel asked absently.

Miles leaned up on his forearms and gritted his teeth. "It's constant."

"The wound is healing, I see, and I'd bet the Blarney Stone you won't have any more problems with that infection. Serene's been taking good care of you?"

Miles nodded.

"Everything else all right?"

"Anna has been giving Serene a difficult time because I'm here. I'm thinking it's better for everyone if I go."

"That's not new, unfortunately. I tried talking to Anna myself, but Serene insists she isn't a threat to us. I suppose she's a good old woman at heart, but I still hold reservations."

"I'd just as soon get out of your hair and save you and Serene the trouble."

"Don't push it, Coulson." Sam rose from the edge of the bed. "You're not nearly ready to leave. Your leg wouldn't even be able to support you back to the beach, let alone across the country."

"It's not me I'm worried about. It's Serene."

"She's faced the death of her father, and now she has to manage the family responsibilities on her own. That's a lot for any young woman to handle, especially one who just announced her engagement."

"She's getting hitched?" Miles didn't know why, but the news nearly knocked the wind out of him.

"Her father arranged it. That night you came into town, they'd just finished a big dinner to make the announcement. Now that her father is gone, I don't know when the wedding will take place."

"Ah, hell. I'm not good with the timing."

"She's a strong woman. All of the Moneto women are strong. She'll get through it."

"What does she need an arrangement for? She's a looker, all right," he said with a laugh. "And marriage arrangements are outdated, anyway."

Samuel put the remainder of his tools back in his bag.

"It's not about appearances. It's about arranging a secure future for your child. Probably better this way. Saves a lot of hearts that would come pounding on the door. It's a real shame that her father isn't here to see it."

"Yeah." Miles stared at the ceiling, feeling his stomach knot up. The girl had more heartache than he could figure, and her father's death must have been the toughest blow of all.

Miles remembered when he lost his own father. The notification came in the form of a brown envelope he'd received while lying in a trench somewhere in North Africa. It was one of the worst moments of his life.

Samuel slapped him on the shoulder. "I think we're about done here. I've got that chair for you downstairs. If you want, we can go give it a ride."

"Not today."

"You need to get up and move."

"Not today, Sam." Miles muttered a thanks and turned over, his mood becoming fouler by the minute.

"I'll let you slide for now, because I have other patients today, but have Serene come for me if needed. Otherwise, I'll be back in a day."

Miles pulled up the blanket to his chest and found himself annoyed, almost angry, that Serene never mentioned her upcoming marriage. Chewing it over, he tried to reason it out, but it did nothing except make him wonder more about her. What the hell was he thinking? He was practically engaged himself, and he hadn't thought one iota about Josie in days.

Where was this guy she was supposedly going to marry? Didn't she trust him enough to let him know that she was harboring an American at her house?

Or could it be she was ashamed of getting married? He had never been good at reading girls, and she certainly seemed like a complicated one. Beautiful, but too complicated for his Minnesota blood.

He turned over his pillow and pounded it with his fist a few times.

A drifting mind is a drifting heart. The phrase popped into his head. He remembered his mother had said those words when she tucked him in for the last time, the night before she abandoned them. Dad never spoke much about why she left, but growing up, Miles pieced it together through bits of town gossip. His Ma had a drifting heart for Mr. Jacobs, who lived down the road in a small red shack. The last he heard, the two of them hitched a ride to Florida.

Drifting got you into trouble, and he certainly wasn't going down that road. But when Serene touched his arm, he couldn't get her softness out of his head. She nearly knocked his socks off when she came to give him that soup.

Let it go, Coulson. Another man already had his claws in her. It would be her husband's job to figure things out.

He had to get out of here.

****

The villa had quieted for the night, but Serene paced the kitchen floor, her hands clasped together in the prayer sign at her mouth. The look on Marcus' face when she'd proposed the deal stuck with her like the seal on a contract with the devil. Arrogant. Self-satisfied.

She squeezed her eyes shut. In her own small way, she had won a horrible victory of sorts. Marcus got what he wanted, and she could assure herself that the restaurants stayed in their family. If only she could be certain that he would keep his end of the deal, she would have felt better about it.

A loud thud and then smaller pounding sounds came from the top floor, interrupting her thoughts. And then silence. She ran up the three flights to her mother's room and, breathless, tried to push the door open, budging it only slightly. When she peered through the opening, she found Miles slumped on the floor beside the door, his body holding it closed.

Serene's heart beat faster. Slipping her hand in, she pushed him over enough to get the door open a little further. No, not now. Not again. Please God. She squeezed through and knelt beside him, putting her fingertips to his neck. One beat, two beats, and then his eyes opened slowly and closed again before his gaze steadied on her.

"What happened?" she said in a sigh of relief.

Miles lifted his head, squinted, and then shut his eyes. "Tried to get up and walk around."

Anna shuffled up to the door. "What's wrong? I'll get the light."

Pushing her robe sleeves to her elbows, Serene prodded his torso to a sitting position. "Here," she said to Miles, "put your arm around my neck."

Like a drunkard, Miles flung his arm around her shoulder. Serene winced, trying to hold strong against the weight of him.

"Be careful, *Signorina* Serene," Anna commanded. "Easy with him. He's too heavy, and you still need to bear children."

"We're fine, Anna. You can go to bed."

"I can't leave you like this."

"We're fine," Serene said in gasp. "You can check on Margot and Harry to make sure the noise didn't wake them."

Anna mumbled something in Italian that Serene couldn't hear, then left.

"She worries too much," Serene whispered. With a grateful nod, Miles half-hopped on one leg while leaning on her.

"Is it too much on you?"

Serene gulped a dry breath and shook her head before they finally made it to the edge of the bed and collapsed at the bottom. Serene hesitated, then scrambled onto the mattress, and braced him from the back. Tugging on his waist, she tried unsuccessfully to pull him toward the headboard.

Hearing him laughing, Serene swatted a dribble of perspiration from her forehead. "What's so funny?"

"I'm not accustomed to hearing grunting from a woman."

"Oh," She leaned up on her knees and tied her robe tighter. "Then can you push yourself a little? I can't seem to—"

"Yup. I think I can make it."

Relieved, Serene swung one leg off the bed, straddling his back, then realized the compromising position she'd put herself in and returned to her knees. Deciding how to get herself from the bed in a feminine way, she noticed that Miles' shirt had scrunched up to the middle of his back. A white eagle, the size of a playing card, its wings outspread, was painted at the base of his spine. The whole bird, except for the bottom of its claws, showed above the top of Miles pants. Its dark, solid eyes had a determined, almost vengeful gaze. The center of its belly held an American flag.

"It's glorious—"

"What?"

"The bird painted on your back."

"The eagle? Something a bunch of us did on draft day. At the time, I didn't care much for the needles, but it seemed like a better idea after downing a few beers. My buddy chose the picture. Said I didn't have the sense to pick something appropriate. Probably right." He turned slightly to glance at her. "He also said girls are supposed to go for that sort of thing."

"Do you mind if I touch it a little?"

"Go ahead," he chuckled. "No one's ever asked me that before."

The red paint held a slight sheen, which begged her fingers to run themselves over it. The satin colors came alive on his skin, the ink smooth and cool to her fingertips. Getting closer, she rubbed along the edges of the wings, outlining each intricate marking, then grazed down by the eagle's claws. The muscles in his upper back were barely a breath away, the warmth of his skin inviting.

Miles dropped his head a slight bit, as if waiting for her fingers to wander to other places. Serene stopped, but her heart sped. He reached his hand behind him and touched her thigh. "You don't have to stop."

"I do," she murmured. The air in her lungs threatened to evaporate completely if she touched more of him. She abruptly slid his white shirt back down over the eagle and scooted both legs off the edge of the bed. "Did you hurt yourself when you fell? Do you need me to get Samuel?"

"I think I'm fine." Miles pinched his eyebrows together as though questioning. "It can wait until morning."

She busied herself adjusting the pillows behind him as he starting pushing himself back toward the headboard. With each thrust, his pajama bottoms moved down a little, until finally they left little of his lower torso hidden.

"Oh my goodness," Serene blurted, her body frozen.

Startled, Miles followed the direction of her eyes.

"Excuse me," he said, with the expression of a gentleman, but his face brightened to the shade of autumn apples. He seized the blanket and pulled it up past his waist. "I'm sorry."

Heat worked its way all the way down Serene's legs. She turned slowly and grabbed a poker, jamming it into the biggest log she could find in the dying fire. Urgent desire ran through all of her limbs.

"May I have something to drink?"

Serene dropped the steel poker in the bin. She summoned up the lightest manner she could muster and faced him. "Only if you tell me where you were trying to wander off to in your nightclothes."

"To get something to drink." He said it without a bit of expression, and the absurdity of the episode hit Serene full force.

"What about the water on the table?" She pressed her lips together to stop the giggle in her throat, but her shoulders started shaking. She hunched over and let it out, knowing it was useless to try and stop it.

"If I'd taken that water in the first place," he explained scientifically above her laughter, "and didn't try to get up, I wouldn't have fallen and then—you wouldn't have charged in here like that and found me on the floor. And then I would not have been able to see your pretty face laughing at me."

Awkwardly, Serene lifted her head. "I'm sorry." She gulped. "Yes, here, have some water."

Grinning, he chugged down almost the entire glassful without taking a breath, watching her eyes, her beautiful eyes, dance with amusement.

She put the glass back. "I'm sorry. You looked so serious asking for the water after, well, you know."

"I should never have gotten up in the first place."

"No—uh—I was just a little surprised to find you lying at the door. You're not going to try that again, are you?"

Miles thought for a second and then decided to lay the truth on her. "I wanted to walk, walk anywhere, just walk. I tried to get up, and then I just fell. My legs are like yarn."

"It just means you're not ready."

"A few weeks ago I was on the front, running, shooting, in combat every hour of every day, digging trenches, unloading ammo trucks, and now.... One leg won't get me too far. I'm twenty-six years old. I shouldn't be just lying here. I hate the thought of not being able to help my country. And now Samuel wants to stick me in a chair?"

As he talked, he watched the amusement fade from Serene's face, and he was sorry he couldn't keep his anger in.

"The wheelchair will help you. You're lucky it's not permanent. Others aren't quite so lucky."

He shook his head. "It is so frustrating."

"I know."

"How could you know?" he exploded. "Have you ever held the guts of your best friend in your hands? And then left his dead body lying there while you seek help for yourself? And now I'm just lying here like an invalid, still not able to do anything myself."

"You're right," she said softly. "If you just give it a little more time."

"I've given a few years of my life already. And I feel like I haven't done a damn thing to help end this war."

Serene lowered her voice. "In all of this, you

saved me from that horrible, disgusting man. Doesn't that count?"

At the sound of desperation in her voice, Miles submerged his anger instantly. "Did he touch you? That soldier in the restaurant?"

Anna came through the door, oblivious to their conversation. "Please, *Signorina* Serene, come to bed. The rooster will be crowing soon."

"I was just leaving," she said turning back to him, her dark hair hanging careless, rumpled by her efforts at getting him off the floor. "I'll get Samuel tomorrow."

Miles studied her eyes, which held the glassiness of a still pond. "Did he touch you?"

"No—he tried, but—you—you stopped him."

Raising himself up on an elbow, Miles didn't even want to guess what that soldier would have done to her. He couldn't tell if she was being truthful, but, Jesus, she looked so innocent. "I was out of it—I didn't know if I was too late."

Her cheeks flushed against the flimsy pink robe. "You weren't."

"Will I see you in the morning?" he asked.

His question went unanswered as Anna guided Serene out of the room. How many men had wanted her for the wrong reasons, he wondered. He almost began to understand the old woman's protective attitude toward her.

Sitting up, Miles plumped the pillow. Her fingers on the bottom of his spine had talked to him like no other woman's touch had. He thought he had honest-to-God died and gone straight to heaven.

He liked her. He'd admit that. Who was he kidding? He'd fallen for her harder than a walnut. Turning over, he wrestled uselessly with the pillow. He couldn't get comfortable.

As long as he was in the same house with her, he wanted to get to know her better. There had to be a reason she hadn't mentioned her engagement. Even in his little town of Hazel Run, when a girl got hitched you could hear her screaming clear across the farm and showing every Tom, Dick, and Harry the ring. Serene didn't wear one, though. But since it was an arrangement, maybe she didn't even know the guy. Or maybe she wasn't happy about it. Out of respect, he wouldn't ask her unless she wanted to tell him. He wasn't about to tread on another man's girl, anyway.

The smell of lilacs lingered in the room, staying with him as he fought to clear her from his mind. They were different people from different countries during a world war. Nothing must happen between them.

Settling back into the pillow, he did figure out one thing. Serene was the kind of girl you wouldn't take on a car date. You'd bring her home to meet the parents, because you'd know right away that she was the one.

The one? Holy Jesus. Had he gone completely out of his mind?

Without even realizing it, Serene had wound herself around him, making him rethink his own happiness.

He rolled the sides of the pillow into his face.

He needed to get back to Josie and run the farm, and eventually settle down. The mundane tasks that he had detested before he entered the service were the things he wanted now. A simple life doing simple things. More than ever in his life, he wished he could sit on the porch and chew things over with his pop. See how he would have handled things.

When he got home, hell, he would even clean out the chicken coop with a smile.

And he was going to walk out of here if it killed him. He had to walk away from it all, and from her.

Chapter Ten

"Anna?" Serene placed her cloth bag on the kitchen table and slid her arms from her drenched coat. Removing the few items from the bag, she was struck by how the scarcity of foods in the piazza worsened by the day. "Anna, I'm home." When she took off her hat, a spray of rain dribbled down the back of her neck, and she shivered.

"She's not here," Miles called from the parlor.

"It's not safe for you to be down here." Panic energized Serene's limbs as she rushed into the adjoining room and found Miles sitting in a wheelchair, facing the long windows full of streaming rain, his back to her. "What if someone sees you?"

"I'll stay upstairs from now on, if that will make you feel better."

Serene smoothed back her wet hair and adjusted the bottom of her sweater. "Here. Come sit with me in the kitchen. *Caffè* cleanses the soul." Serene didn't wait for an answer but swung his chair around and wheeled him into the kitchen, parking the chair at the table. "Did Sam have to wrestle you into the chair?"

"Practically, but the sooner I can get moving, the sooner I can get home."

"It will take the pressure off your injured leg. Why would you not like it?"

"I'm not as handsome in metal," he said dryly.

Serene smiled as she lit the stove. More than you know, she thought. Even in a cross mood, he had a charm about him. "You know what I mean."

"I'd be much better out of this contraption and on my feet."

"You will be soon enough, especially if you don't try to walk again before you're ready." With her back to him, she took two cups from the shelf. "I may not be there to rescue you."

"Did you rescue me last night? I can't remember."

Serene bit her lip to keep from smiling. "Next time maybe I'll send Anna."

"You wouldn't."

"I would."

"But what if it were you I needed—to rescue me?"

As Serene put the two cups on the table, she fought the blush coming into her cheeks. "It'll just take a few minutes for the water to heat up."

Harry bounded into the room. "How'd you get downstairs?"

"Hey, buddy." Miles patted him on the arm. "Samuel helped me down. I'm almost all fixed up." He slapped the upper part of his bad leg.

"Can I wheel you around?"

"No," Serene cut in. "He's got to improve his health first, not do more injury to it."

Miles winked. "Later, how about I show you how this chair works?"

"I'm going to join the *Balilla*," Harry said, his eyes bright. "You get to wear a uniform and learn how to fight like a real soldier."

Serene scowled at her brother. "It's called the *Gioventù Italiana del Littorio*, not *Balilla* anymore. And Papa has had this talk with you before, Harry. Nothing has changed. An organization that teaches fascism to young boys is not a place for you."

With a pout, Harry dug his hands into his pockets. "When can I be a soldier?"

"Do you know where Anna is?" Serene asked,

hoping to veer him off the subject.

"She went to the factory."

Uneasiness swept through Serene. Why the factory? The only factory she knew of was the Sturinis', but that couldn't be. "You don't know why?"

Harry bent closer to Miles' leg, the argument forgotten. "Can I see it? Where the bullets were?" His eyes bulged with curiosity.

"I don't see why not." Miles shot Serene a questioning look. "Is it all right with you?"

Serene nodded. "Don't touch, though." Since their father died, Harry hadn't had a man in his life, except Samuel. It made Serene more than grateful for this attention to her brother from Miles.

Harry flashed her an I-know-and-you-don't-have-to-tell-me glance.

"Are you sure you're ready for this?" Miles teased. "It's ugly under these bandages."

"Uh-huh."

Serene poured the steamy coffee. "It's a war injury, not a monument."

"Here goes." Miles started to lift his pant leg, just as the back door burst open with a gust of pelting raindrops.

"*Mamma mia!*" Jumping from her chair, Serene pushed at the door, fighting its heaviness and the strength of the wind. At the same time, she yelled for Harry to get the bucket as the rain blew freely in onto the tiled floor.

Miles backed his chair into the door, and after one good shove, their combined weight got the door closed. She leaned her back against it to regain her breath, and mouthed a thank you.

"The whole floor is covered!" Harry exclaimed, returning with a wooden bucket.

Serene threw several checkered towels on top of the water seeping toward the center of the floor.

A Daughter's Promise

"Can you hold this?" Without waiting for an answer, she plopped the bucket onto Miles' lap.

Harry and Serene crawled on their knees, scooping up the drenched towels, piling them one by one into the bucket. She dried off the wall adjacent to the door and the few chairs that had gotten sprayed.

"That's all of it." Serene took the last towel from Harry and threw it into the bucket.

Miles reached over from his chair and took her elbow, helping her to stand up. In that instant, the wheelchair rolled in the opposite direction. Serene's elbow slipped from his hand and she landed on the floor, her legs sprawled apart, one shoe flying through the air to land a few feet away on the floor. Dumbfounded, she struggled to sit up, unable to decide whether to cry or laugh. Just the thought that Miles might have seen her panties made her face burn with embarrassment. At least she had on the nice ones with the lace top. Silently she said a small thank you to God.

Harry was laughing so hard Serene thought he might fall over, while a grinning Miles held his hand out to her. "Let me help you up."

"You think this is funny, too?" She bit the inside of her cheek. "I guess it's my turn to be rescued from the floor, no?" she challenged, stretching to retrieve her shoe.

From his growing smile, he had to be taking in all her foolishness. The strength in his eyes warmed like a newly lit fire. She hadn't noticed before the dimple that settled comfortably high in his right cheek. Way down low, her insides fluttered.

"Are you hurt?" He barely got it out before breaking into a deep, contagious laugh.

From the wet marks on her wool skirt to her unraveled hair, Serene knew, as sure as maple syrup came from a tree, that she must appear a mess.

Crinkling her nose at him, she fought the laughter that clogged her throat. "I'm fine." She scrambled to her feet, knowing her pride stung more than her bottom. "But dry clothes would help."

"Good luck," Miles said and cleared his throat.

All the way to her room on the second floor she could still hear him laughing. Flouncing onto the bed, she dug her face into the pillow, where she laughed until her belly ached. Then she jumped up, unzipped her skirt and glanced downward, thankful again for having put on nice underwear that morning.

Pulling on a fresh skirt, she reached for a rose-colored, button-up sweater from the chest of drawers and held it against her bosom. Disappointed at the way the color looked drab against her skin, she opted for a maroon blouse. She ran a comb through her damp hair, then twisted it into a low bun at the nape of her neck. Not satisfied with her reflection in the mirror, she re-twisted the hair, glanced in the mirror again, and decided it wasn't going to lie any better, no matter how many times she re-did it.

"Silly," she murmured.

Rummaging through the small velvet box in which she kept her jewelry, she found her favorite red lip stain, coated her lips and pressed them together, then did a quick sign of the cross and prayed the little quiverings deep in her stomach would go away.

But she knew they wouldn't. Not as long as Miles Coulson was near.

****

Miles had maneuvered himself back to the parlor and sat with his head tilted up to see the family pictures on the fireplace mantel. Hearing her footsteps on the stairs, he wheeled around.

"Better?" At the sight of her sweater curving around her breasts, his palms moistened. He bet he

112

could fit one hand around her tiny waist.

"Much."

He cleared his throat and pointed to a picture of Maria and Anthony, dressed in their finest attire, standing in front of the villa. "Your mother was beautiful."

"Mmm."

Serene leaned over him, her hip grazing his arm as she removed the frame from the mantel and handed it to him. He surveyed it for a moment. "You look a lot like her. And a lot like the picture in her bedroom."

"That's what my father said."

"Do you remember her much?"

Serene pulled up a skirted ottoman and sat down. "She died when I was fifteen, but I still remember the parties. Oh, those glamorous parties. All the society people were invited. The women dressed in their finest gowns, and the men put on dinner jackets for the evening. See the gown she has on?" She scooted the ottoman closer, pointing to the picture. "I helped her make it for the party."

"Tell me about it," Miles prompted.

"Yellow. It was her favorite color. Once she had the dress on, she twirled around and around—it was like waves of sunshine spilling all around her. I can still remember the scent of her perfume. She always smelled so good when she held me in her arms."

"Like lilacs?" His voice was husky.

"Mmm." Serene nodded, as if it were everyone's favorite.

He put the picture aside. It wasn't her mother's dress that stayed in his head as he listened to Serene unravel her memories. It was the way her green eyes danced their own waltz as she told him. "Tell me more."

"My mother was a woman ahead of her time. Even as a child, I knew she was different."

"What do you remember most?"

"Her independence," she said softly. "She didn't care about the same things as the other society women. She only cared that we felt loved."

As Miles listened to her memories unfold, he found himself moving closer, wanting to kiss her so God-awful bad. Instead, he cupped his hand over hers and waited, sensing she wanted to tell him more.

"That last day I saw her," Serene continued, "she asked me to take care of my siblings and my Papa. I think she wanted us to know that the world was good, even though she knew..." When she raised her eyes to meet his, a tear dropped onto her cheek. "She knew she wasn't coming back to us."

He felt the trembling in her fingers. "She sounds a lot like you."

"Me?"

With their faces barely a breath apart, Miles was consumed by her scent, her softness. "You risked your own life so that I could survive. I'd bet my farm that's something your Mama would have done." Slowly, he smoothed his fingers along her hairline. "I'll always be grateful for that."

"I'd do it again if I had to," she murmured.

With the weight of a feather, his mouth brushed against hers, tentatively, questioning. Feeling her body respond, he pressed his hand against her back, bringing the swell of her chest closer.

"Serene?" Anna called from the front entrance. "We have a visitor."

Serene tugged her lips away and leapt from the ottoman, immediately smoothing down her sweater and skirt. "You have to hide! Oh my—we have to hide you. If they find you here—"

Miles sat up straighter. "Who is it?" he whispered.

"*Buongiorno*, Serene," a deep, distinct voice said

behind her.

Like a bird before flight, Serene turned toward the voice. "Marcus."

Groomed perfectly, Marcus strode toward her. The satin patch on his eye shone like onyx.

Before Serene could speak, he seized her into his arms and slammed his mouth against hers, moving and groping, pushing his tongue between her lips. The taste of ugliness seeped into her as she struggled to break free. But as quickly as he took her, he shoved her from him harshly, and slid the back of his hand against the wave of her cheekbone. "I thought you had more sense than this."

Stunned, Serene dared not move, but fought to keep her voice steady. "What do you want?"

"You think this will bring your father back?" With a narrowed eye, he shot a hate-filled glance in Miles' direction. "Taking that *porco* in?"

"Miles is not an animal, and we don't refer to people in my home that way. He tried to save my father's life—and he saved me, too."

"So you think you must hover over him like a mother watches a baby?" Marcus pursed his lips as if to spit on the floor. "Shame your family and your precious father's memory?"

"You're not understanding—"

"I understand perfectly."

She gripped his sleeve. "That night, the night my father was shot, one of the Germans almost— had his way with me."

"He touched you?"

"No, yes—he didn't hurt me, but only because Miles got to him first."

Marcus smirked. "He wanted you for himself, *no?*"

With a shuddered breath, Serene dropped her hand and backed away from him, searching for any kind of compassion in the blackness of his eye. "We all lost a lot that night, Marcus. Even you must be able to understand that."

"You want to shame my family, too?"

"By helping another human?"

"No, Serene, not another human. An American." He said it flatly. "Taking as much as he can from you—from us." He gripped her shoulders, then let her go and stalked to the opposite side of the room. "Your Papa wasn't enough? You should be grateful that Anna came to me with this."

"He should have known from the start," Anna cried out and ran from the room.

Miles wheeled closer. "What are they saying, Serry?"

Throwing his wet beret onto the table, Marcus strode past her to the wheelchair. He leaned down slowly and grasped the arms of the chair, eye to eye with Miles.

"Well, *Serry*," Marcus drawled in perfect English, his eyes locked on Miles, "is that what he calls you? Did he tell you how many poor Italians he killed? Did he tell you how many of my friends—your friends, *Serry*—he shot down cold?"

Miles shoved Marcus' hands away. "Defending my country." He attempted to stand, but his leg wouldn't support his weight, and he crumpled to the ground. "Just like you."

Serene ran to him and helped him hoist his body up and back into the chair.

"You will never be like me," Marcus hissed. "We are loyal to our own until our very last breath. You'll never know what it means to take your own life rather than hide in the enemy's home, taking from them, pretending."

"Stop it, Marcus!" Serene yelled, gripping his shoulders. "I'm the one to blame. Miles didn't have a choice—he was dying. Take your anger out on me, not him."

"Back off of her," Miles warned with a coldness that made the room go still.

Without a flicker of emotion, Marcus moved Serene aside, and stepped closer to Miles. "She is mine. She listens to what I say. So you, as you say, back off."

"If you have a problem with me being here, it's between me and you. Not with her."

"Then so be it." Marcus fingered the leather waist pouch holding his knife.

Unbridled hatred flamed between the two men.

Miles didn't take his eyes away. "Go ahead and try. I'll show you what my country is made of."

"No," Serene gasped. "It was my decision, not his. If you have any feelings at all, Marcus, don't do this. You'll regret it, I promise you."

As if contemplating, Marcus slipped out his cigarette case from another pocket and jammed a lean butt into his mouth. The flick of the metal lighter snapped the silence. "Regret that I took a waste of a life? Or was that your attempt at a threat?"

Serene watched the cigarette tip brighten and then slowly dull. "He'll stay as long as he needs to."

"If you still want to be my wife, stop this and get rid of him. The moment my father finds out, the arrangement will be off. You will get nothing from me or my family." He threw the cigarette into the fireplace, lifted her chin with one finger and said softly, menacingly, "Our deal will be off, and you'll get nothing."

Serene searched his good eye for a hint of feeling, but it resembled a newly dug black hole. "Can you at least understand why I need to help him?"

"There isn't any reason good enough to keep him here. That man, and his people, took too much from us already."

Miles slammed his hand on the chair handle. "You know what you took from us? You know how many of our boys died? God dammit! Up until a little while ago, I would've died and left this God-forsaken place and you in it, but Serene convinced me otherwise."

"She made a bad decision."

Feeling broken, Serene hated herself for allowing Marcus to belittle her decision. "You have to understand…"

"I won't understand, and I won't allow this to happen, Serene. Neither will my family." He lifted his beret from the table. "If you want to respect your father's memory, you know what you have to do."

The door slamming behind him hammered the finality of his words into her ears.

****

Serene leaned against the door, her heart aching for security and love from a family she could trust. She forced her body to take a slow, soothing breath. Feeling Anna's presence behind her, she spun to attack. "How could you do this?"

"You must understand, *Signorina* Serene," Anna explained.

"Understand? You say you love me as if you were my mother, but a mother wouldn't betray her own daughter."

"I was doing what I thought was best for your family. You understand, no? Marcus is your betrothed. He should know everything."

Serene barely heard her. She felt glazed over, as if she were a nondescript object in the room. She ran her fingertips down the door, struggling to stop the anger from seeping into her whole body. How could Anna have betrayed their *family*? When she exposed the Monetos' secret, she had endangered the entire family.

Slowly Serene's anger turned to fear. God-awful

A Daughter's Promise

fear. Would Marcus tell? If he did, he would have to admit to others that he was engaged to a woman who harbored an animal, as Marcus had put it. Serene prayed that his pride would prompt him to keep his silence. Otherwise, she knew the next knock on the door could leave them all dead.

With a shiver, she stepped from the door and faced Anna. "We've been found out, and now we are in real danger. You brought on the thing you were afraid of most. You need to leave before anything terrible happens."

"I have nowhere to go. Naples is torn up, and my sister has fled from there."

The burst of misty air as Anna opened the front door made Serene wish she were the one going. Leaving them. Leaving her life behind. But even as heartless and scared as she felt at the moment, she couldn't let Anna go in the cold rain. "You can stay until you contact your sister, but then find someplace else to go." She thought of Margot and Harry. They needed to be protected, too.

Hearing Anna retreat to her room, Serene hugged her arms to her body and leaned against the door, letting her face absorb the dampness. She wanted to stay in that spot forever and never have to face the humiliation of claiming such a disgraceful man as her betrothed.

"You all right?"

The sound of Miles' voice sent a new wave of emotion through her.

"A little ashamed, I guess." Not bringing herself to admit how truly desperate she felt, she shut the door and returned to the parlor, where she curled into the nearest chair and hugged her knees to her chest.

"Of what?"

Serene forced a chuckle. "Him. Me."

"It's him that should be apologizing. Probably

119

makes him feel like more of a man to handle a woman like that."

"He's never been like that with me before, at least not that callous. The pressure he has at the factory after it was bombed—it's complicated—"

"There is no reason on this earth that a man can't be decent to a woman."

"Sometimes he is rough with people." She smiled faintly. "I believe he's good, deep down."

"Listen, Serry, I don't like to tell people what to do, but if I were you, I'd get far away from him. He means trouble."

"Our parents made an agreement. Through our arrangement, he vowed to protect me."

"Through threats? Is that how he protects you?"

"You don't understand."

He understood completely. The guy was a no-good son-of-a-bitch who had no right having a girl like her. "I know what love means. What I saw from that man you're supposed to marry was not love."

"People marry for different reasons," she stammered. "Things are different here, not like they are in America."

Minutes passed before either of them spoke, and the silence killed him. The last thing he wanted to do was hurt her, but the venom in Marcus' eyes when he spoke to her had stuck him like a vicious thorn. He couldn't leave it like this. "I didn't mean to judge you. I care about what happens to you."

"My future is settled. I can't change anything."

"He can't hurt you for changing your mind."

"My father arranged the marriage years ago, when I was just a child. It's a good decision for my family."

Jesus. "You would really go through with the marriage? After what just happened?"

"I'm committed. I could never live with myself if I defied my father's wishes now."

"You can't get out of it?" He asked, incredulous at the honest-to-God horror on her face at the thought of dishonoring her father. "It's *your* life. Your family doesn't have to live with the guy day after day."

"My father thought this was best for me. My family needs this marriage. If you knew the whole story, maybe you would understand."

He took her hand, warming the coolness. "Then tell me. Maybe I can help."

"No one can help."

"Do you love him?" Miles couldn't imagine anyone caring for the brute, let alone loving him.

"My papa signed an agreement and gave his word for my hand. It would be immoral to break it. Not just me but my family would be looked upon badly. My mother had a hard life before she met my father, and this is the way he wanted to protect me from the same."

He studied her. "But do you love him?"

Serene dragged her hand away, and hopped off the chair, pacing the length of the room. "I have to do this."

"It's a simple question."

"Yes, I love him. Is that what you want to hear?"

Miles didn't believe her any more than he believed the war would end that very day.

Chapter Eleven

The sun hadn't yet risen when Serene awoke. Marcus' threat loomed before her in the semi-darkness.

She turned the choice over, her emotions drained empty. Would he go so far as to alert the authorities or anyone else, including his own father? Marcus had his temper, but with the money at stake, he wouldn't be that vindictive. At least, she prayed not.

Serene glanced at Margot sleeping across the room, her sister's face barely visible beneath the thick curls.

Stretching her legs, Serene felt the soreness in her muscles. It had taken her and Margot nearly a half hour to help Miles back upstairs, with her sister chattering all the while. About her day. About Samuel's job as a doctor. About her plans to be a nurse. Serene hadn't the strength to tell her to be quiet; she had her own new worries about Marcus.

She replayed the night in her head again, letting her thoughts float to Miles. When he'd asked simply if she loved Marcus, she knew he could never understand her obligation. He lived in a country where pure choice was encouraged even by the government. Choosing a person to love and be loved by came as easily as breakfast. In her world, family obligation was much stronger than any amount of freedom.

Rubbing her cheek on the pillow, she stared out the window. Wiry tree branches rustled in the wind, colliding and twisting around each other, slamming against the window as if searching for a new direction.

Watching a single branch spiral upwards, she tried to forget Miles' breath on her cheek, her neck, her skin. His kiss had warmed her in private places, personal places that she hadn't known existed. Absorbing herself in getting the man well had only brought them closer, making it harder to think about his leaving.

Many thoughts burned in her head. She would use Cucina Moneto as her sounding board. Maybe seeing the dining room again, facing the ghosts from that night, would provide the solace she needed to bring her father's death to closure. The prospect of seeing the restaurant again scared her a little, though. Could she really expect a visit there to be uneventful? According to Franci, who had agreed to be caretaker until Serene was able to assume the responsibilities, the Germans had never returned to the restaurant.

She swept away new tears and rummaged through her clothes, settling on a plain white sweater and wool skirt. As she dressed, her heart lifted a little at the possibility of repairing the damage and re-opening the restaurant. But all the plans she dreamed about required the dowry money; the meager savings they had left continued to pay on the debt. With a sigh, she decided it didn't hurt to take inventory of the impending repairs needed to get Cucina Moneto up and running.

The kitchen would have no stock, but she hoped the main market would have vegetables, at the very least. Maybe she could even prepare a meal.

After slipping on her shoes, Serene hesitated at the foot of the stairs, then decided to run up to the third floor. She hadn't even given a thought to the pain Miles must have endured in his leg from moving in and out of his wheelchair the previous day. It was the rest of him that had put her in tangles, and now she was searching for a legitimate reason to talk with the man. Couldn't she check on him as normal adults do, without second guessing her own motives? Exasperated at her indecisiveness, she peeked in to find him sitting in the chaise, his bad leg out straight with his foot resting on the edge of the bed.

"Up early?"

He didn't turn his head from the window. "I have a lot on my mind, I guess."

"I'm going to the restaurant for a little while. Do you need anything before I leave? Or maybe I can help you get into the wheelchair so you can move around?"

"I really don't want anything, except an explanation." He shifted his gaze to her. "You said there's more to it, and I'd like to hear what it is. Right here. While it's just the two of us. I'd like to know what he has over you."

Her vision centered on the painting of her mother. "It's not important to anyone except me."

"Treating a stranger badly is one thing. I can handle that, but I hate to see—I mean, I can't walk away knowing you will let him treat you that way."

She folded her arms, surprised by his quick anger. "These matters have nothing to do with you."

"Like heck, they don't. When I'm the cause of him barreling in here like that, threatening to screw up your life, I damn well want to know the rest. I understand what good, decent people are, but Marco, or whatever his name is, doesn't seem to care about you or the responsibilities you have running this place. He doesn't understand. That's all I'm trying to explain. And for all its worth, if I didn't have this bum leg, I would've fought for you myself."

"Fight? This isn't about fighting. This is about what *I* want." As a way to let out her own anger, she asked, "Are *you* the one marrying him?"

Her question hung in the quietness, only to amplify the awkwardness between them.

"I made a promise, and it's something I have to do." Her words came out in a rush.

"Whatever it is," Miles said, "is it important enough for you to want to spend your life—your entire life—with him?"

"Arrangements are binding," she blurted. "It's an oath you give from your heart. It's a very hard thing to break, especially if it was done by a man who adopted you and gave you a life you wouldn't have had otherwise."

"You're adopted?"

"Yes, when I was a child." Talking with someone else about it seemed odd, yet at the same time it was familiar and right to be sharing it with him. "The moment my adoption certificate was sealed, the plans for my marriage were sealed between our fathers. They were like brothers, and that's the reason Marcus was so desperate. Breaking the arrangement by either family would cause shame, and it would affect our businesses. We would all suffer."

"There's more, though, isn't there?"

Serene paused. She hadn't told Margot or any of her family about the money. "I can't tell you the rest."

"Whatever it is does not change the fact that he treats you badly, and I want to protect you from him. I owe you that much, at least."

"You don't owe me a thing. Your thinking that is truly an insult. I don't need protection from a man I'll wed in less than a year."

"In my country, a man protects the people he cares about. If he didn't, *that* would be an insult."

"You're different from him," she whispered.

"I have to go, Serry, and you know it, too. What

happened yesterday before Marcus came here—it was wrong."

Wrong? The most glorious, wonderful thing was wrong? She backed away. "Don't say that."

He chuckled, sourly. "It wasn't proper, kissing you like that. I knew you were engaged, and I should not have touched you."

Hopelessness overwhelmed her. "You didn't do it alone. I was part of it, too."

"I'm sorry for it, Serry. I promise you, it won't happen again."

Before she could stop it, tears crept into her eyes. On instinct, she leaned in just enough to close the space between them. "Don't say you're sorry. No one has ever made me feel that way."

"You really want to continue with it? Knowing you're marrying Marcus, you'll continue this with me?"

Barely hanging on to a thin string of self-control, Serene took his hands. "I—I don't—"

"You're not that kind of person, Serry, and I don't think my Minnesota blood could handle stepping in on another man's girl. I can't be responsible for what happens in your life. I need to go, and you need to move on with your life."

With a tremor in her bottom lip, she faced him squarely, exposing every single one of her vulnerabilities. "And we'll just forget what happened?"

"Yes."

****

Outside her mother's room, Serene adjusted her skirt, smoothed a palm over her hair and mustered the strength to go downstairs. With another reason to find comfort at Cucina Moneto, she yanked her coat from the hook. Whispering coming from the parlor prompted her to detour a little and she stopped, keeping out of sight.

Samuel stood by the fireplace, arms folded. Across from him, Margot sat tensely on the velvet settee.

"This will not just go away, Margot. You have to tell them."

Still wearing the same blue wool skirt and white cardigan as the day before, Margot shook her head.

"No, no, I can't."

"Someone has to tell them. "

With their voices barely audible, Serene strained to hear.

Margot's head dropped between her knees, her curls loose and big around her shoulders. "But I've ruined everything," she cried. "Papa would be so ashamed."

"Your family should know," Samuel persisted.

"They can't see me like this."

"What is it, Margot?" Serene stepped quickly to her sister, her heart beating fast. "Is it that bad?"

With a sob, Margot threw her arms around Serene's neck, squeezing her tight as she gulped for air. Serene leveled her vision on Samuel, his face reddening to the color of burgundy wine. Gently, she lifted Margot's head from her shoulder. "Please tell me what it is."

"You have too much to think about already. With Papa's death—and now the man we're helping—it's too much." Her bottom lip shuddered. "It's a sin," she whispered.

"I can help you." Serene rubbed her knee, tempering her patience. "We've faced the worst already. What could be that awful?"

"She's with child," Samuel announced, leading to a suffocating stillness in the room.

"You're—what?" Sitting back on her heels, Serene gaped at her younger sister, barely eighteen. "A child? But, how did this happen—" she stopped herself, knowing how foolish it sounded.

127

"I take the responsibility." Samuel stood straighter.

In shock, Serene didn't hear him. She wished for the ability to think with the clarity of a parent, something in which she had no experience.

Margot peered up at her, eyes wide open and still glassy. "I've ruined everything for us, haven't I?" She moaned, putting her arms around her head.

"No, no, you haven't. I'm just surprised." She didn't even know where to begin, but the sheer unexpectedness of the situation hit her with the force of a small blast. Of course she'd do what she could to help her sister, but gaining her own understanding had to be the first step. "How far along?"

Samuel scratched the back of his neck, his color returning to normal. "She looks to be starting her fourth month."

"I've known since before Papa's accident, but I was afraid—"

"You know you can come to me with anything." Serene resisted the urge to chastise her for waiting this long to tell them.

Margot wiped her watery nose with a handkerchief. "I was afraid."

"None of us have to be afraid when we have each other. Look what we've been through already, with Papa's death. I wouldn't have survived that without all of you."

"This is worse—everyone will be so ashamed of me."

With an unsteady smile, Serene brought her sister's head closer to her chest, wondering how to mimic what her Papa would have said in this exact moment. "We'll just have to make them understand, won't we?"

"We'll get married, of course," Samuel declared. "As soon as it can be arranged."

"I won't marry you just because, just because I'm with a child."

"That's nonsense, Margot. You know how I feel about you."

Realizing the conversation was slipping into personal territory, Serene suggested, "Why don't you both get some rest? No one has to make any decisions right now."

"You need to at least think about it," Samuel pleaded, not taking his attention from Margot. "It's the right thing to do."

Serene sucked in a breath and stood. "I'll let you two talk some more. Will you be all right, Margot, if I go to the restaurant for a little while?"

Margot nodded. "Is this your first time back there since—since Papa's death?"

"Yes, I guess it is."

"I know how important getting the restaurant back together is to you," her voice cracked. "I'll help you, Serry, I will."

"How about we think about one thing at a time?"

"I'm so sorry about this, about me and the baby. You don't need to worry about this, too. That's why I couldn't tell you."

Serene wrapped her arms around her sister's warm shoulders, letting her cry until her body settled. "Don't you ever be sorry about this." She pushed back a small cluster of curls from her forehead. "All your baby needs is love, and he already has it. I'll help you bring him or her into this world."

****

As Serene pushed open the front door, its ear-piercing creak echoed through the dining area of Cucina Moneto. She walked in slowly, her platform shoes thumping away the silence. She pulled open the front window drape to let the bright daylight stream through the front windows and cast squares of light on the restaurant floor. With a furtive glance, she confirmed that everything seemed secure and in place.

She roamed through the maze of tables to reach the spot. Biting the inside of her cheek until it ached, she bent down. The dull, maroon stain marked the stone floor in a misshapen oval. She put both palms on the center of the oval, feeling the coolness of the stone mixed with the warmness of her father's memory. Her lips quivered, but she had promised herself on the bus ride there that she wouldn't cry.

She closed her eyes for a brief moment and then scrutinized the rest of the room. Most of the chandeliers and sconces had been shattered, leaving the walls and ceiling with burn marks, but the glass and debris was gone. Some of the tables had one or two chairs; the rest were gone. She had to remember to thank Franci profusely for keeping intact what was left.

Passing her hand along the curve of a chair back, she closed her eyes, desperate to bring back the warm atmosphere of chatter, and the smell of fresh-cooked lamb, but upon opening her eyes she found the room still devoid of life, almost eerie. She pulled her coat closer, determined to push away the coolness and stay and live through the memories.

As she started for the kitchen, her foot caught on a loose chain, half of it wrapped around a chair's leg. Lifting the chair, she released the chain to find two small metal tags dangling from it. She recognized them as identification tags worn by U.S. soldiers. Slowly she walked toward the kitchen, holding the tags up, trying to decipher the name. In the light of the kitchen, she was able to read the inscription more clearly. *Pierson Walter P.*

Holding the chain more tightly in her fist, she did a quick sign of the cross before she looped the chain over her head and secured it under her shirt.

She ran her fingers down the wooden counter, her hand resting on the single pot remaining out. The aroma of lemon cleaning oil hung heavily in the air. She sighed, remembering that she had wanted to check the food stock. As she opened the pantry door, the familiar creak of the front door stopped her in mid-motion.

Serene waited.

At the sound of footsteps approaching the kitchen, her breath quickened. Moving silently, she wedged her body into the two-foot sliver of space between the counter and the icebox. Then, trembling, she closed her eyes to shut out the memory of the night they murdered her father. It was the same sound. The same click, click, click of the soldier's boots on the stone floor before he slammed her against the wall. And now, the same fear threatened to stop the breath in her throat.

When the door to the kitchen opened, she dug her nails into her thighs and crouched further into her hiding place. "Serene, are you here?"

Relief pounded at her temples, and she stood straight. *Marcus.* "What are you doing here?"

"Expecting someone else?" He held out his hand to help her out of the space. His firm grip probably matched his mood, but she vowed not to let him rattle her.

"Are you here to threaten me?"

Obviously ignoring her challenge, he strolled to the other end of the counter. "You won't need to be in this kitchen once we're married."

She tried to discern his intentions. "Of course I'm going to keep the restaurants, at least one of them, this one preferably, and work it exactly as my father did."

"You will be at home."

"What did you come here for, Marcus? Does this

mean you want our marriage to go forward?"

"I want to apologize for the way I acted," he said briskly. "I couldn't understand why you would protect that American in your home."

"That man tried to save my Papa from death, and he helped me, too. He was injured and needed our help."

"So you let him stay in your *home?*"

"You have no business making those judgments. I did what I thought was right."

"And you don't tell me?"

"I thought it would be safer to keep it in our family."

"Then you must have little trust for me."

"It doesn't have to do with trust, Marcus. It has to do with being scared and wondering if the Germans would plow right inside our home and kill us all. And the more people who know about something, the more easily the Germans will find it out. Don't you understand? I risked my entire family to take that man there because my Papa wanted it. And now you question me on my motives?"

"It's the way I feel, Serene, and you need to respect that."

Feel? Serene thought. He couldn't possibly feel anything, let alone jealousy. "I couldn't just cast him off and let him die." She breezed by him and headed through the door into the dining room. "I'd do it again, if I had the choice."

"We need to settle things, Serene." He followed, and they sat at the center table. "We need to come to some sort of agreement. I do want to marry you and hold up my end of our—as you call it—deal."

"Things have gotten complicated."

Marcus deliberated, and then said, "It's the circumstances that have put us here. That man has no business being in our home."

"*Our* home?"

"It will be ours, once this silliness is over."

"What are you saying?"

"If you came to my house and found another woman, it wouldn't matter if she was American, British or even German. It would be a woman that I kept secret from you. And in wartime, you're risking your life having him there."

Serene had to admit that he made some sense, even though the apology was certainly out of character for him. "If I had told you right away, would you still have acted the same as you did last night?"

"I don't know how I would have reacted. But having Anna come, in desperation, to tell me, and finding him living with you, eating your food, and I can only imagine what else—"

"Nothing else. Samuel comes to check him, and Margot and I do the in-between nursing. That's it." She hurled the words back at him, her temper beginning to boil.

"I do trust you, Serene."

"It was wrong, the way you reacted, whether you felt that way or not. You could've talked with me about it first. Treating anyone the way you treated Miles—and the way you treated me—is inexcusable."

His face tightened. "If you want me to, I will apologize to him for that before he leaves."

Serene ignored the obviously insincere gesture. "He's not leaving until he's ready. He's not a threat, and I won't throw him out. If you don't think you can keep his existence a secret, then you should tell me now."

The tiny blood vessels at Marcus' temple bulged. His patch glinted in the strip of sunlight coming from the window. "He can stay until Samuel says he can leave. But in return, you must marry me six weeks from today. I've already told my parents, and they've arranged the mass at Santa Cecilia."

A shiver ran down Serene's arms. "Should we get married so close to my Papa's death, and when the world is in such turmoil?" *When I'm in such turmoil?*

"Obviously, when you take such risks with your family, you don't care much of what others think."

"You don't think I was scared, taking that man into our home? It was the most desperate decision I've ever had to make. But I did it because my father needed me to do it."

"And now your father needs you to do this. Your family will be comfortable, and I'll take care of things."

She gazed into Marcus' face and wondered what it would be like for all of them if she didn't go ahead with the marriage. "It would be better if we waited."

He took a thin gold band from his pocket. "If you don't marry me, the money will be wasted and you'll get nothing for your family."

It wasn't a question; it was a statement of finality. It was the moment where there was no turning back. Serene stared at the maroon stain on the floor, her tears blurring the image of her father lying there. She felt the weight of all the debt he had left behind with no money to pay it.

And now Margot's baby needed a future none of them could give.

In desperation, her mind moved to other possibilities. Maybe if she sold off some of the restaurant equipment. Or maybe took a loan to pay off the current debt. But who would give a loan to a woman, let alone a woman during war time? She had no collateral, other than the villa and the restaurants themselves, and no business experience that would count for anything with a lender.

Marcus held the ring out, its gold shining dully against the dim room. For such a tiny object, it controlled her life like nothing else. She knew that, as surely as his eyes were searching her now for an answer.

It was like being sucked into quicksand, and she felt herself grasping at the sides, searching for a way out but finding nothingness. Then, at the bottom, all she found was a man staring at her from the other side of the table, waiting.

"What will it be, Serene?"

At that moment, a surging anger toward her father tore through her. How could he have done this to her?

Chapter Twelve

"I miss Anna," Harry announced, finishing the last bite from his plate. "She should be here with us."

"She's going away for a while," Serene said absently. Her insides knotted uneasily as she stared at her hand, where the engagement ring had sat only a few hours earlier. Just having the ring on her finger had proved so painful that she'd slipped it off the second Marcus left the restaurant.

"Why?" Harry demanded.

"I told you why, last night."

Margot's dark eyes studied her. "You could've at least asked her to join us for the meal."

"It's better for us if she doesn't. We have to be careful about things now."

"You think Anna will hurt us? You even said yourself that she was like a mother to us."

Serene picked up her dish. "That's not the point. She betrayed not just me but you and Harry, too."

"She made a mistake and told Marcus," Margot retorted. "If he's going to marry you, why would he turn us in?"

"If we can't trust someone in our family, what is left?"

"I told her she could stay," Margot blurted.

"What?" Serene gasped. The dish slipped from her fingers and smashed on the tile floor.

Anna came running into the dining room. "What happened?"

Margot pursed her lips together and threw her napkin across the table. "I am old enough to decide who I need as my mother. With this baby, I *need* a mother now. You can't take that from me, Serene. You're the eldest, but just because we're without Papa it doesn't mean you can decide everything."

"I want her to stay, too," Harry chimed in from the other end of the table.

Serene's gaze teetered from Anna to Margot. "Did you think I would change my mind because you said so?"

"I don't know what to expect from you anymore. You made this rash decision without even asking us."

"Asking your opinion is unnecessary, and that's not the issue here. Anna told Marcus without our permission. Luckily, this time, no danger came. But what happens next time? They killed Papa because he did what we're doing now."

"You betrayed Harry and me by trying to send her away. She is more of a mother to me than my real mother."

The anger in her sister's voice made Serene's cheeks grow hot, as if they had been slapped.

"*Signorina* Serene, can you forgive me?" Anna asked. "I was looking out for you, something your mama always told me to do. I was very, very scared for you. I know I promised, but when *Signore* Marcus came to me and held my wrists, demanding—" Her hand flew to her mouth.

"He came to you?"

Anna backed away. "I promised him I wouldn't tell. I said too much already. Please don't ask me for more."

"Tell me, Anna. I need to know."

"He saw, that night of your father's funeral. He saw how you were acting when his mother asked about the soldiers at the restaurant. He came to me the next morning when I was at the market. He tricked the truth out of me. I swear on God himself,

137

Signorina Serene." Her eyes pooled with tears. "I couldn't tell you. I was scared for my life. And if he should ever find out that I told you..."

Serene slowly took in what she was saying, her own air of sophistication crumbling before them. Why hadn't Marcus just asked her if he suspected something? "I, I..." She stuttered, trying to regain her bearings. "It shocked me that you would go to Marcus without talking with me first. But now I understand."

"She thought she was doing right," Margot said defiantly. "Isn't that what's most important?"

Anna came closer. "He didn't mean to lie to you, *Signorina*. Why would he do that on purpose?"

Serene knew why. Marcus couldn't trust others. He couldn't even trust the woman he supposedly loved.

"He cares deeply for you, *Signorina* Serene. You must believe that, but sometimes—he seems dark inside, like a bad man."

"We'll be married soon, and there will be no secrets." The statement slid unsteadily from her mouth. She knew there would be secrets. Marcus couldn't live any other way.

Margot's voice intruded on her thoughts. "I need Anna to stay and be a *nonna* to my baby."

"You're with child, *Signorina* Margot?" Anna grabbed the table and eased herself into a chair. "You have a wedding planned, *si*?"

Margot shook her head and put her hand on her belly. "No, but someday I'll marry Samuel, move to Ireland and meet his family."

"He's different from Serene's father," Anna murmured, rubbing her hand across Margot's stomach.

"What does she mean?" Margot asked, bolting her eyes to Serene.

"My real father left Mama when I was just a

138

baby."

"Papa's not your real papa?" Harry asked.

"He's always been the only father I know, just in a different way than to you and Margot."

Harry shrugged his shoulders and asked to be excused, seemingly not affected by one of the biggest confessions in Serene's life. She chuckled inside at the contrast and watched him go.

"Did her real father die?" Margot asked.

"Your Mama met Angelo Costadina while she was still in school. When Serene came in her womb, the boy tried to stay and make good with your Mama's family, but it didn't last long. They never gave Angelo a chance, so he left and has never been heard of since." Anna paused, as if trying to put it into the right words. "What your Mama did brought a lot of shame to their family name, especially because it was a boy that lived outside of Rome. It truly crushed her. Even after she married your father, she sent letters trying to reach him—for your sake, Serene—but nothing ever came of them."

"Were my grandparents really that awful?"

"Shame causes grief to many people, but as ashamed as your grandparents were, they gave you and your Mama a home, Serene, but not their hearts."

"But it was better with Papa?" Margot asked, her elbows on the table, fully engrossed in the story.

"When your mother met your father," Anna added, "I had just started working for your father. He brought home this lovely *signorina* with a beautiful daughter with eyes like emeralds." Anna seemed to reminisce for a second and then said, "I used to think your mother's voice sounded like soft air."

"Within six months of meeting, your parents were married. Your father made quite an impression on your Mama's family with his feel for business things. Your Mama told me about it once and then never spoke of it again. Nor did she ever see her parents again."

Margot frowned. "Didn't they at least want to see Serene?"

"Papa saved her," Serene murmured, "and me, from the horrible life they would have given us."

"Your Papa loved her so much. That is why he planned ahead for your marriage, *Signorina* Serene, so you would be safe and have a good life, and not have these worries your Mama had."

"And it happened to me instead," Margot said miserably, sitting back in her chair. Unwed and with a child. "I'll take the shame for the family."

Serene hugged her sister. "We would never, ever abandon you as our grandparents did, or stop loving you. Your baby is unexpected, surely." She chuckled. "I have to admit it was a huge surprise, but you have to know this baby is welcomed as a new member of our family. You can be a bit dramatic at times, but your baby is part of us, and we're a part of him—or her. So don't ever forget that."

"You mean that?"

"More than anything."

"Then will you let Anna stay to be this baby's grandmother? She can help prepare for your wedding, too."

Serene gave them a strained smile as she glanced down at her empty ring finger. "If you both promise no more secrets. We're in this together. No matter what happens, we'll be there for each other?"

But it was Serene keeping the biggest secret of all, because she knew no one could help her with that.

****

Serene slipped up to the attic, just as she had when she was a girl, and found the wooden trunk with the tarnished hinges. Her mother's initials,

MM, were engraved on a front plate in the top center of the trunk. Straining to open the lid, she fell back to catch her breath. Inside, she found the large tissue-wrapped package. She flipped back the edges and lifted out her mother's wedding dress. It was a simple ivory dress with a wide matching ribbon of satin across the front, intricate lace edging the petite wrists, and a high neck decorated with a string of pearl droplets.

She turned the dress over and undid the twenty-two buttons going down the back. She had counted them when her mother showed her the dress so many years ago, and she'd never forgotten the number. A surge of excitement hit her and, smiling, she knew she had to try it on. Quickly she stripped off her sweater and skirt and then slowly, gingerly put on the dress. She spied the long, oval mirror in the corner and used a rag to wipe away some of the dust. The dress hung at midcalf, loose around the middle.

"Mama, is that you?" A small voice echoed from behind.

Serene turned to find Harry standing at the top of the stairs, holding the banister. "Oh, Harry, it's just me. Come see. I'm trying on Mama's dress."

"You look like her, just like that picture," he said. "You're like an angel."

"It's just the dress, but our mama was beautiful."

"How come I can't remember her much?"

"You were very small the last time you saw her." Serene skirted up the bottom of the dress, knelt down in front of him and put her hands around his waist. "Come. Close your eyes."

"Why?"

"Just do it, and you'll find out."

Harry squinted and then let his eyes relax.

"Mama used to always hold your cheeks in her

hands and tell you what a big boy you were."

"Wasn't I only a baby?"

"Shhh and listen. When she touched you, her hands were soft and could take away even more pain than a scraped knee gave. And when she would laugh, which she did so much, the corners of her mouth crinkled up. Her hair was the color of honey and ran all the way down her back, but her eyes were the opposite, dark like yours. She used to rock you at night, I remember, and sing for close to an hour each night until you finally fell asleep in her arms. For one song, I can't remember the name, but you used to laugh until you complained that your belly ached enough that you couldn't go to sleep."

Harry's eyes flew open. "The song about the fish who could dance."

"Oh, that's right. Let's see. *Have you ever gone a-fishin'*...mmm, that's all I remember."

"When do they dance?"

"I don't know. We'll have to ask Margot for the rest."

"Then I do remember some."

"Of course you do." Serene pointed to his heart. "She's been right in there all along."

"When you get married, will you leave us the way Mama did?"

Serene's eyes swelled at the innocent question. "She didn't leave us on purpose. She was very sick, and God took her to be with him. I'm sure she's watching you and can't believe how you've grown."

"I guess," he said, lowering his head. "I miss her."

She watched his bottom lip tremble and felt her own insides breaking. "I miss her, too." After a few minutes, she asked, "What are you doing up here, anyway?"

"Promise you won't tell Anna?"

Serene nodded and wiped away the single tear

on his cheek.

"I have some treats hidden in the corner. I come up once in a while, but not every day, I promise."

"That's not so bad. Sometimes I need a space of my own, too. That can be a secret just between us." Serene hugged him. "Maybe coming up here will stop you from pestering *Signore* Miles too much."

"He's leaving tonight. He asked Margot if he could borrow Mama's suitcase."

"What?" She hesitated, ready to launch into questions, but instead, scrambled for her clothes. "He can't be; he's not better."

"Give him some rum cake. That always makes me feel better."

Serene laughed, but he was probably right. "I need to change my clothes. I'll be down in a few minutes."

The last thing she wanted was for Marcus to be the reason for Miles' leaving. Was it because of the words they'd had only that morning? After rewrapping the dress in tissue, she returned it to the trunk and closed the lid, then donned her clothes.

She stopped at her mother's door to see Miles placing his personal things into her mama's embroidered traveling bag. The intricately stitched floral pattern brought a flood of memories racing into her head. Her mother had used it to travel back and forth to the hospital. Serene had helped her pack it again and again.

Light blue nightdress with a matching robe.

Rose-scented soap.

Bible.

Her heart sped up when she noticed a pair of wood crutches beside the wheelchair. "Are you leaving?"

Miles placed his belt and suspenders in the bag. "I hope you don't mind if I borrow the bag. My own pack got messed up real bad. I'll return this one as soon as I get back to the—"

"You don't mind carrying a bag with roses on it?" She tried to smile.

"Unless you have another, I don't mind."

"You're really leaving?"

"Yes." He shoved the remainder of his items into the bag.

"Were you even going to say goodbye?"

"I wanted to make it easy for all of us."

"But what does Samuel say about it?" She didn't care if she sounded like she was pleading for him to stay.

"He was here this morning. Got me those crutches. Listen, I figure that if one leg got me here, it can get me out of here, too." He turned to face her. "You know as well as I do that I need to leave."

Serene would not let herself cry. "I spoke with Marcus," she blurted. "He met me at the restaurant."

"Did he treat you like a civilized human?" He paused. "I'm sorry. You know how I feel about him. I have no business saying a word about it, but it's hard to help myself when I care about you."

"He said you could stay as long as you like. I think he felt bad about what happened."

Miles raised an eyebrow. "That's very generous of him, with no prodding from you, I'm sure. How did that come about?"

"It doesn't matter. What matters is that you and your leg get well."

"I need to go, Serry. It's not good, me being here, for you—or for me. I'm grateful for all of your help. I really mean that."

"Can you wait until I can arrange it with the proper authorities?" In her head she knew it would probably be safe, as Samuel had explained, if they contacted the U.S. government through the underground.

Miles smirked. "You're sure Marcus didn't arrange it for me already? It would be a quick way to get rid of me."

"They would have stormed in here last night, if he had told anyone." She came closer. "Don't go. Please don't leave me—us, I mean. Don't you want to get well first? And it will give me time to see that you leave safely."

"I'm not leaving you. I'm going back to my country where I belong. You have a family here that needs you."

"I need..." She let the rest float away.

"What? What do you need?"

Miles watched her struggle, both of them wordless. Did she need *him?* The night before, he had practically unraveled the sheets, trying to toss and turn away his feelings for her. No matter how much he had been determined to leave and cut her loose without getting more involved in her life, the more he became consumed with her.

"Here, I want to show you something." He reached for the crutch and stood, bearing his whole body weight on the wood. "How do I look?"

"Does it hurt to lean on it like that?"

"If I adjust my weight, it's not too bad."

He hopped a little to reach her, then steadied himself with a hand on her shoulder. "If I stay, you and I both know what would happen." He paused, wanting his words to reach into her soul. "I have to go—for both of us."

"You're right."

Miles came closer, letting his hand drift down the centermost part of her forearm. "About which part?"

With their bodies barely touching, he felt hers responding and molding against his. She lifted her face, her gaze full of her wanting. As he breathed in a trace of lilacs, the silkiness of her hair brushed against his cheek, and he glided his lips down the side of her face, ever so slowly, lower, feeling the slightest tremble at the base of her neck.

Serene arched her neck back. "You should wait until we can locate the right people to bring you to the U.S. ships."

Pressing his body gently against hers, Miles lost his ability to make a sensible decision. He brought his lips down on hers, feeling her fall into the rhythm of his touch. "How long will it take to contact someone?"

"Samuel said a day or two," she whispered.

Leaning back, Miles swallowed hard and tucked loose strands of her hair behind her ear. He wanted her as much as he wanted anything in his life. "If it was another time, another place, it would be right for both of us."

Serene cradled his face in her hands, her eyes wet. "It can never be right. I have another life I have to live."

Dropping his crutch, he closed the little gap left between them. Circling his arms around her, his gaze stopped on the metal chain around her neck. "Is this a dog tag?"

Serene slipped off the chain. "I meant to give it to you. I found it at the restaurant."

Miles lifted the chain dangling from her fingers and let the metal plate settle in his palm. Walt Pierson. "My buddy. He died in my arms that night, before I got to your place," he said roughly. "I was going to bring this to his parents when I got home."

"He must have been a good friend."

"As good as one could be in this Godforsaken time. Thanks for this." He squeezed the chain in his hands. "I thought I had lost it."

"I don't believe you can lose anything you care about. Sometimes it may get misplaced, or broken, but it's never truly lost." A few seconds passed before she added, "I hope you won't lose us when you go back to the States."

He watched her face redden. "Us?"

"Our friendship, I mean."

"Do you want letters? That's what friends do. They write letters about their lives and their families. They talk about the success of their crops that year or maybe share a cake recipe. Is that what you want?"

Serene backed away, her eyes pained. "I just thought—"

"That we could fill each other in, every once in a while? Sure. I'll let you know how my cornfields are doing."

He didn't laugh and neither did she. Seeing the torment in her face, and feeling the burn in his gut, he couldn't imagine having her as a friend and not having more. God help him, he had to leave.

"I just need to leave, and you can go back to your planned life."

"I can't have more with you," she cried. "Don't you understand? What I want, what I really want, was sold away years ago."

"What is it you want, Serry?"

Her eyes searched him, as if searching for an answer that he couldn't give. "My Papa gave up a lot for me to have this marriage."

Fumbling for his crutches, Miles struggled to get closer. "I have no right to ask you to change your life, or choose another path, or do whatever you don't want to do. But for whatever it's worth, I care about what happens to you. Your father seemed like a fair, decent man. He would have done anything, that night in the restaurant, to save anyone except himself. I can't imagine him wanting this for you."

"My father's dealings on this earth left me with no choice."

Wanting to make her parents happy wasn't a

good enough reason, for his Minnesota roots. He understood family commitment and honor. Heck, he'd seen what his own father lived through. But with Serene, something about it went against his grain.. There was more to it, and he swore he'd find out what it was.

Chapter Thirteen

Still breathless after leaving Miles, Serene barely made it downstairs before she heard Genna Sturini's voice streaming from the kitchen. She wanted to run away. Right at that moment, Serene wanted to walk out the front door and not look back.

Instead, she slipped into the washroom and leaned against the back of the door. She took in a long, steady breath and exhaled slowly. Hearing Genna's voice mingled with Anna's, discussing the wedding, Serene knew she was getting closer to the moment with Marcus that she feared the most.

Seeing a glimpse of herself in the small mirror beside the sink, she rubbed her fingers on the dark shadows rimming both eyes. She took a comb from the drawer and paused, not wanting to comb away Miles' touch or smell. Instead, she smoothed her hair down with her hands. From the basin, she splashed water on her face and tilted her head back, letting the coolness run down her neck and onto her chest.

In a heartbeat she could change it all. Tell Everto to keep the money, lose the restaurants, and start over on her life. But as the pressure in her head subsided to a dull ache, she decided it could never happen.

Placing both palms on the pedestal sink, she closed her eyes and summoned enough courage to enter the kitchen. Through the window, she could see Marcus perusing the perimeter of the yard. Not now. She didn't have the strength to handle Marcus and his mother at the same time.

"Ah, there you are, Serene," Genna said.

"Marcus told me the grand news. There is so much planning to do in such little time. But even with the time constraint, I think we can turn this into a social event."

In one sweeping glance, Serene took in all of Genna's perfection. Polished hair. Red-stained lips. A black wool suit with matching pumps, black gloves resting on the table beside her.

Serene kissed Genna on both cheeks. "A small service would be fine."

"Nonsense." She took a cup of coffee from Anna. "First, you need a dress."

"She has her Mama's dress," Anna said.

"I do believe your mother was rather fashion conscious back then, but I remember her dress as being plain—elegant, of course. I was quite a young girl then, newly married myself. Are you sure you won't get something new? Perhaps you could wear my dress? It was the most beautiful thing, with delicate embroidery lining the middle."

"I have my mother's," Serene said crisply. "If it needs mending, I'm sure Anna will do it."

"Whichever you choose, make sure it compliments your best features, especially those colorful eyes of yours."

"What's this about needing a dress?" Marcus asked from the back door.

Genna took a sip of coffee. "As you know, Santa Cecilia has been planned. Would you like me to have our guests back to my home? I hope you don't mind, but I've arranged it all with my cook."

"Did you ask Serene first if that's what she wants?" Marcus asked, kissing Serene on the forehead. "It's her wedding, too."

"Sit," Anna said to Marcus. "Have something to eat."

"And Anna, of course you'll need to be a part of the planning," Genna said nonchalantly. "I won't

150

take no for an answer."

To the side, Marcus whispered in Serene's ear. "What did Anna have to do to get back into your graces?"

Ever so casually, Serene playfully touched his cheek, as if they were lovers. Smiling, hating the moment, she whispered back, "You lied to me. You forced the truth from her about Miles."

Feeling the heat of Marcus' stare, Serene kept her own eyes on Genna, who continued to speak about wedding plans.

Did Genna even realize a world war was going on outside their doors, a war in which Serene's father had become a casualty only a few weeks earlier? Genna discussed the approaching wedding as if it would be the celebration of the century rather than an arrangement. But watching the woman smiling in her own haughty way, Serene was sure of one thing: Marcus hadn't mentioned a word about Miles. "There won't be time for a honeymoon," Genna spouted, "with Marcus having to go back to the factory, but possibly you could stay at our villa for a few nights. Have you decided if you'll live there? I naturally thought you would want that."

"We haven't talked about it, Mother," Marcus said, "but with the baby coming, I think Serene wants to live here."

Genna's gasped, her startled movement sending a splash of coffee trickling down her black jacket. She wiped her mouth with a napkin and seemed to regain her composure. "You're going to have a child?" Her small black eyes probed Serene as if pregnancy were the most horrible event to have happened since the outbreak of war.

"Mother, it's Margot's baby, not Serene's."

"Oh—it's not—my goodness! I thought—"

"*Signorina* Margot needs her sister here, at home," Anna said.

Genna turned sharply to Serene. "What would your father have said? She'll need your help, and with the marriage approaching, I hope you'll still be able to handle your responsibilities to my son. He has had his hands full with the rebuilding of our factory."

Pressing her lips together, Serene badly wanted to tell Genna that it was none of her concern. Instead, she filled her own cup with coffee, and when she offered Marcus another cup, he touched her elbow and gave her a sly smile. "I agree. I think Serene should stay right where she is needed most, at her home. Once Margot is settled with the baby, and Harry has grown, we can move out on our own, but only if she wants to do that. Don't you agree, Serene?"

"Yes, I'd like to stay here," Serene answered quickly. Returning the coffeepot to the stove, she tried to figure out Marcus' reasoning. He couldn't be defending her, could he? His smug expression told her he probably had the idea planned out from the beginning. For his mother's benefit, Serene added, "Margot's baby will not add a burden on this family that can't be managed."

Genna frowned. "I believe your father would have been ashamed, but on behalf of his memory, our family will still do what we can to help out."

Serene wanted to slap her. She wanted to show her, right then and there, how wrong she was, how spiteful she sounded. Instead, not wanting to tarnish her own ability to be a real lady, she bit the inside of her cheek to gain control before discussing the subject.

"And what will you do about the restaurants?" Genna asked.

"They're salvageable, and I'm going to try my best to bring them back to what my father had. Everto seems to think this war will break soon."

"You can't work on them once you're married, my dear."

"That's what I'm planning to do." Serene held her breath, knowing Marcus' position on the matter. It was as though they were acting in a theatre and this was all a story she was participating in rather than her life.

Marcus cleared his throat. "Of course a woman should be able to pursue her own dreams, but only if there is nothing else to keep her mind occupied."

"What would that be?" Serene challenged him.

"Children. A household that needs food and clothing and mending."

"Women don't take jobs outside of the home," Genna said, in a proud tone. "Marcus' father has always supported us by working outside the home, and I stay inside to take care of all those things you mentioned. There's no greater joy than watching your children grow to be men."

"It's different for me, since my father isn't here to carry on our business and the traditions we set. It's my turn."

"It's in her blood to follow her Papa's steps," Anna retorted.

"You two have plenty of time to decide these things," Genna said, ignoring Anna's remark. "But I'm sure, once you are settling into your new lives, things will change."

"My mother's right," Marcus remarked, turning from the window. "We don't have to decide anything yet."

They've already been decided, he thought, leaning back on his chair and smiling. Not because his mother supported his wishes, or because Margot was going to have a baby. He smiled because the oak table at which he sat would be his, as would the villa and all the money from her father. And selling off her father's restaurants would bring in more money to finish his plan to buy land in the hills and start his own spaghetti factory. Never again would he have to smile to the other workers while his father cast him aside when it came to the bigger responsibilities of running the factory. Time after time his father had walked past him without so much as a slap on the back or an appreciative word.

The reason was simple, as Jack Sturini had explained to Marcus on several occasions. He claimed his son had to grow in business sense in order to handle the major decisions. Running one of the largest spaghetti factories in Rome required someone with strong determination, someone capable of dealing with deadlines across the country. And apparently, according to his father, Marcus took the easy way out too many times. Marcus despised the accusation and vowed to prove his father wrong. He clasped his hands together behind his head and listened to the women chatter about his wedding. The only goal he had was to build the biggest empire he could and put his father's factory under.

His thoughts were broken by the arrival of Samuel, who took off his coat and bid a hello to the group. Marcus noticed Serene's eyes dart from Samuel to Genna and knew his mother had to be wondering why a doctor was arriving in the middle of the day, carrying his medical bag. With folded arms, Marcus prepared to watch them scramble. How he would have loved to tell his mother that an American soldier was hiding in that very house, waiting for Samuel's medical attention. Be patient, he thought. If the truth came out too quickly, his mother would never let the marriage take place.

"Samuel, it's such a surprise to see you," Serene said, kissing him on both cheeks.

Marcus exchanged a handshake with Samuel. Watching Serene squirm was entertaining, especially when she was always so composed.

"Come, sit," Genna said to Samuel, "and let's talk about this child on the way." She focused on his medical bag. "Are you here to give someone medical attention?"

"No. To see Margot, actually."

Genna eyed him. "What is the occasion, if you took time from the hospital?"

"I come and go, especially with our child on the way."

"I do think Margot's father would have had concerns with it. An immediate marriage must be planned. I'm only saying that because Anthony isn't here to say it."

"She's a stubborn girl, but once Margot says yes, we'll marry as soon as the war has ended."

"You'll wait all that time to legitimize that child? It doesn't have to be a big ceremony, of course. Maybe I should talk with her and get this straightened out. Anthony would've dropped on the spot if he knew one of his daughters had a child before marriage."

"With respect to you, Margot and I must decide what is best for this baby."

"She is only a child herself. How much can she know about these things?" Genna scolded. "I'll stay a little longer and set Margot straight about some things."

Samuel reddened. "Again, with respect, *Signora* Genna, I appreciate your advice, but we can make our own decisions, with or without anyone's consent. Margot will stay with Serene until the war has ended. It's safer for her to be with her sister rather than living with a doctor who is never home."

Genna stood and grabbed her gloves from the table. "I was only doing what Anthony would have wanted. It's getting late and my husband needs his meal. Marcus, take me home."

"I suppose it *is* getting late," Marcus said. "Too

late to make any more decisions."

****

It was Thursday at sunset. And that meant the special mass given by Padre Angelo at Santa Cecilia for fallen soldiers. Whether it was a British, American, Polish, or Italian soldier, it didn't make any difference. As dangerous as it seemed, the Germans never bothered the doings in a church unless there was a reason. It always touched Serene in the deepest way to have her community pay homage to men who had never lived on their soil. And she guessed Franci must have told the Padre the entire story of the American soldier, Clay, being killed at the restaurant at the same time as her father. What a wonderful and decent man Franci was.

Serene bit her lip, having already thought again and again and decided to go alone to the service, without Anna or her sister. For purely selfish reasons, she needed the time to be alone. Samuel said he had new information for someone to pick up Miles, but at the moment he was preoccupied with Margot. Shaking her head in frustration, she shoved her arm into a coat sleeve, reminding herself to talk with Samuel when she returned.

The church was less than a mile away, and walking would give her the much needed air and space she'd been craving. It was her usual ritual to go with Anna, so at the last second guilt got the best of her. "Anna, would you like to come with me to the vigil?" she yelled toward the kitchen.

Anna came into the room, rubbing her hands on her apron. "You go. I'll stay here with Harry. Margot is with *Signore* Samuel. Say two novenas for that poor man who died with your father."

"If it hadn't been him, it could have been Miles instead."

"You care for him, *no*?"

"Of course, like a nurse for her patient. I just want to see him get well."

Anna scowled. "Your face tells a lot more."

"No, it's not like that. He brought me closer to my father, in an odd sort of way. There is nothing else to tell, so I'm going to the mass."

"Will Marcus be at the mass?"

"No." Serene took Anna's hands. "And if he pays a call here, please tell him I'm not feeling well." If Marcus found out that she attended the special mass when one of the soldiers being honored was American, it might make him angry enough to give away their secret of Miles being at the villa. She didn't want to stir the waters that had finally seemed to settle. Or what Marcus apparently considered as settled.

She stepped outside, debating about whether to invite Miles to the mass. There were still Germans around, hiding bombs, waiting for villagers or remaining soldiers to make a wrong move, and she didn't want Miles falling prey to them. Taking a risk like that, being seen in a public mass right before he was going to leave, seemed ridiculous. Still, she cursed herself now for keeping it from him. Clay was his friend and, whether he should attend or not, Miles would have wanted to pay his respects. She turned back through the door. He was a grown man and had a right to know. If he chose to argue it, she'd be ready.

"I need to tell you something." Her eyes narrowed on him as he sat in the wheelchair beside the fireplace.

He glanced at her coat. "Have you arranged it? Am I leaving now?"

"No, I am." She paused. "To church."

A shred of relief passed over his face. "Sitting through a service isn't that bad, not bad enough to put that sour face on you. When I was young, my father used to tell me to keep myself busy during the lecture by saying a prayer for each of the rafters in the church's ceiling. Is it a holy day or something?"

It was Serene's turn to laugh. "Each Thursday a mass is said for the soldiers who have perished in the war. Tonight, I think it may be for your friend Clay and a few others."

"You waited until now, when you're walking out the door, to tell me? Of course I'm coming with you." He lifted his rear end off the chair, trying to bear weight on his legs.

"No," she said, holding his shoulders lightly. "That is exactly why I couldn't tell you. I know he was your friend and you did a lot for each other to come this far. But taking you there, in front of all those people, risks everything. But I couldn't go without asking you if there is anything you want me to—say to him—say to his spirit, I mean."

"I don't know, really. He was a good man, and without him I wouldn't have made it out of Anzio."

"How about I tell him that?"

"We bunked together a few months, and then in those hours he got us to Rome, I got to know him better than any of my family. He lay on the ground next to me as those Jerries trampled over us. Just the sound of his breath was assuring, you know what I mean?"

Serene nodded her head slowly, struggling with tears. She didn't want to pretend she understood. Unless she had lived it herself, she couldn't possibly understand. The pain in his eyes drew a picture in her head far worse than she could imagine on her own.

He took her hand. "You really don't want me to go?"

The intense blue of his eyes threatened to wear her down, fighting what little strength she had left. "I don't think you should."

"Even if you need me there?"

"I don't—"

"Clay was my friend, but it was your father, too. You may want someone else there with you. If not Anna or Margot, you can take me. I'm not suggesting anything else, just that you might need a friend. I'll disguise myself. No one will ever know."

Serene's heart lurched. "I'm a grown woman and going to mass is something I do all the time. This one can't be that different, can it?"

"You know what I mean," he said with a huskiness that pulled her insides to him.

Serene heaved in a breath and took her hand away. "No, I don't. And I don't want to know. I *can't* know."

For a few seconds, neither of them spoke. Was it really too dangerous, or was she just desperate to keep him at arm's length? After their last encounter, she didn't trust herself anymore to stay away from him. "Sam will be here later," she said softly. "He mentioned earlier that he had details about your leaving. Maybe as soon as tomorrow you'll be able to return to the States."

"Will I see you before then?" he asked stiffly, "or shall we say goodbye now?"

It was as if he challenged her feelings, right there, right when she was her most vulnerable. Struggling to calm the tremble in her throat, she pushed out the words. "Of course we'll have a chance to say goodbye."

Miles looked away from her. "Tell Clay he was the one of the best damn buddies."

****

Still hashing over whether to follow Serene to her church, Miles hobbled to the window and watched her silhouette disappear in the dark shadow of the street.

Even in the short time they had grown to know

each other, she listened to what he had to say. He'd even told her about his father, a part of his life he had never shared with anyone. And from someone else, he might have expected judgment about how he handled his relationship with the old man, but not from Serene. She was different. He could talk with her about anything or about nothing. Dammit, he cared so much for her, but that was as far as he would take it. And if he couldn't have more with her, he'd take the friendship over nothing.

When Anna came into the room, her more-than-usually grim expression piqued his curiosity. On a whim, he asked, "Did Serene leave for church?"

Anna put down the plate of fruit and nuts. She muttered something but Miles couldn't put together the mixed English and Italian.

"She went alone?"

Making a tsk-tsk sound, Anna shook her head fast. "*Non capisco—*"

"I wanted to go with her, but she convinced me that it wouldn't be safe."

Harry came into the room and ran to Miles. "How is your war injury?"

Miles pulled his attention from Anna, knowing in that minute that, for a reason he couldn't yet figure out, it had been a wrong decision to not accompany Serene. He should have followed his intuition and gone with her, and to heck if she would be mad at him. "It's fine. Just fine. Want to help me into these crutches and I'll show you how good I've gotten on them?"

Harry's eyes widened.

"Can you bring them to me?"

After handing him the crutches, Harry helped place one under each of Miles' arms. "There," he said, beaming.

Anna said something and clapped her hands three times.

Harry glanced at Miles. "She's just happy you'll be walking on these, and then you'll be able to leave." He gave him a sheepish grin. "She doesn't like you here," he whispered.

Laughing out loud, Miles braced himself on the crutches. He hopped the first step, and then the second, and still smiling, hopped quickly to the other side of the room.

"Wait until Serene sees."

"I showed her a little bit already." Hesitating, he added, "Did she really go alone to church?"

Harry thought for a second. "*Si*, I think so."

"I'd like to go, too. Can you ask Anna to take me to the church?"

He relayed the request in Italian to Anna.

Anna replied so quickly, Miles could hardly catch any break between her words. And then she said, "No-o-o," making the tsk-tsk sound again.

"Tell her I have missed the church, that it would mean the world to me to attend the service for my friend." Anna was the old religious sort, and he knew it could help him to bring God into it.

Harry relayed the message. She answered, threw her hands up in the air, and left the room. "She said it's too dangerous. The Germans might see you. But I know you wouldn't let them hurt you."

"Thanks for trying." Miles kept his tone even for the boy's sake.

Harry lingered, then came closer and whispered in his ear. "I can take you."

"Buddy, I can't ask you to do that. You heard Anna, it would be too dangerous, not just for me, but for you, too."

"I can show you the way, and you can go on your own from there. I don't think Serene would mind."

The advice of a child sounded more logical than all the thoughts Miles had considered for the last month or so. Letting Serene go without him was the first mistake. Giving up the fight with Anna to join her would be the second. Serene must have wanted him to go. Why else would she have come back to tell him, minutes before she left, when she hadn't even mentioned it before. Girls just had a roundabout way to doing things. "How far is it?"

"It's less than one mile, straight up the main road. Serene walked, but you won't be able to make it on those crutches."

"I've performed more miracles than that," he said. "Can you draw me a map? And I'll take it from there."

Chapter Fourteen

Clutching her rosary beads, Serene apologized to God profusely for not concentrating on the mass and begged his forgiveness. She twiddled her fingers and prayed. And stood. And prayed again. All the while, her heart moved further away from the altar at Santa Cecilia's and away from the Padre's kind words about Clay and the other soldiers. And back to Miles.

When she knelt, a small noise pulled her eyes to the back of the church, toward the main door. A man hobbled on crutches down the center of the aisle toward her. As he got closer, she recognized her father's gray overcoat and black, wide-brimmed hat. *Miles?* She put her fingers to her lips to prevent herself from gasping out loud. She put her chin to her chest, her heart beating fast.

She lifted her gaze again to the sanctuary, as if not recognizing him. She concentrated on Padre Angelo holding the host in the air, thankful her dark veil covered the burning in her cheeks.

As Miles slipped into the pew beside her and removed his hat, the tip of one crutch banged against the wood bench. The Padre's eyes slid down to meet hers, and the pit of her stomach jumped.

She was surely going to hell.

Miles knelt down on the kneeler, and she knew by the clean scent that he was right beside her, close enough to touch. *Pray.* Look to God for peace, she chastised herself, keeping her eyes riveted to the sprays of colored glass behind the altar. The most sacred part of the mass was occurring, and she had a hard time pulling her concentration away from the man beside her, the man whose mesmerizing blue eyes had the ability to see into her soul.

They finally stood for the Lord's Prayer, still not looking at each other. If only for that one moment, they stood like man and wife. Serene's breath stopped when Miles' hand touched hers lightly, the same way it had that fateful night in the restaurant to show her he was alive. With her chest pounding, Serene moved her hand closer, so the backs of their hands were touching. The warmth of his skin sent a shiver of exhilaration all the way to her temples.

When the prayer ended, Serene dared to catch a glimpse of him from the corner of her eye. He stared straight ahead, seemingly engrossed in the mass. Fear and excitement scrambled in her head. Why had he jeopardized his freedom and their safety to come there? His compassion for his friend drove him there, she was sure, but it didn't cushion the new fear that grew in her heart. Trying to get him out of there at that minute was impossible, and the end of the mass was an eternity away. An eternity to be with him. For once, she didn't want to push the thought away. In a full church, with lots of eyes and ears, they were still alone, if only in her mind.

As if he read her thoughts, he turned to her and winked, that simple wink he had done so many times before, the same wink that shimmied her belly into a knot. She bit her lip to keep from smiling at the grin that sat on his lips.

When the line started forming to receive the Lord's body, Miles pushed back against the pew, to let the others pass. The line paused, just as the side of Serene's knee grazed his thigh.

With the slightest movement, she felt the tip of his fingers rub against her knee within the folds of her skirt. Fighting the urge to respond, or touch his hand, she kept her eyes locked forward. She stepped slowly over his bad leg, ever so gently swaying her hips toward him. As she exited the pew, she heard his chest empty of air.

Returning, she said her prayer, under the baritone of the *Ava Maria* being played on the organ, and then whispered in his ear, "You shouldn't have come."

"I couldn't have done it without Harry. He's a real good kid."

Serene frowned. "Harry? What does he have to do with this?"

A man in front of them cleared his throat and Serene lowered her head.

Miles leaned over. "He drew a map with all the right points, cows and farms and olive groves. He wanted to come, but I didn't think it was a good idea."

"At least you showed some good judgment by leaving him at home."

"Was it good judgment for you to come alone?" He wasn't going to be apologetic that he came. Showing his respect for Clay was one reason, but protecting her was more important. If it put a beacon on himself for the Germans to find, so be it.

When the last hymn waned, the Padre gave the final blessing.

A man came from behind and kissed Serene on both cheeks. He whispered something in her ear and Miles watched her face grow pale. The man stared Miles down, but he didn't make a gesture to shake hands or make any other greeting. He continued his conversation with Serene in Italian, glancing back and forth between Serene and Miles. As Miles listened, the voice sounded so familiar, but he couldn't identify it.

Serene nodded briskly and then came back to Miles. "I knew it wasn't right for you to come. People are already questioning who you are."

The desperation in her face immediately made him sorry for putting her in that situation. He didn't care what happened to him, but for all the help she had given him, he would never want to put her in that kind of jeopardy. "It was probably wrong of me, but in some crazy way I thought you might need me." He reached over to touch her shoulder, but she snapped it away from him.

"We must leave now."

Miles put his hat back on and followed her to the door. Others passed them, some gazed, others stared. One step, two steps... He didn't know walking down a few steps quickly would be so difficult. But as long as he made it down those steps without a chair, he didn't care how long it took.

Outside the perimeter of the church, they faced the dark road. Serene walked a little ahead of him, but he didn't miss the few tears she wiped from her cheek. Miles wobbled behind her, trying to think of anything to get her to talk. "Our church back home is an old wooden schoolhouse," he rambled on. "It's not used for a school anymore, just Sunday masses. But it does the job. Confessions, marriages, baptisms. All of it."

"Sounds nice," Serene murmured. She strolled away and then stopped abruptly. "How did you get here?"

"By these crutches."

"All this way?"

"A mile? That's hop, skip, and jump where I come from."

"Where is it?"

"What?"

Her hands went to her hips. "The wheel chair?"

"Oh." He grinned. "How did you know?" He used one of his crutches to point to the woods along the outside of the church grounds. "Over there."

She stalked to the bushes, as if not believing

him.

"Aren't you going to yell at me some more for coming here?" he called after her, but not before she disappeared behind the largest bush. When she came out, pushing the chair, with olive leaves stuck to her coat and hair, he would have fallen in love on the spot, if he hadn't already.

"Sit," she said, her finger pointing to the seat of the chair.

"Not until you tell me why you're so upset. Do you see anyone running after us?" He tried to lighten the dread on her face. "It's good of you to be worried about me, but I can take care of you and myself at the same time."

Serene turned her face from him and folded her arms.

He hopped closer and pulled one of the small leaves from the shoulder of her coat. "Did the service bring up memories of your father?"

"No, it wasn't like that."

He shook his head back and forth. "Coming here was stupid, I know. I guess I thought in some odd way that you would have liked me here, since we did share a lot that night."

"I did need you there," she blurted.

Miles fought the urge to kiss away the new tears that surfaced in her eyes. "You should have just said so," he said in a low voice. "Then you wouldn't be angry with me."

"I'm not," she said. "It's just, well, a lot has been happening, and I'm confused and overwhelmed."

Leaning closer, he kissed her lightly, slowly taking her lips with his own, tasting the sweetness he'd sworn he would never taste again.

Their eyes met and she caressed his cheek.

"We'd better get back," she said. "I'll help you home."

"Right."

As she eased him into the chair, she teetered and lost her balance, her upper body falling into him. Laughing, he maneuvered her into sitting on his lap.

"Aren't I too heavy?"

Miles grinned and started wheeling the chair. "I can handle both of us."

Feeling her closeness against his skin, he couldn't take his eyes from her. And each time the chair hit a patch of rock, the bumpiness jostled her hips against his thighs. He wondered how much a guy could take, of having a beautiful girl on his lap while his hands were busy wheeling a chair.

"You're sure I'm not hurting you?" she asked.

"Put your arms around my neck."

A large bump thrust her against him, her lips landing within an inch of his cheek. When she threw her arms around his neck, her scent and softness consumed him all at the same time. His self-control was somewhere blowing in the wind, and it seemed natural to kiss her, so he did. Just a little one wouldn't hurt. On her neck. Her ear. Oh, and her chin...

"Isn't that better?" he mumbled, stopping the chair.

"Mm." She tightened her hold on him, her mouth coming down on his slowly, lingering as if it belonged there and nowhere else. "But I can still walk."

"I know," he said, laughing softly.

****

Marcus paced the floor, his fists clenched, a white towel wrapped around his waist. Perspiration dotted his forehead and the bridge of his nose. He had been pacing since he learned that Serene had masqueraded her American around town, in his own church. His mother's friend had seen them and questioned Marcus for forty-five minutes while he tried to calm her about it, making excuses for Serene. His mother would certainly cancel the wedding if she knew about the soldier, but there was too much money at stake; he couldn't let that slip through his fingers.

What was she thinking, being disloyal to him in public? Didn't her golden Papa teach her anything about respecting a man? And this was even after he, Marcus, had made such an effort to give her another chance. Did she think that story of hers would work on him? He had almost laughed at her, sitting so prim and serious at the table, pretending she wasn't afraid of him. None of that mattered, really. He would take the money, and she would be the casualty.

Then it hit him. Could she have bedded the American? No. He shook his head, going to the other side of the room. He was dead sure she was a virgin. The girl had too many morals.

He interlocked his fingers and pushed them out, sending out the rhythmic sound of his knuckles cracking. Then he flexed his biceps and squeezed, examining the contour of the muscles. Women loved that. They even made love to him because of his body. Feeling the burn of the muscles contracting started to ease his mood a little.

He had to admit that riding Serene's gorgeous figure would be fun for a little while.

"Are you going to drop that thing and come get me, or what?" Ava's husky voice called from the doorway leading into the bedroom. Her long black hair streamed down around her shoulders, a few strands strategically placed to cover the center of each bare breast. She crooked her finger and wagged it his way.

Marcus perused her up and down, his eyes lingering on that special woman's spot he loved to taste. It was barely covered by white lace that rose high on each thigh. The twinge in his groin made him cast the towel aside. At the same time, he forgot all about Serene Moneto. For the moment.

****

"Anna, the meal is delicious." Miles sat back in the chair with a satisfied smile. "I'm gonna miss your cooking."

Serene relayed the message to Anna in Italian, still feeling his eyes on her. Since their return from church, his gaze had followed her every move. Even as she helped prepare the evening meal, she felt him watching. All the way back to the house, she had tried to think of a reason to dislike him, any reason that would take away the sting of his leaving. But for the entire mile, sitting on his lap, feeling his closeness and watching his arms move the wheels, she couldn't think of a single one.

"You outdid yourself this time," Samuel said, reaching for some polenta.

"*Grazie.*" Anna cast a worried glance toward Margot. "*Mangi, mangi.*"

"Ugh." Margot groaned, holding her stomach. She twirled pasta on her fork. "I wouldn't be able to eat if I tried. I'm not hungry."

"The baby needs nourishment," Samuel said.

"But the sick feeling in my stomach..."

"It's all normal," Samuel said. "Take deep breaths. "In. Out. In..."

Margot took in an exaggerated breath. "It happens more when I eat."

Serene caught the confusion on Miles' face and realized he had no idea what they were saying in Italian. "She's not feeling well."

"Are you taking Miles to his home?" Harry asked Samuel, before stuffing a piece of bread in his mouth.

"Yes, in a way, I am." Samuel directed his gaze to Miles. "We can go over the details in a little while,

170

but someone I know can get you to Anzio. From there, I'm afraid you'll be on your own."

"I can find my way. Once I get back to the States, I want to pay you for all your trouble."

"Think of it as a going-away present. If you can handle the travel, I think we can get you out of here tomorrow night. Medically speaking, I believe you can make the trip."

"Me, too. I'm ready."

Samuel slapped him on the shoulder. "If nothing happened to you tonight in a public church, I think you'll make it back. You agree, Serene?"

"He's walking now. Wasn't that what we were waiting for?" She picked up her full plate and brought it to the sink.

"Don't take it personally, m'friend," Samuel said. "She is under a great deal of stress with this wedding coming up. All women get like that."

Serene mustered the most realistic smile she could and came back to the table. "My marriage has nothing to do with anything. And, Samuel," she said with an accusing tone, "don't put your nose where it doesn't belong."

"You need my nose to get this man out of here."

Harry giggled.

Gulping the last of his wine, Miles poured another drink. "What's the plan?"

Samuel pushed his plate away. "A man I met a few years ago got into a little trouble and needed medical help but wouldn't go to the hospital. I won't go into details, but I ended up treating him, and now he's willing to do me a favor and take you to Anzio."

Returning to the table, Serene raised her eyebrows. "You trust him?"

"As much as you can trust a man on the other side of the law." He took a sip of wine. "He turned himself in to the government some time back, and now he's a soldier. A good trade, I would say, for his crime. He's lucky they didn't kill him."

"What was his crime?" Serene asked.

"Murder. But don't let that worry you. He's a good man now, and he owes me a big one."

Miles glanced at Serene and back at Samuel. "If you trust him, I'm in. When?"

"Tomorrow, about seven, right after dark. Take only what's necessary. He'll bring you to the shoreline where you first landed. We believe there are American troops there. You sure you're ready?"

"Yup." Miles leaned back and ran his hand through his hair.

"I'm going to be sick." Margot wailed. She pushed back her chair and fell sideways to the floor.

Samuel jumped from his chair more quickly than the others and helped her up. "Let's get her to bed," he said. "Bring some water," he called back to them. Anna poured some water from the jug and followed to the bedroom.

Harry's face whitened. "What happened?"

"The baby makes her feel uncomfortable," Serene said in an even tone, not wanting to worry him more. "It's normal for her to feel like this."

"Will Margot die like Mama did?"

"No," Serene said quickly, her eyes wet with tears. She held him close, wanting to squeeze away all his fear.

"Then why is she so sick?" his small voice demanded.

"All new mothers feel sick once in a while," Miles explained. "It's natural in the first few months."

"Oh." Harry seemed to accept the rash explanation.

"Since I'm leaving tomorrow, buddy, do you want to show me that barn? I've been dying to see it."

Serene gave Miles a grateful glance.

Harry pondered for a second, and then his face lit up and he turned to Serene. "Can I?"

Before she answered, Miles cut in, "Only if your sister agrees to go."

Serene's heart began to beat faster. He raised his eyebrows, as if waiting for her to accept the challenge of spending more time together. Serene wanted to argue with Harry, but she couldn't crush him. She couldn't trust herself to spend time with Miles, but it was no reason to deny little Harry some fun. Besides, her brother's persistence and rush of energy made it simpler to just give in and accompany him to the barn. She sent Miles a wistful glance and then answered Harry, "Only for a few minutes. We need to come back soon in case Margot needs us."

Chapter Fifteen

"You want to see the barn that much?" Serene asked, crossing her arms. As she took a breath, the cool night air made her shiver.

"Only if you'll show me." On crutches, Miles followed them outside, to the back of the villa.

"I will." Harry bounded ahead of them into the yard.

Fixing her gaze on the clear night sky, empty of smoke or planes, Serene wanted to make the moment stay forever. Even the stars shimmered against the dark backdrop. "Do you hear that?"

Miles gave her a questioning look. "I don't hear anything."

"Me neither," Harry added.

"Exactly," she murmured. "No gunfire, no bombs. Just quiet." She sauntered across the moist grass, feeling its cushion beneath her feet. She took Harry's hands and swung in a full circle with him, laughing. "Who knows for how long?"

"It must be the beginning of the end," Miles said.

Harry let go of her hands and ran across the grass, beating them to the barn. "Are you really leaving?"

"Looks like it, buddy."

"Are you gonna miss us?"

Serene tousled her brother's hair. "I'm sure *Signore* Miles has more to think about than us. He'll be busy with his own life when he returns."

"I'll be back on the farm, fixing it up and getting the corn ready for next year's harvest."

"Your family must be missing you."

"I suppose so. I have some cousins that I'd like to see when I get back. I think one of them just had a new baby."

"Like Margot."

"Yeah." Miles laughed.

"Do you think they'll send you back to the war?" Harry asked. "Then you can come back and see us."

"Not sure, buddy. Maybe if my leg gets all the way better."

As another question formed at Harry's lips, Anna called his name from the back door, making his face drop.

"He'll be right there, " Serene answered.

The door slammed and Miles grinned. "Now I've really gotten you into trouble."

Serene mouthed a "thank you" to him for bearing all the questions. She knew Harry was going to miss him.

"She's always mad, but I like her," Harry said, waving his hand. "C'mon. I only have a few minutes." He unlatched the barn's double doors. A rooster scurried out. "Two stalls over there are for cows, and that one is for Margetta, our horse. She has the whole barn to herself now. Except for a couple of chickens."

They stepped inside and met the clean scent of hay. Serene ran her fingers through Margetta's soft, dark mane.

"Do you ride her much?" Miles asked.

"Mama did, I think." Harry opened the stall gate. "Serene used to ride her, too, a long time ago. And now I'm learning. Geraldo takes care of him, and sometimes he comes to show me how to do that and the riding. He says they are equally important, caring and riding."

"He's right. Can we go riding together sometime?"

"You shouldn't put his hopes up like that," Serene whispered. "You don't know if you'll ever be back."

"Don't listen to her. I know you'll be back," Harry winked. "You're part of our family now."

Miles playfully punched his shoulder. "You take care of everyone after I leave, right? You're the man now."

"Harry?"

At the sound of Anna's second call, Harry's smile faded. "I forgot..."

"She didn't," Miles said.

"You'd better go, Harry." Serene patted his head, fighting the urge to laugh. "Say goodnight to *Signore* Miles, and you can say goodbye to him tomorrow."

Harry ran out of the barn, and they both burst out laughing.

Serene shut the stall gate. "You were so patient with him."

"He's a good kid."

"He likes you a lot." *And so do I.*

In the few seconds of quiet, they stood looking at each other, each as if waiting for the other to say something that would keep them there longer. She didn't want the night to end. Just a few minutes more, she promised herself, and they would go in.

As she relatched the barn doors, she said over her shoulder. "Did you ever ride?"

"At nightfall. We used to ride after the chores were done. Pa would take me out to the cliff overlooking the lake. We'd ride for hours, and then come in with barely enough time for shuteye before starting our work again the next day."

There was a long pause before Miles asked, "What about you? Did you ever take her out? I mean, before things got bad with the war?"

Serene sighed. "Before, when things weren't so busy here, but it's been a long time. Harry told you

176

about Geraldo. He takes care of her and teaches Harry to ride. He brings Anna apples when he comes. I think he has a fancy for her."

"One day I'll come back and take you riding, if you want."

"I'll be a married woman, then. That wouldn't be proper."

"I suppose not. I expect Anna will see to it that you keep things proper. Will she stay with you once you're married?"

"Marcus said—yes, she will. With the baby coming and Harry needing me, there doesn't seem to be a choice. We'll live in my home for a little while." With a dull smile, she gestured to the yard. "Why don't we go take a look around?" Not waiting, she whisked by him and headed toward the outskirts of the property that lined the woods, knowing he was only a few steps behind her.

"My parents planted many of these trees. Papa thought the oaks made it more peaceful out here."

"Talk to me, Serry. You know I can't leave you like this." His breath dusted the outer part of her ear. "You know I care for you, no matter how much you think it could never work."

Serene nodded quickly, without turning, and walked a little further from him. "I'll have a new life and a new purpose." She clenched her teeth together to stifle a sob. "Nothing else will matter."

"Your life will be just beginning. Of course things will change, but you'll be all right. You're a strong woman."

Serene faced him, her eyes filling. "And you have Josie to go back to."

"Serene—don't."

"I helped you when you needed it. That's the only way God intended us to be together."

He tilted up her chin and used a finger to smudge along the bottom of her lip line. "You must love him, for you to pledge your life to him like this. Because of that, I could never be the cause of you leaving him. But if you tell me you want *us* more than you want him, I'll tell the world."

Serene's mind whirled. Could she explain that her father's lifetime of work and savings now hinged on her marriage to Marcus? She pressed her forehead against his chest. She couldn't.

Miles dropped one crutch and grabbed her shoulder, crushing her against his chest. "Please tell me what it is, so I can understand. What could be so awful that you keep it bottled up and let it eat at you?"

"I can't tell you. I won't. Please don't ask me." She pressed both palms on his chest.

Neither of them moved as he stared down at her. The yearning was there in his face, in the curve of his eyes as they centered on her. It was the same desire that had been building inside her.

Their lips were held apart by the strength of a feather. All of her senses ignited, Serene's breasts swelled with anticipation as she pressed them against his chest. He groaned and brought his lips down on hers. She kissed him back, tasting him, their bodies clinging to each other. She tugged on his lips with her teeth and then kissed him again, deeper, feeling his tongue mingle with her own.

Serene played with the top two buttons of his shirt, distracted with the realization that there was nothing either of them could do to stop it.

Miles pulled his mouth from hers. "We—"

Before he could finish, Serene put her index finger to his lips.

"No," Miles said. "I can't destroy what you already have planned." He held her face in his hands. "I won't. You mean too much to me." He stroked the tip of his thumb down the side of her face and pushed back a few strands of hair that fell near her eyes. "We have a friendship that is worth everything to me."

Serene froze, immediately snapped back into reality. Humiliation crept into her face as she realized what she had nearly done. Her lips still tingled as she took her hands from his shirt. "I didn't mean to make it worse." She stumbled back from him, her eyes glazed. How could she have been so foolish as to think things could be changed. "I'm sorry," she said, shaking her head. "This isn't fair to you."

Covering her mouth, she turned from him.

"Fair? That's hardly it. I wouldn't be able to live with myself if I took you from the life you have planned. Dammit, Serry, you know what I mean. Your father gave his life for me and now, in a way, if you didn't go on the plans he made for you, it would be like I was dishonoring his memory."

His words spun through her head. Could she tell him that she loved him and wanted him more than any other soul on earth? She hated him for making her feel that much love, showing her how to see it, breathe it, and then making her walk away. If she let herself go any farther, she would be running into his arms, begging him to love her in the same way she loved him. But she had no right to expect anything from him.

"I won't be there to say goodbye. I could never say it, never watch you walk out that door. I can't, Miles."

With a sob, she ran to the only place she could find comfort.

"Serry?"

Only the low chorus of night bugs answered him.

"Dammit. I didn't mean to hurt your feelings." Miles stumbled onto an overgrown path and expertly made his way through the beginning of the woods, grateful that even with his bum leg he was able to somewhat maneuver in the dark. The full moon against the dark sky cast grayness on the trees, and for once he acknowledged all the army training was worth more than he'd ever imagined. He used the crutch tip to guide himself through the brush.

"Serry?" Annoyance invaded the pit of his stomach. She ran as if it were his fault. He clutched the handle of the crutch and caught his breath, cursing her, and cursing himself more for having to let her go.

The path ended a few paces away and Miles stopped as his crutch knocked against a hard structure. Dragging the tip across the wood, he moved closer, and a few branches prickled his cheek. Once he found her, he swore he would carry her back to the house and then lay out the truth for her. She was engaged, and he was leaving because of her. *For* her.

In one fluid movement, he gripped one arm on his crutch and ripped some branches from the trees and tossed them out of his way. He stood back, squinting in the darkness at the back of a little house and following the roof's outline against the bright moon. "What the—" He moved more branches out of the way as he felt his way to the other side, reached the door, and swung it open.

"Serry? You in here?" His voice was more demanding than he cared it to be, but his patience had thinned considerably. He waited a moment and then, teetering on his good leg, he tried to balance but instead toppled through the door, somehow twisting enough to land on his rear end, his bad leg still outstretched in front. "That went smooth," he murmured to himself.

After a few minutes, he heard a scutter from a few feet away.

"You make me crazy, you know that? You make

me care about you, not like a man should care about a woman, but the way a man wants to care about her. But you have a commitment, you understand?"

By the little slivers of moonlight coming in between the wall boards, he realized she was sitting in the opposite corner of the small room.

He closed his eyes and prepared to wait. He would sit there all night if he had to.

As Serene listened to the steady rhythm of his breaths, she knew that running from him was cowardly. Even if he didn't reciprocate, she at least had to tell him that he made her feel safe and alive. The love that she never wanted had somehow found her. He could never know about the money or her true purpose in marrying Marcus, but she needed to face him and face the truth, so they could both move on.

She crawled to the other side of the room and sat next to him. Their thighs barely touched, but the electricity of having him there, in her little house, began to overwhelm her mission.

"I could never betray my family, but then I started feeling things for you." She shook her head, trying to make sense of her thoughts when she felt his hand rest on her knee.

"I would never ask you to do that." He started to get up, but Serene held his arm.

"When I saw you walk into church on those crutches, it was then that I fully understood how much I care about you."

"I won't ask you to give up your marriage," Miles turned and held her. "You have to make that decision alone."

"I c-can't," she sobbed, "and it's such an awful feeling."

"That's why I need to go home and let you live your life."

She felt his breath, cool against the tears on her

cheeks. She let her fingers wander down the side of his face, and across his mouth. Using her forefinger, she nudged open his lips, her eyes closed, and felt his mouth caress her finger.

He took her hand and brought it to his chest. God, she had to let him go, but from the pounding in her chest, she knew it was too late.

The thread of control she had mustered was stripped away, and she gasped when his lips came down on hers. Wordless, he blanketed her within his arms and brought her closer, crushing her to his body.

In the patch of moonlight streaming in through one of the small front windows, Serene let her body move with his. With their faces close, his eyes searched her for an answer. They both understood what he was asking. One night. One chance to claim each other.

"You sure?"

A deep "Yes" moaned through her lips as she anchored herself around his neck, kissing him, letting the waves of exhilaration ride through her as her body took its natural course.

Miles pulled his shirt over his head and smoothed it over the wood floor. Serene stroked her fingertips across his chest, then helped him ease his trousers down.

A throb of want spread over her as he released each of her sweater buttons.

"You are beautiful." His voice was a mere husk.

Smiling between kisses, Serene hoped she would never wake up from this sweet dream. He drew her down slowly, resting her head on the shirt. She reached for him, hesitantly, before her hands wandered over him, searching and learning.

"You don't need these where you're going," he said hoarsely, as he lifted her bottom slightly to peel away her skirt and stockings.

Kneading her breasts with his lips, he grasped and released each hardened nipple, then slid downwards to her flat belly. Not wanting him to stop, she pushed his lips lower, hearing him moan in response.

She smiled into his soft mane. All of her femininity exposed to him, she wanted him more than she had ever wanted anything. Every inch of her waited, breathless, alive with desire.

When they were spent, she wrapped her legs around him, daring him not to leave her. He was finally hers. If for just that moment, he was hers. And she felt like shouting it to the world. Instead, she purred a sigh of contentment.

She kissed the tip of his nose. "Am I imagining all of this?"

"I don't think so."

What seemed like seconds later, Serene awoke to the sound of rustling. She sat up, forcing her drowsiness away as her heart began to pound faster.

"I need to go," Miles whispered in her ear.

Serene tried to see his expression, but the moon had shifted and she could only hear the quickening of his breath. Snatching up her sweater to cover her breasts, she suddenly felt like one of those loose piazza girls. Sniffling, she scrambled up and ran her hand across the wood floor searching for her skirt and panties.

"Please don't cry," Miles said, handing her the panties.

She grabbed them from him, her throat quivering. "I couldn't let you go without at least telling you that I love you. I wanted to be with you and love you like you're mine, just for a little while, before you have to go." The words scrambled desperately from her.

"I'm sorry for all of this. You were upset, and this was a mistake. I'm so sorry, Serry." He opened the door. "This was a mistake and my fault, all my fault. I shouldn't have let it happen."

Serene's chest tightened. A mistake? She fumbled with the buttons on her sweater. "I don't understand. Please don't leave me."

"I have to. It's already too hard to leave here. We can't be like this now, when in a few hours we'll be saying goodbye."

Before she had a chance to say any more, the door closed.

Chapter Sixteen

Serene held her breath, tiptoed to her side of the room, and slipped into bed, fully dressed. She peered over to Margot's side; her figure lay motionless.

She exhaled slowly. What had she done? Her stomach quivered with panic. She closed her eyes and waited for absolution from her conscience, but found none. Tonight she had committed the worst sin of her life. A sin she had *wanted* to commit.

Turning over, she put her hands under her pillow and faced the window. Her heart raced with love and sorrow. She couldn't stop her lips from curling up at the thought of his warm body against hers. Little quakes rose in her chest. She wanted to cry and sing at the same time.

How could she face her life in the morning? Face Miles.

They shouldn't have let it happen. He had been right all along. She'd practically pushed herself on him. But how she had loved every minute. She sat up and brought her sweater up to her face, taking in his lingering scent. Fresh, like the outdoors. Her body began to tingle all over again.

She turned her pillow over, patted it, and forced herself to lie down and focus on something else. Black, vengeful eyes came to the forefront. Marcus. She bolted upright, her hair glued to the sides of her face with perspiration.

He could never know.

She sank back down, disgrace gnawing at her. The realization of it hit her with such force that she almost skipped a breath.

"I'm so sorry, Papa," she whispered to the air, and hugged her knees to her chest. "In my heart, way down deep, I don't know if I can live without him."

****

Marcus ran his index finger down Ava's taut belly. She stirred and stretched, and let out a purr. When she coiled back into the fetal position, he lifted her away from him and slid quietly off the bed.

He put on his beige trousers and grabbed a cigarette from the case, lit it and paced. He had decided not to confront Serene about the church incident. Instead, he needed to make sure the pig was out of their lives for good. Luckily, after a little research, Marcus had found the perfect man to do the job, an ex-soldier from Mussolini's army. The man was hiding in the underground, but was willing to do shady work for the right price. There was even talk that he had crossed paths with Samuel at one point, but Marcus hadn't learned the details. Didn't matter anyway. If the two men had known each other, the plan would run that much smoother. Oh, yes, Marcus thought, any amount of money he'd pay to get rid of the American pig would be the right price. He clenched the cigarette between his teeth as he buttoned his shirt. Now, all he had to do was sit back and watch the sweetness unfold.

He rummaged through his pile of clothes for his watch. Six in the morning—not too early for the day he had planned.

Kneeling down, he scanned under Ava's bed for his shoes. He wanted to arrive in time to offer an apology to Miles for acting like a bastard himself. The absurdity of it made him laugh bitterly. But in Serene's eyes, the goodwill gesture would transform him into the perfect gentlemen and husband.

On his way out, he stopped by the bed. Ava lay still, unlike the woman she had been in the middle of the night. So creamy. She knew of his marriage plans, but still planned to service him. He rubbed his thumb across the remnants of lip stain smudged at the outer corner of her mouth. One of the better girls, he mused. He almost felt bad that he had to let her go for a few weeks, at least until he settled up the dowry business.

****

Serene's eyes popped open at the sound of an engine. She flew to the window and watched a dark green truck pull up in front of the villa. An Italian flag was painted on the side. One man got out, dressed in an Italian military uniform.

"Anna!"

Margot jumped up from the bed next to her. "What is it?"

Serene ignored her and grabbed her robe from the hook and raced to the kitchen.

The knock at the front door shattered the quiet morning air and Serene bolted for the main room.

"Anna, wait to open—"

But Anna had already opened the door. The man was about thirty or so, short, with hair and eyes the color of coal, and he strode into the house as if he were in charge, removing his hat as he entered. "I'm a friend of Samuel. Is the soldier ready?"

"You weren't supposed to be here until tonight," Serene stated. "Where is Samuel?"

"Those weren't my orders."

The man's eyes didn't budge, but Serene noticed perspiration gathering on his face. "Are you sure?" Had Samuel changed the plan?

"I'm following orders from Samuel McCarthy."

"I understand, but the pickup was supposed to be tonight."

"If he doesn't go now, he doesn't go."

Serene sent a furtive glance to Anna, a spasm of uncertainty coming over her. "I understand. He'll be ready. We just weren't expecting—"

Miles came to the last step. "I'm Miles Coulson."

After a brisk handshake, Miles cast a glance Serene's way, but to her it lasted an eternity. "Can you tell him I need to gather my things? Maybe Anna here can make you some of her finest coffee."

Serene translated, and Anna led the man to the kitchen.

Transfixed by each other, Serene and Miles stood a few feet away, with only the stair banister between them, she in a pink robe, he in her father's shirt and a pair of rumpled trousers.

"Did you get any sleep?" Serene asked with a coolness she hated to hear from her own mouth.

"No. You?"

Her bottom lip quivered. "It's going to be a long trip."

"Last night—"

"There isn't much more to say," she said softly. "As you said already, we have our own lives. For a little while, we both needed someone. I needed someone to help me through my father's death. I'm grateful to you. Really."

Miles ran both hands through his hair and clasped them behind his head. "Is this how you want it?"

"Is there another way?" She stared straight at him, into him. *Don't leave me. It was the most wonderful night of my life.* His features swam together in ripples, and Serene wondered when she had started to cry.

He reached for her hand, but she wouldn't accept it. If he touched her, she wasn't sure she would be able to get her bearings back enough to say goodbye. "You should get your things."

"Serry, we can't leave it like this."

She wiped her cheek. "Last night, what you said, it was all I needed to hear. We have a wonderful friendship. Please don't say any more."

"How can I ever tell you what all of this has meant to me? The care you gave me, taking me in when things were bad."

"I did it because my Papa cared—and then you turned out to be the most wonderful—"

He reached for her arms. "If it weren't for you, Serry, I would have died. And for my entire life, I will thank you for that. Wherever you go, remember that. The friendship you gave me will stay with me forever."

With a sob coming from deep within her, Serene moved her thumb gently over the scar on his eyebrow and wondered if the ache of emptiness would stay in her heart forever.

****

Miles fought the wetness in his own eyes when he returned to his room. "Pull yourself together," he whispered. He had to make it through the next few minutes and summon up the guts to leave her.

He found his field coat and trousers pressed and folded, lying neatly on the chaise. Shaking out the trousers, he turned them over. No hint of the damage. Anna must have replaced the entire leg. Even the shredded pieces near the bottom were mended perfectly. He laughed, realizing that he would probably miss the old gal.

The pant leg fit over the last bandage that circled the top of his shin. His head throbbed relentlessly, outweighing any twinges in his shin.

Inside the front pocket of his torn-up pack were Josie's picture and an unopened letter from her. He had thought the picture lost somewhere on the field, and he had forgotten about the letter, received just a few hours before the attack. Scrutinizing the picture of the smiling girl holding a sign that said "I love you," he realized that in an odd sort of way he felt affection for her, but not the longing he'd known when he was on the front. Were those feelings desire, or loneliness? He couldn't now remember. But he knew one thing—never again would he have that longing for anyone except Serene.

He ripped open the letter and read the Dear John. She'd found herself another man and wouldn't be waiting for him when he got back. Miles sat on the bed, in a bubble of disbelief. Josie had left him out to dry in a letter. Couldn't she have waited until he returned? Either way, it didn't matter to him anymore. Probably better this way, so he wouldn't have to find her shacking up with some draft dodger. He crinkled up the paper and threw it across the room.

He shoved the rest of his belongings into the bag he had borrowed, including his torn-up pack and a C-ration he'd never eaten, put Walter's dog tags with his own around his neck, and gazed around the room.

Just as he picked up his bag, Samuel came in. "You ready, Coulson?"

"You know, you could scare a lion away with that voice at this early hour. I thought it wasn't supposed to be until later."

Samuel smirked. "The driver couldn't make it later in the day, so I agreed. I didn't think you'd want to wait another week."

"The sooner in my book, the better. I got a life to start living."

"Then let's get going and have a look at that leg. You have a long journey ahead."

"So I've been told."

Samuel pushed up the leg of Miles' trousers and unwound the bandage. "I do see a little new pus around the one edge. I'll give you something for the trip, but you should see a doctor at your next landing. I'm assuming you're going directly back to the States?"

"They won't let me back on the front with a bum leg."

"You'll go back to your farm?"

Miles rallied all the good spirit he could. "Bringing it back to a profitable state will take a lot of my time. Lots to do around there since my father passed."

"Grand for you. But we'll miss you around here. Especially Serene. She's a bit shy, but I think she has some feelings for you, m'friend. That's what her sister says, anyway. It's woman talk, you know. I'm sure women talk their gibberish, gossip, whatever you want to call it, in all parts of the world."

Miles laughed, feeling his stomach churn. "She's getting married herself. I don't know what she would want with me, anyway."

"Marrying Marcus will change her, I'm afraid. He's a bit too big for his britches, but I think with a regular woman to come home to and the family life, he'll come around. Like we all do." He started to ease the bandage around the top of Miles' shin and wound it around a few times, working up his leg. "Serene will help settle him down."

Miles' throat felt dry. "She'll be fine. She's a strong woman."

"That she is, m'friend."

"What about you? You gonna marry Margot?"

Samuel put the stethoscope to his ears and inside Miles' coat. After listening, he said, "I love her, all right, but she said no, the first time. She thinks I'm marrying her purely for the baby. After being with her for so long, it stings a little, but there's not much more I can say to change her mind. But she can't push me away that quickly."

"My advice is to keep asking."

"Oh, I will, but for now she'll stay with Serene until the baby comes."

"She'll come around."

Samuel smiled, putting all his supplies back into his bag. "Now don't go taking any more bullets."

"Doc, you patched me up good."

Miles put his hand out. Sam took it, and the two men embraced.

"If you go back to the front somewhere, you be careful."

"I'm planning to start my life, not try to end it again. But if the army has other plans for me when I recuperate, I'll go along."

Sam shut his bag, pivoted to leave and Miles grabbed his arm.

"Watch after her, Sam, will you?"

Sam raised his eyebrows, started to ask something and then stopped, nodding. "As you said, Coulson, she'll be fine."

****

Watching Miles actually leave the house was the last step in their journey together, and Serene dreaded it as if it were a terminal illness. For the twenty or so minutes while she waited for him to come downstairs, she watched Alberto, the driver, as he ate a bowl of noodles and soaked up Anna's garbled stories about the past.

"You ready, Alberto?" Samuel asked, coming down the stairs.

"*Si.*"

"You know the route?"

"*Si.*"

"Will you let us know when he arrives?"

"*Si.*"

"Do you need food or drink?" Anna asked.

The man shook his head no, shifting from one foot to the other, his shirt now spotted with perspiration. Serene wondered if the man was nervous about the trip or about something else. She trusted Sam's choice, so she forced herself to put her uneasiness aside.

"Sorry I kept you waiting." Using crutches, Miles dragged his one leg only slightly behind. "Samuel is very thorough in his examination."

"Don't blame anything on me, Coulson."

Serene took a deep breath at the sight of him. His cream-colored hair was slicked back behind his ears. Overwhelming desire tugged at her insides. She pulled her robe closer to her body, remembering the feel of his fingers running through her hair. Her arms shook, and she couldn't tell whether it was from desire or the realization that he was leaving.

She watched him track the room until he found her. Over the olive-green uniform, his eyes were painted the color of a faded blueberry. Her lips opened; even her skin ached for him.

The driver took Miles' bag and headed for the front door.

Anna kissed both his cheeks. "You be a safe boy."

Samuel laughed at Miles' struggle once again with the language. He touched Miles on the shoulder. "She told you to go out and have some ale when you get home."

Laughing, Miles patted his stomach. "Tell her I've already filled out my uniform some from her cooking."

As if she understood, Anna laughed brusquely and used her hand to shoo him away.

Seeing Harry come into the hall, Miles gave him an outstretched hand. "Take care of your family, sir. Try to convince Serene about the Billy."

"It's *Balilla*." Harry laughed. "Don't forget to write me a letter."

To no one in particular, Miles said, "And tell Margot I said goodbye. I haven't known this family long, but I do know that Margot is still in the sack. She'll make a good mother."

Samuel roared as he held the door open, letting

the driver go back to the truck. "You're right about that, m'friend."

They both knew Serene's turn had come. She took in a deep breath and touched his arms in a stiff embrace. She hugged him the way she had rehearsed in her head over and over, the way a mother would hug her son going off to war.

"I don't care who sees," he said gruffly, pulling her closer. He pushed her chin up with his fingertips, and bent his head to kiss her.

She took his lips, his body, all of him, into her heart for the last time. Feeling the rapid beating in his chest, she fought the urge to mold her most intimate part against his. When their lips parted, his warm breath on her neck made her body shiver.

Wrapping her arms around his neck, she buried her face into his jacket. "I'm not ashamed about what I said to you last night or what happened between us." Her voice cracked. "It's a sin, I know, but it was the most beautiful—"

"Ashamed? I don't think I'll ever have that kind of love again."

Trembling, she stood back a little, clinging to her emotions with the delicacy of a spider web. "But you were right. We made the most logical decision."

"*Jesus*, Serry. I want to tell you so bad that I—"

"You're all set, then?" Sam said, coming back into the house.

Serene let go of Miles, letting her one finger intertwine with one of his pinky fingers. She couldn't let him go.

Slowly, he released her and went to the door, putting one foot on the outside pavement before hesitating and turning back. His eyes were red, and she clutched the stair banister to keep from running to him. How much she loved him would be a secret she'd take to the grave.

Carrying a bottle of whiskey, Marcus passed

him at the door and gave him a friendly slap on the back. "I came to give you a goodbye, Coulson."

Serene stood up straight and froze.

Miles jerked himself away. "Change of heart about me?"

His answer was Marcus' deep kiss on Serene's cheek and an arm around her waist. "I realized, Coulson, that I'm proud of her for taking the responsibility for you. I thought it was about time that I offered my apologies for the undiplomatic way I acted. "We're all in this for a cause, *no*? Why don't we share a bottle to celebrate?"

"No, your change of heart doesn't rub me the right way." Miles offered an apologetic glance to Serene and then shifted his gaze back to Marcus. "You hurt her, and I'll hurt you. You understand me?"

"Have a safe trip," Marcus drawled.

Serene watched the driver help him in and her knees weakened. As the truck's engine started, she braced herself against the wall.

"Don't worry. Serene. Just think of this as a wedding present from me. No more worries about your American. He is well now and gone for good. Your only thanks is to marry me."

She couldn't hear him. Her throat ached and she made no effort to wipe the tears spilling freely from her eyes. She started for the door, but he grabbed her by the shoulders.

"No—oo." Just as the jeep had gone out of eye range, she tugged her arms free.

Marcus forced her against him. "You won't be afraid anymore."

Afraid? If only he knew it was numbness, not fear, that took over her sense of purpose. The love she had for Miles was all she would ever know. She had never wanted love, but now she clung to it with every bit of life she had left in her.

Chapter Seventeen

Miles sat in the back seat of the truck, not able to focus on anything except the picture of her face, the fear in her eyes.

They drove through the outskirts of Rome, through hilly terrain, and then out to a more flat, unpopulated area. They had been on the road for nearly an hour, heading north, or so he gathered by the direction of the sun. He had no idea where they were, but he did know Anzio was south.

He could almost feel Marcus' hands on her, and it made him want to puke.

Damn him.

He couldn't do it. He couldn't leave her like that.

"Take me back," he called to the driver.

"*Non capisco.*"

"Samuel. Take me back to Samuel."

"No."

At a fork in the road, the truck turned sharply and drove down into a ravine covered with woods and brush. No visible road was apparent.

"What the hell—"

The driver grunted something and kept driving, up the incline, deeper into the woods, snaking through a mass of trees and headed for a clearing about a hundred yards away.

The truck halted in the center of the clearing, a green field encased in trees.

Miles called to the driver. "Why are we stopping?"

The driver sat motionless, as if it were perfectly logical to be stopping in a place that seemed like

196

nowhere. Miles strained his neck to see in back. Nothing. More trees. No sign of the beach or troops or anything.

Another dark-haired man, a few inches shorter than the driver, emerged from the woods, one arm in back, the other waving to the driver as if they were friends. He smiled, but Miles could practically smell the falseness of it.

The driver got out and stood in front, his back to the truck. The two men talked in earnest for a few seconds, the second man still keeping his arm behind him.

"What is going on?" Miles put one foot out of the jeep, leaning on his good leg.

The new man came to Miles' side. "*Via! Se ne vada!*"

"I don't understand."

"*Via! Se ne vada!*" He yanked at Miles' jacket, pulling him from the truck.

Caught off balance, Miles fell to the ground on his stomach. "What do you want?" He pushed himself up on his elbows. From the corner of his eye, he saw the second man raise a thick piece of wood. Miles blocked the blow with his arm, only to take the brunt of it across his forearm and chest.

Struggling against grogginess, he took in a haggard breath and swung at the man holding the wood.

The driver and his new friend yelled back and forth in Italian. Miles fought to understand, but the only familiar word he heard was Marcus' name.

Another whack came to his head. And then one across his cheek. Miles flattened against the ground; blood oozed from his forehead and warmed his cheeks, trickling down into his mouth. He spit it out and pried his eyes open. The two men had turned into four.

He couldn't raise his head. Nor could he move

any of his limbs. He opened his mouth to call for help but no sound came. With the heaviness in his chest, he wasn't even sure if air was moving in or out.

If he wasn't dead yet, he could feel death coming.

The turnover of the truck's engine startled him enough to cause one finger on his right hand to move spontaneously.

And then a slam to his bad leg. The impact of the hit made his whole upper body shudder up from the ground and collapse into a heap. Pain scorched the area below his knee, and then in the same instant it came, it was gone.

Oh, my God, they cut off my leg.

****

Miles forced one eye open. The other was swollen shut as though weighted by a brick. He lay face up on the ground and could see only blurry patches of stars in the early evening sky.

Shifting his body on the ground just enough to ease the pain in his back, Miles found an old woman kneeling beside him. Dressed all in black, with a black veil, she held his hand and chanted something in a wrinkly voice.

With his free hand, he tried to swat away the pungent odor of garlic. A hunk of it hung from a string tied around his neck. He yanked at one of the cloves, only to feel the string chafe the back of his neck.

"Don't move," A man's voice spoke from behind him in broken English.

Miles squinted. "Who are you?" he mumbled between swollen lips.

"Don't try to talk," the man said.

"Did you do this to me?"

"No," the man whispered. "Save your strength."

"Where are we? Are we near Anzio?"

"No. No—Turni."

"He was supposed to take me to Anzio, but then he whacked the hell out of me with a piece of wood."

"We thought you were dead. We sent our son for the doctor, but he's been gone two hours and no sign yet."

The woman stopped chanting and squeezed his hand tighter.

Miles jerked at his necklace of garlic. "This is so heavy. Can you take it off from around my neck?"

"Do as he says," the man ordered the woman in Italian. To Miles, he said, "My wife is a healer of nature."

"What's your name?"

"Nunzio Cazzio, and this is Evita."

Miles closed his eye, reliving the argument he'd heard between the men. Marcus. That bastard was behind it. His mind bolted to Serene, the last image he had of her. How could he have left her? The reality of his mistake wrenched his stomach.

What seemed like hours later, he heard new voices approach.

The woman took a blanket from one of the newcomers and draped it over him. "You come—our cottage."

Two men picked him up and carried him. He didn't have the coherence to talk, or ask where he was going, but deep in the woods they finally stopped at a small place—from what he could see, the whole house was probably no bigger than his kitchen back home. Through the haze in the one eye he could still open, it resembled more of a shack, dwarfed by the forest's tall trees to the back and sides.

They carried him across a front porch and into the house and laid him on a narrow iron bed in the rear of the house.

Miles cringed when the old woman ran a cool

cloth over his forehead, and his mind drifted to his night with Serene. He had to go to her. Trying to lift his body up but unable to bear the weight on his arms, he fell back and slammed his head against the iron headboard.

"Easy," Nunzio said.

"I have...to get back."

"You're not going anywhere."

He had to get back there and warn her. Would Marcus attack her the same way if she didn't conform to his wishes? The thought jabbed his gut as he fell asleep. Serene came alive in his dream, wearing a wedding gown, waiting only for him at the altar. But when she reached the end of the aisle to claim him, she laughed and turned from him, tears running down her face, as she put her hand out to Marcus.

His eyes opened to the blackness of the room, illuminated only by the small candle beside the bed. His heart pumped and ached. He couldn't get up without pain jutting up his leg in waves. Maybe he didn't lose it, after all. He couldn't remember. Leg or no leg, he would get Serene away from Marcus if it took his last breath.

****

"We have so much to get ready." Margot sighed, lying on her back, her hand behind her head.

"*Who* has so much to do?" Serene asked absently, opening the chest of drawers. The box had to be there somewhere; she had just moved it the week earlier.

"You know I can't be much help with this watermelon in my stomach."

"It's hardly a watermelon, more like a grape, at this point." Serene sifted through some garments and pulled out the box, her sister's quibblings becoming a distant noise. She dropped to her knees and opened the black lid with shaky fingers.

"Serene, are you listening? What do you have there?" Margot got up from the bed and peered over her sister's shoulder.

"They're from Mama."

"They're beautiful. Try them on."

Serene hesitated, then lifted the gloves out. Reaching into one of them, she slid out the note from her mother and shoved it into the drawer.

"What was that?" Margo asked.

"Something Mama gave me a long time ago."

"What does it say?"

"Nothing important." Serene slipped her hand in and marveled at the perfect fit. "They're for my wedding day."

"They're like princess gloves." Margot curtsied. "I'm at your service, your highness."

"Once I'm married, I will be at least a queen." Serene tossed a pillow at her.

Margot caught it, her smile fading. "Why can't you tell me what the note says?"

"If you must know, it's a letter about my arrangement. Mama asked me to marry who Papa wanted, that's all."

"*That's all?* You say it like it doesn't matter that you didn't have a say. Or did you?"

"I trusted Papa's judgment."

"So then you would have picked Marcus, if you had the choice?"

Serene smoothed the glove along her forearm. "Probably."

"I don't believe you."

"Well, believe it or not, it's my future. Serene put her hands on her hips, determined not to let Margot see her heart falling into pieces. Since Miles had left, she could hardly sleep an hour at a time without waking in panic. Missing him hurt too much to even talk about it. "Don't I look happy?"

"Sometimes you do." Margot twirled a curl that

dangled from the center of her forehead. "Maybe I just worry too much because I'm your sister. But if you're not happy with Marcus, don't marry him."

"Nonsense. There is no decision."

"Stop being so—so old." Margot said flatly. "It's almost 1945. Times have changed since the old days. Don't marry him just because they asked you to."

"I'm not. And besides," she added, "it will be better for our whole family."

"You can't be worried about me and Harry? Papa has us taken care of. With money, I mean. At least that's what Samuel says."

"He's wrong." Serene spit back. "It's just that, well, we have to be careful with things until the war breaks. With the restaurants being closed, we can't have the things we're used to, but Samuel was right, Papa took care so we wouldn't have to worry." Once I walk down the aisle.

"There is someone else who can make you much happier."

"Who?" Serene knew exactly who.

"You can't fool me. You could fool everyone else, but not me. I know how you felt about each other."

"That's nonsense."

Margot smoothed her hand down her belly, hidden behind a loose pale blue shirt, then coaxed Serene down beside her on the bed. "Even from two different worlds, it could have worked."

Before Margot finished, Serene cut in. "What makes you think that's what I wanted? It's the farthest thing from my mind."

"I saw the two of you in the yard, after Harry left."

Margot's matter-of-fact accusation put Serene's stomach in a spin. "It wasn't anything. He wanted to see the barn, and I showed it to him." She hesitated, then added, "We went to see the dollhouse, too."

"*Si?*"

Serene hopped off the bed. "He touched me...oh, Margot, we—"

"You did? He did? In this house?"

At the sight of Margot's open mouth, Serene lost all seriousness, and started laughing. "Of course not."

"You, the perfect Serene, committed the most sacred act without a marriage blessing? "

Serene's smile dropped, and she sat suddenly on the bed. "It just happened. I didn't mean it to. Oh, I guess I did. I don't know what I'm saying."

"Did he feel the same?"

"I don't know. At first I thought he did. The way he acted, I knew he cared for me. I guess I wanted it so desperately that I imagined things." For the two weeks since Miles had left, since something so wonderful had been ripped from her heart, she had carried on a façade of happiness that would never be real.

"He had to let you go because he's a gentlemen. You are betrothed to someone else, and so is he."

Serene admired the honesty in her sister's brown eyes as she fought to keep the pain from showing. "Margot, no one can ever know. Especially Marcus. The way he feels about Miles, it would be the end of everything."

"You've always been the one to take charge, even after Papa's death." She smoothed back the side of Serene's hair. "Let Marcus do that for you now." Margot's tone softened. "Miles has his life to go home to. Now it's time for you to start your own life and get that business of Papa's running again."

A rush of adrenaline hit Serene square in the chest. She would never be able to get on with her life in the sense that Margot was implying.

Serene forced a smile. "There's no going back. Only forward, right?" Deep in the loneliest part of her soul, she knew that if Miles Coulson walked through the door at that very moment, without hesitation she would take him as her husband, her soulmate, and her lover.

Anna billowed into the room carrying one large box and one smaller one. "I have some things for your wedding day."

"Let me see," Margot said.

"For your wedding day, *Signorina* Serene."

From the glint of pride in Anna's eyes, Serene didn't dare tell her that she had tried the dress on already.

When Anna held up the creamy gown from the big box, visions of her mother came into her head. She was dancing with her father, both of them laughing. Could they be real memories, she wondered? It didn't matter, she thought, holding the gown to her body. A piece of her mother would go with Serene to the altar.

Anna smoothed the bottom of the gown.

"I kept it stored away all these years for one of you."

"Mama was so tiny," Margot exclaimed.

Serene's eyes flickered, and she compared her waist to the gown. "I think it may need mending. Don't you, Anna?" She knew for a fact it would need to be altered a little, but Margot was practically jumping from the bed in excitement.

"Let's try it on, and I'll measure."

Stepping into the dress, Serene slipped it up to her waist and slid her arms into the sleeve holes. Margot fastened the trail of satin buttons running down the back.

"What do you think?"

"Just like your Mama. Come to the mirror."

At the sight of herself in the mirror, Serene took a step back. She was her Mama. Her own mane was more dark, but it still held the same shimmer.

"And this, too." Anna opened the smaller box

and took out a halo of the same creamy material, with intricate lace attached as a veil. She placed it on Serene's head, leaving her hair loose to skim her shoulders.

Anna stretched back a little material from each side of the gown. "You're so tiny. A little taking in and it will fit just fine. Step up on the chair, so I can pin it."

"What was my Mama like on her wedding day?"

"As nervous as a cat having a babe. She loved your Papa so much."

"Papa loved her, too." Serene moistened her lips, watching Anna put pins into a gather of material at each side. Her mother had once told her that a girl's wedding day was worth the wait for your heart and body, but for Serene throughout her entire life there had been no waiting, everything had been given to her. Now there didn't seem to be anything to wait for, or even hope for.

"You look like someone stole your milk." Margot took the veil from Serene and put it on her own curly head. "I'll make a beautiful bride, too, someday, don't you think?"

"If you would say yes to Samuel, you would."

"I can't. And you know the reasons."

Plucking the last pin from between her teeth, Anna stuck it in toward the back of the dress and motioned Serene down from the chair. "Careful of the pins."

"We'll all be beautiful brides and have the lives that we dream about."

Margot twirled around, the veil still on her head. "When a girl is ready, she knows it, and I don't know it yet."

"You are living in sin," Anna said, frowning.

Serene laid the dress on the bed, biting back tears. "Sam will wait. He loves you." When she gazed up, Margot was staring at her.

"Why are you crying? Because I won't marry Samuel? That's just plain silly."

"It's nothing, Margot, really."

Margot didn't appear satisfied with the flippant answer. "Are you sure *you're* ready for this?"

"Nonsense," Anna swatted away the comment. "She's just happy, as every bride should be."

Happy? *Happy*? Is that what they thought? Serene felt like her heart had been torn up. Fighting back the last stranded tear, she murmured, "Of course, I'm happy."

Chapter Eighteen

Using the two makeshift wooden crutches Nunzio had pieced together with tree branches and rope, Miles slowly lifted himself from the cot and hobbled the few feet to the kitchen table. Slowly he let himself down onto a chair, and waited for the pain in his head to subside.

As he watched Evita's lined hands move expertly around the table with preparations for dinner, he wondered how the hell he could still be alive. When they lugged him from the clearing, Nunzio and Evita had put him on a cot in the corner of the main room, sectioned it off with a piece of material used as a curtain, and then essentially revived him from the dead.

Evita had used herbal cures, what Miles considered hokey-pokey recipes, including a chunk of garlic that made his nose burn hotter than if he had eaten one whole. Stubborn as a cat, she made sure Miles took all the herbs. Nunzio translated for her once, in his own rusty English, telling Miles that it would make him stronger than a woodsman. Miles thought her screws were loose, but Nunzio had assured him she had a way with greenery and it wouldn't do him any harm.

Now, feeling both legs intact and the wounds on his head and back healing, Miles believed him, and also believed that he would survive long enough to get back to Serene. As he lay there recovering, she was in his dreams, in his thoughts, drifting in and out of his mind like the sun peeking through the clouds.

Miles knew now, more than ever, the mistake he had made. He hadn't even given her a real chance to choose. Maybe if he had just given her time to talk about it. He'd just slept with her and left—left her with that monster. It killed his gut to rehash it. Leaving her was a decision he would regret for as long as he lived.

He had to get back to her.

A few times, he had thought about asking Nunzio for paper to write her, but he couldn't risk it. If Marcus learned that his plan had failed and Miles was still alive, who knew what he would do in retaliation. Go after Nunzio and Evita, too? Blame Serene somehow? Just the image of him touching or hurting Serene made Miles' heart pump harder.

He wanted to get to Marcus first, on his own terms, and make things right. Miles knew the man was capable of murder, capable of any cold-blooded act.

It was almost time now. Miles had to be ready.

Evita brought his attention back when she handed him a knife and an onion. She gestured for him to cut.

"What do you have cooking?" he asked.

She nodded and gave him a broken-toothed smile. That meant potatoes. Whether they were boiled, fried, or roasted over the fire, Evita made potatoes. And always mixed with vegetables of all kinds. Peppers. Lettuce. Tomatoes. Sometimes corn. But always potatoes.

"We have a guest tonight," Nunzio announced. A stream of cool air followed him and his son Antonio in the front door.

The father and son immediately started their usual heavy conversation, complete with many hand gestures, none of which Miles could understand. Antonio was about Miles' age and seemed frustrated all the time.

When it was over and Antonio stormed out of the house, Miles asked, "Is everything okay?"

Miles was grateful that Nunzio could at least speak a little English, enough to communicate the basics.

"He wants to give his hand to this girl Veronica. I say no."

"What's wrong with that? Don't you like her?"

Nunzio frowned, not seeming to understand Miles. "No, no. Not good. He's leaving for the war soon. She will be a widow."

"Tell him that if he loves her, to just do it. He'll regret it later if he doesn't, I promise," Miles said.

Another half hour passed before Antonio returned and brought in his beloved Veronica. Evita continued stirring the pot of potatoes, but Nunzio muttered a hello, followed by a small kiss to her cheek. Veronica's knee-length dress was the color of a cherry.

God, how he wished he understood Italian. A scene like this in his small town back home would've generated a week of gossip.

Miles stood to greet her. Besides the usual pain in his temple and back, he had only one deep throb in his thigh. They nodded introductions, and she kissed Miles on both cheeks. "Antonio told me someone did this to you? No?"

Her accent was thick and a little garbled, but he could grasp the question. "Hallelujah! You speak English."

Veronica laughed, splitting widely the same cherry red color applied precisely to her lips. "Not so good."

"I'm stronger every day," he said. Her dress was so tight across her middle, he was sure he could bounce a coin off it.

"We'll find the person who did this," Nunzio stated. "I watch that field every day. No one's been

Christine Clemetson

back. Leaving a man to die there is what a coward does."

Miles kept silent. He hadn't revealed his knowledge about Marcus, fearing Nunzio and his son would go after him. That was something he would do himself. He hadn't mentioned any of his past in Rome, feigning he was abandoned in battle and was being transported to a U.S. camp by someone in the underground.

"*Mangi*," Evita said, taking the pot of potatoes from the woodstove.

After Nunzio finished the prayer, Miles spooned out some potato clumps and passed on the bowl. At supper, they spoke completely in Italian during the meal. Miles smiled politely or laughed when the others did, but for the most part he didn't understand a stitch of their conversation.

As Veronica babbled on, filling the table with incessant chatter, he was drawn from his own thoughts like lightning hitting a tree. In the onslaught of her story, he could have sworn he heard her mention the name Serene. There had to be dozens and dozens of girls named Serene in this country. It could never be *his* Serene.

He was toying with a piece of vegetable when he heard Veronica say her name again, and he dropped his fork and took a gulp of wine. And then she mentioned Cucina Moneto, and he spit out the wine.

All the eyes at the table darted to him, Veronica holding her fork in midair.

Miles wiped a cloth across his face and knew he owed them some kind of explanation. "You surprised me. I've been to that restaurant. A bunch of us boys were stationed near Rome."

Veronica studied him, her red pout unmoving. "I work there a long time and do not remember you. You are an American soldier?"

"It was a long time ago that I was there at the

restaurant. Her father—helped me with something."

"Serene was there all the time with her Papa. Now she is the one to take care of things."

Evita glanced up from her plate and frowned. Miles sensed she didn't like English being spoken, but he wasn't about to stop now.

Miles' heartbeat quickened. "I know her. I mean, I knew her."

"You do?" Veronica put down her fork.

"Terrible what happened to that family," Nunzio said. "First the mama, and then only a few years later, the father. He built that restaurant from the soil."

"*Signore* Anthony was good to me."

"He was a good man," Miles agreed.

"I was at Cucina Moneto this week," Veronica said, taking a bite of potato. "Serene re-opens it after the wedding," she said. "Not the best time, but it is good for her. She misses her papa so much."

"Is Serry okay? I mean, is she okay with the wedding? Is it soon?"

Evita slammed her fork on the table. "*Italiano.*"

"You understand, we should speak Italian at the table," Nunzio said, glancing to his wife.

It was nearly two hours before Veronica begged her goodbyes and stood with Antonio just outside the front door, kissing him goodbye.

Miles had waited outside in a darkened corner of the house, making his way out the back entrance without anyone noticing. With rain hammering his face, he half-walked, half-hopped after Veronica on his crutches.

"Can I talk to you?" he called above the rain.

Veronica turned, stepping back a little. "Who are you?"

"It's Miles. From inside."

She wrapped her arms around her body. "What is it? You scare me."

He maneuvered his crutches to get a little closer, despite the risk of having her call for help. The beads of rain dripped down the back of his neck, but he ignored the shivering. "Can you bring me to her?"

"To who?"

"Serry. I need to get back there. Will you take me? I don't want to get Nunzio and Evita involved."

Veronica wiped wetness from her eyes and wrapped her arms around her body. "I do not know who you are. You maybe hurt her or something bad. Antonio told me they found you near dead in the field. What did you do for a beating like that?"

"It's not like that. I can't tell you the whole story. I hope you'll trust me."

"I do not even know you. A strange man asks me all these questions, and I am a woman by herself in the dark."

"No one can know."

"We should get Antonio." Veronica charged away from him, her heels teetering in the mud.

"Please," be begged, taking hold of her forearm. "Don't tell them. If they know about Marcus, they could get hurt, too."

Veronica ripped her arm away. "Marcus Sturini? If you know him, you know he does not hurt anyone. He loves Serene. They will be married."

"I'm afraid for Serry," he yelled above the thunder of rain.

Her eyebrows raised. "Serry? You call her that? I was curious about you, but now you talk like a mad person. I need to get the bus."

"The bus is near here?"

Without a glance back, or even the slightest perceived interest, she kept going.

"How far is it?" He followed her, his hands slipping on the wet crutches. He couldn't let her go without trying to find out more. "Serry has a little house in the woods. One she used to play in when she was little. I know she didn't show many people."

Squaring her shoulders, Veronica finally stopped. "How do you know that?"

He took the window of opportunity to press further. "She showed it to me. Right behind her house..."

Unmoving, Veronica stood for one endless minute, as if contemplating his morality. She narrowed her gaze on him. "You do not tell the truth."

"I need to know how she is, that's all," Miles said in a low voice, slapping rain from his face. "And to warn her about Marcus. He's the man who did this to me."

The expression on Veronica's face turned smug. "He would never do something like this," she blurted, "not to you or anyone. That is how I know you are wrong."

When Veronica swung back around and marched away, the rain had begun to slow. Miles watched her disappear into the fog. If she told Marcus, he might have just given someone a death sentence.

****

Rejuvenating Cucina Moneto gave Serene a certain sense of renewed purpose. Each day, listening to the silence, she craved the sound of clinking glasses and laughter. She wondered if the place would ever come alive again. Or if *she* would ever come alive again.

Trailing her hand down the glass on the hutch, she took out the first plate and closed her eyes for just a minute, allowing herself a small glimpse of Miles' light blue eyes. Letting her mind dwell on him was her only true salvation. It had been almost a month, and she hadn't heard a thing. No letter had come. No indication of anything, not even if he had made it to one of the U.S. ships. She'd thought he would let them know something, anything. Samuel couldn't find out anything, either.

She forced her mind from Miles and took a breath, analyzing the china in the hutch. She'd take everything out, sort through it, and see what they would need. A lot of the dishes had been broken that fateful night.

As she took out the first plate and traced her finger along the silver edging, her mind wandered to the scar across Miles' eyebrow, and how his lips crinkled up slowly when he smiled, and... She swallowed hard. "Keep going," she muttered.

"Once you tell me what needs to be done," a man's voice said from the direction of the door.

Serene found Franci standing at the front door. She put down a plate and sighed in relief, tears springing to her eyes faster than water out of a jug. "Oh, Franci."

He grinned. "I thought I heard someone over here."

They embraced and Serene felt as though the warmth of her father had returned. "I was hoping you'd come over. How is your shop?"

"Fine. Everything is fine," he said. "Whatever help you need here, I can lend you what I have. I know someone who can repair the floor and the holes in the wall. You say it, Serene, and I'll give it to you. I know how important this place was to your Papa."

As she embraced his hands, she let her gaze fall on the bloodstain for just a second, then brought her attention back to Franci. He had helped her at the worst minute of her life, and she would never forget it. "You've done so much already."

Franci smiled, and the lines around his eyes deepened, as if he understood. "Do what's in your heart and get this place on its feet again."

"I'm here to help," Veronica interrupted, sailing

in the front door, her long red hair swinging around her shoulders haphazardly.

The two women exchanged kisses on the cheek, Serene holding onto her for an extra second. "What a nice surprise, Roni."

"I'll leave you to the woman talk," Franci interrupted gently, heading for the door. "If you need anything, anything at all, I'm right next door. Are you ready for the floor to be cleaned?"

Serene smiled at him, nodding, her eyes filled with tears. He must have known she needed to see it one more time before he fixed it.

"What are those tears for, Serene Moneto?" Veronica laughed. "You're one lucky woman, having all these men falling at your toes, wanting to help."

Her friend's ease with certain topics always mystified Serene. "It's not always what it seems."

"Marcus is the only important one." Veronica seemed to contemplate something, then pulled off her gloves. "I've seen the way he dotes on you. He's good to you, *no?*"

Instead of answering, Serene decided to sidestep the question. Divulging her true feelings about Marcus would ignite more questions, the very same questions she wasn't ready to answer to herself, let alone to another person. "Someday Antonio will ask for your hand, too. Just be patient and he'll come around. You know he loves you."

"I have been. I took the bus to his house for the evening meal a few times, and I suppose I was hopeful." She met Serene's eyes. "Has there been any other man with you? I mean, have you ever wanted a relationship that didn't happen?"

Feeling the bigger nudge of Veronica's prying, Serene laughed a little. "You know me better than most. If there was anyone else—you would know about it. Why do you ask that?"

"If another man asked about you, would you

want to know?" Veronica fluttered around the kitchen, nervous as a mouse. "I mean, now that you're going to give your hand in marriage?"

"What nonsense is this, Roni?" The oddity of her friend's question heightened Serene's curiosity, and she stopped taking stock of the china. "Have you had too much grappa?"

"Too much thinking, I guess. Antonio will be going to war, so whatever feelings he has for me will have to wait."

Her own weariness was getting in the way. The poor girl was simply worried about Antonio. "You can postpone all the ceremonies until he gets back, but feelings never get postponed. He loves you, Roni. Accept that for now, and know that he'll make things right once this war ends."

"*If* he comes back..." Veronica mused.

"He will."

"What if I make his family a meal before he leaves? His mama is sour toward me, but if I make a nice evening meal and bring it to them?" Thoughts crossed Veronica's face like fast-moving clouds, almost as if she was grasping for something. "Maybe you could help me? It's out in the country, in Turni, near that huge ravine."

"I know who they are. Papa used to send food to Nunzio when times were bad. I can make something for you to bring."

"It would mean a lot to his family if you came with me. They have a guest staying there, so it would be good for everyone."

"What guest?"

"A stranger, really. Antonio's papa found him in a field. It wasn't far from their house. The man didn't really say what happened, except someone attacked him and left him for dead."

"But he survived?"

Veronica took a stack of plates from Serene.

"Antonio's mother is very spiritual, and she also knows a lot about using the old remedies, from plants and things, so she gave him those and said a few prayers. He came around and now he's recuperating. I'm sure Nunzio would be grateful to see you—"

"Do you want me to talk to Antonio? Is that why you want me to go there? I don't think he'll listen to me about your marriage."

Taking another few plates out, Serene pushed through the door into the kitchen, Veronica following. "I've started a pile near the basin."

Veronica scanned the kitchen. "Smells good. You made that all for yourself?"

"The eggs and potatoes are already cooked, but now I don't feel like eating. Go ahead and fill your belly. The rest I'll bring home later."

With a spoon already dipped into the bowl of eggs, Veronica continued. "I just thought it would be good for you to get out. You've been through a lot since your Papa. We'll take the bus and make a small trip out of it."

Serene eyed her friend. "I can't put any more sense into Antonio than you can."

"Would you try, at least?"

Deep down, Serene knew her focus should be on the restaurant and proving to Marcus that she was able to run the place by herself. But now, seeing the determination on Veronica's face, she couldn't say no. "Maybe in a few days?"

"I'm keeping you to your promise." Veronica smirked. "It's awful for me to say, but he's kind of cute, too."

"Who?"

"The man staying with them."

Serene laughed. "Is that what this is about? Do you like that man?"

"No, I just thought you would enjoy meeting

him. He's different from the boys here. And he's from the United States."

"Maybe if things don't work out with Antonio..." Serene's voice trailed off, her mouth suddenly dry like cotton. From the United States?

"You haven't lost your touch," Veronica said with a mouthful of eggs. "Once you re-open, people will come from all over, just like when your Papa was here."

Dipping the first plate in the basin of sudsy water, Serene wanted desperately to ask the name of the man. It couldn't be him. "I hope I'll get to keep cooking. Marcus doesn't think it's a good idea that I will take control of the restaurant after we're married."

Veronica took a wet plate from Serene, and wiped it down with a towel. "But that's what you want."

It couldn't be him. "This is where my family is. Right here in this kitchen. I won't give it up..."

"Marcus must know how important this is to you. Any of us will help you in any way we can. You know that, don't you? Times are hard, but not too hard for friends. Luigi has been asking when he can come back and cook. Your father helped a lot of people in the past, and they want to help you now."

"You have been such a help already," Serene said, fighting distraction as she plucked another plate from the stack. Thoughts and worries collided in her head. If Miles was still in Italy, wouldn't she have known? Sam had never said otherwise, either. "All three restaurants meant a lot to Papa. Once I finish here, I have to work on the other two—" She wanted to know something, anything, more about the American, but she bit back the questions. Veronica would be all over her with the curiosity of a monkey. "We'll get there, slowly, but we'll get back to normal, whatever that is."

"Marcus is a gentle man; he'll see your point."

Maybe Miles never made it home? Serene leaned on the icebox, fighting the dread that was growing in her stomach. Who would've done that to him? Her head began to swim as though a wild river rushed through it, and then she buckled and the plate slid out of her hand, smashing to the tiled floor.

Bending beside her, Veronica took hold of her shoulders. "What is it?"

The spells had happened before, and a nap usually made her feel better. "I'm fine. Just a little tired."

"Come, sit."

With a hand gripping the chair to steady herself, Serene grimaced. "It's nothing."

"I think all you need is to put some meat on you. You're as thin as spaghetti. Come sit here." She patted a chair. "I'll get us some of those eggs."

Before Serene could object, Veronica whirled around the kitchen and prepared a full bowl for her friend, while Serene dropped her head between her knees to let the wave of queasiness pass. The picture of Miles lying beaten nearly to death in a field practically took all the air from her lungs. "I've just been working too hard—this restaurant needs so much."

"You can't do it all, my sweet." Veronica put the bowl down, then rubbed her back. "Besides, soon enough you'll be home having babies and making eggs for your husband. You'll be too busy to worry about these little things."

Serene's body trembled. One way or another she had to find out if Miles was in Turni. "I don't know if that's what I want."

With a pause, Veronica scooped up the larger pieces of china. "Of course that's what you want," she said over her shoulder. "Every girl wants that."

****

219

Serene waited a good distance from the Mary statue in the Vatican. Casually she strolled around the piazza as if sightseeing, searching for him. In wartime, anything could be detected. People were watched all the time, only to disappear later that day or night, or even the next week. Even with the Americans liberating parts of Italy, it still wasn't completely safe. She clutched her purse, with her papers safely intact inside it.

When his tall frame came toward her, she smiled, recognizing Veronica's brother again by the same fiery red hair. Davido was five years older than his sister and did what he could to reunite or save people lost at war. Whether they were from Italy or another country, men or women, soldiers or citizens, it didn't matter to Davido and his friends. He claimed that he worked for humanity.

Underground activities were done with secret meetings and rarely with daylight conversations, but this was different. She didn't have a letter to send or a person to hide, she only had a question, one that she hoped Davido could answer.

They embraced, and Serene didn't waste any time. "That letter you sent for me a while back. Do you remember?"

They kept smiling. To onlookers it would appear as a casual conversation. "I sent it."

"It was an American address."

"Yes."

"Can you get me the address where it went?"

"We don't keep a trace of such things. You know that."

The smile faded from Serene's face, and she gripped his arm. "Please—I need to find it. I have no idea where to find him."

"Find who? What's wrong?"

"Miles Coulson, the man who sent it. I have to see if he made it out of Italy. That address is the only way I have to track him. I just have to find him."

"I'm sorry, Serene. I don't think I can help you."

"You have to," she said, not able to contain the desperation in her voice. "How else can I find him?"

Davido hugged her, pressing her head against his chest. "Who did you have arrange it?" he whispered in her ear.

"Someone I know—it was through someone my sister cares about deeply. Samuel McCarthy."

"Do you trust him?"

"I think so. Samuel said he'd bet his own life on the man who actually came to get Miles. We've known Samuel for a very long time. I trust him as part of our family."

"Then your friend probably is back in the States." Davido gently let go of her. "In a few months' time, when things begin to settle, it will be easier to look into it."

"This can't wait." Even her breath seemed to buckle inside her. "I have this bad feeling. I just have to find him." She contained the sob sitting in her chest. "I can't tell you why."

Davido glanced away. "Even if I could track it down, where it went from here, how would that help you?"

Even though the address wasn't actually Miles, it was at least a starting point. Maybe if she could contact his girl back home, she could at least find out if he was alive. "I need the address." She didn't need to say anything to Davido about keeping it quiet, even to his sister. One thing war had taught her was the holiness and ferocity of secrets.

Everyone had secrets, terrible secrets.

Chapter Nineteen

"Serene, is that you?" Margot called. "Come upstairs. I've been waiting for you."

Smoothing down her skirt, Serene put her coat on the hook and steadied the nervousness in her chest.

"Be right there." Her stomach still didn't feel right. On the bus ride back from Rome, she had decided to accept Veronica's invitation to go to Turni. She had no choice. It was either that or spend the rest of her life wondering, praying that he was alive. And if he wasn't alive, or if that wasn't him in the field, she wanted to know.

"You there, Serene? Come up here."

When she got to the top of the stairs, Margot grabbed onto her arm and dragged her into the room, forcing her to sit. Her dark eyes were shining as she held out a weathered envelope. "I found this."

With her heart beating faster, Serene touched the crinkled envelope. She froze at the sight of Miles' name on the front. Scanning the rest of the envelope, she couldn't find an army address and no return address.

"Look at the date," Margot prodded, pushing it closer to Serene.

The date on the outside of the envelope was stamped two weeks earlier than her father's death.

"Where did you get this?" Serene gasped.

"I found it under Mama's dresser. It was already crumpled, like he had thrown it out."

"Should I open it?"

Margot giggled. "Of course. It's already open,

and he's not here to say not to open it. Maybe it's a love letter from her."

"Shh," Serene said. She tried hard to swallow her nervousness as she twiddled the letter between her fingers. "I can't. I can't read it. It doesn't matter what it says."

"Don't you want to know? Go on, read it. Or I'll have to read it."

"Isn't it rude to read another person's mail?"

Margot said in an exasperated tone, "Would you rather die of being rude? Or of not knowing?"

Serene bit her bottom lip. "You're right." She hesitated, then quickly opened the top. A piece of paper, the size of a postcard, was folded in half, with words scrawled on both sides. It started *Dear Miles*, and she scanned to the bottom to read *Love, Josie*.

"It's from her—I'll just read the first few sentences." Once she started, Serene couldn't stop, her eyes transfixed on the paper.

...I've been lonely. Too lonely even to be comforted by your letters. The letters always used to push us together, but now I feel differently. I know you always wanted me to get to the point, so now I'm saying, I've found another man who loves me just as much as I love him. We got married two months ago. I wouldn't want you coming home and finding out then. Please forgive me.

"What does it say?" Margot leaned closer.

Dazed, Serene stared at her sister. Doom weighed down on her, hindering her ability to talk. When had Miles read the letter? Had he known all along and lied, telling her that someone waited for him back in the States?

"Well?" Margot chided.

"She married someone else."

"Who? His girl back in the States?"

Serene nodded.

"When?"

"As far as I can tell, before Miles arrived here."

"Didn't he tell you he was planning on marrying her? There has to be more to it than that," Margot said with annoyance in her voice.

"That was it, all along." A surge of adrenaline, fueled by anger, pumped through her body. "He lied about everything."

"For goodness sake, Ser, let me read it. He didn't lie."

"Can you read English?" Serene challenged, holding the letter to her chest. "I'm going to take a walk."

"To run away from it? Why can't you admit that you love him?"

"I don't," Serene retorted.

"You must," Margot said gently, wiping a tear from Serene's cheek. "If you didn't care so much for him, you wouldn't even care about this letter."

Serene didn't trust herself to talk. Couldn't he have simply told her he didn't love her, rather than coming up with a story that he was planning a wedding? He had known all along that Josie had broken it off. Pressing the letter against her thigh, Serene guessed maybe there wasn't a plan of marriage between the two at all.

"I knew there was something between you two."

Heading for the door, Serene stopped. "You don't know anything."

"I know that you are giving your hand to another man, one you don't love. And I also know you let that American go even though he was the first person to bring life into your eyes. I may be younger than you, but I'm not blind, Serene. I saw how you were with him. But you were too stubborn to admit it."

"Stubborn?" New tears choked Serene's throat as she grasped the door handle. "You think that's the reason? Papa arranged it, which doesn't give me a choice."

"You've always been there for us since Mama died. You take care of us and do everything for us. What about you? Do you think Papa would have wanted you to give up the kind of love he had with Mama? The Sturinis will understand if you do this one thing for yourself. Papa would have wanted you to be happy."

Anger and humiliation exploded from down deep in Serene's bones, and she used every millimeter of her strength to contain it. "Happy? You think Papa wanted me to be happy?"

"Of course he did," Margot whispered.

"I have to marry Marcus or all of this goes away." As Serene continued, her tone escalated. "The restaurants that Papa worked so hard to build. The villa. All of it." She took in a shuddered breath. "Any security that we have will be gone."

Margot gently held Serene's arm. "What do you mean?"

"Papa got into debt. The only way we can pay the debt is through the dowry that he promised the Sturini family. I have to marry Marcus for us to get the money."

"What?" Slowly, Margot backed away, her eyes big. "How can that happen? How long have you known this?"

Struggling to submerge a sob, Serene laid it out as simply as she could. "After Papa died, Everto told me. He didn't know, before, about the debt Papa was in." She continued to fill Margot in on the details, letting the truth flood from her mouth like water released from an opened dam.

With a turn, Margot paced half the length of the room, returning with glassy eyes. "But what if you didn't want to marry Marcus and we—we kept the dowry money to pay the debts?"

Serene clutched her arms together in front. "We only get the money if I marry Marcus, and only Marcus."

"What if—"

"I've been over all the options, Margot." Her voice teetered on a shiver. "There's no way out of this. I have to marry him. I mustn't go back on Papa's word."

"This is *your* life, Serene." Margot rubbed her sister's arm, her eyelashes grazing the thick of her cheeks. "If you love someone else, you can't let this happen. Are you willing to be unhappy for the rest of your life?"

Straining to hold in the tears, Serene pressed her lips together. "For all of you, I'm willing to do what's necessary. If that means marrying Marcus, than I'll do it. I can't let Papa down."

****

"Serene?"

A faint voice called to her. As though in a smoky room, Serene couldn't find the door. Feeling trapped, searching, she fell in the darkness, the hard floor splintering into her fingers. Finally, her eyes cleared enough to see the inside walls of her little house in the yard.

Relief washed over her like a cool cloth. She knew where she was, now.

A man's voice called to her. This time it was familiar—oh, so familiar. She spun around a few times before seeing him through the haze. Squinting, she recognized the outline she'd know anywhere.

"It's you," she whispered, smiling. "I've been waiting for you."

It was hard to see in the shadow whether he recognized her. She went closer, just a little closer...

"Serene, wake up."

With a struggle, she pushed her eyelids open to

find Samuel, in a white coat, standing beside her bed. "Where is he?" she asked.

"Who?"

Realizing it had been a dream, Serene settled back into the pillow, feeling the pain in her head begin to move down her neck. "Everything hurts," she mumbled, pressing her fingers against various spots on her head until she found a lump the size of a grape. "What happened?"

Margot leaned over Samuel. "We were talking and then, all of a sudden, you dropped to the floor."

"That knot on your forehead is from the bedpost," Samuel said in his doctor's voice. "You hit the corner when you fell."

Samuel motioned to Margot. "Can you excuse us for a minute?"

"You mean leave?"

With a nod, Samuel explained. "I'm a doctor first. I'd like to talk to Serene alone."

With an air of indignation, Margot marched to the door. "Serene will tell me anyway. Whatever is wrong, I'll know about it."

He put the cool stethoscope to her chest. "Have you had these spells often?"

"The last month or so, I guess. Usually they go away if I take a rest or have something to eat."

"And your monthly cycle? Has it been regular?"

"No. Not really. Too much to think about, I guess." Working on the restaurant had taken its physical toll, but deep down she was worn out emotionally from the façade she had worked so hard to create, pretending to be happy, pretending to take care of everything, and pretending not to be affected by it all. She was already sorry she'd told Margot about the dowry stipulation.

"What is it, Sam?" Serene asked.

His face was serious, more serious than she had seen it even when they told her about Margot's pregnancy. "What is it, Sam?"

"I estimate you'll be having this baby in another seven or eight months."

"You think I'm…"

"Pregnant. At least a month along, probably more."

Alarm jellied her insides. *A baby?* "Marcus and I aren't even married—"

Sam stayed quiet, as if waiting for her digest it all.

Pressing a hand on the center of her flat belly, she knew the truth as sure as the sun shines in warm weather. It all made too much sense, like a puzzle that finally had all the pieces. It had happened in the little house the night before Miles left.

"Are you sure?" she whispered.

"Almost positive."

Floundering for an excuse, a reason, something tangible, she struggled to find a rational story for others. She and Marcus weren't even married.

Hotness rose to her face. "Sam—you can't tell anyone."

"Lie back down and take some more time to rest. I'm not going to tell you not to work at the restaurant, because I know how much it means to you, but only do it if you are feeling up to it."

As she held her breath, letting it out in small bursts, she decided to keep the man in Turni a secret. "Have you heard anything from your contact? If Miles made it back?"

He didn't ask why she wanted to know. He just patted her hand, as if he understood all the truths she'd been hiding. "No, but I didn't expect to."

Then he was back to their doctor-patient relationship. "Come by the hospital tomorrow. They will give you a thorough exam, just to be sure. For now, you need to rest." With a wink, he added, "I'll keep Margot busy for a bit, to give you some time to yourself."

Samuel stuffed the stethoscope in his bag. "Don't forget to go to the doctor tomorrow. First thing."

Not trusting herself to speak, she forced her lips to smile at him.

A baby? The words echoed in her ears, her body and soul already tied to this little being with such a fierceness, such a powerful force, that nothing else mattered. With the hands of fate at play, she had made a new life with the man she loved beyond words or feeling. A man who gave her substance and love, where otherwise she would have lived her life void of meaning.

Letting her legs slide off the bed, she smoothed a hand over her abdomen, wondering when her shape would grow to the size of a pumpkin.

She dropped back onto her side, weeping softly into the pillow, wondering why it was so hard to be happy.

But she knew why.

Miles Coulson had taken her heart with him.

Chapter Twenty

"There is nothing to be afraid of, my dear," Doctor Capelleti said. "Just come a little closer."

Serene tried to squirm back, away from his cold hands, "I know," she chirped out, and scooted a little further down the table, trying to concentrate on the stark white ceiling paint.

The more the doctor poked, the more Serene wanted to squeeze her knees together and jump from the table. When Serene thought she couldn't stand it anymore, he abruptly stopped.

"You'll have this baby in about eight months."

"Are you sure?"

He flipped open the metal chart and finishing writing. She saw a quick smile cross his face and disappear. "I haven't had that question before. Any particular reason?"

"I worry." It was all she could say, because otherwise she'd start to cry.

"Mothers have been having babies for millions of years." He patted her hand. "Eat well, get rest, and celebrate with your husband. I'll see you in three weeks."

When the doctor left the room, Serene drew the hospital gown closer to her body and shivered. At least she had worn her mother's wedding ring to alleviate any questions about her marital status. She hiccupped and bent over, gagging several times before easing off the table. Her feet wobbled, and she caught her hip on the side of the table. Dressing was a struggle, with shirt buttons resisting her fingers and her jacket twisting. Finally, she wiped her mouth with the back of her hand, and steadied herself enough to push back the privacy screen.

She moistened her lips, her eyes warming at the thought of their night together. It had filled her with the most love and hope and joy she had ever known. At the very least, Miles needed to know he was going to have a child.

They had agreed that it had to end. The moment he stepped into that car, it was supposed to have ended, but it didn't. It couldn't. As much as she'd tried, in the last weeks, she couldn't end it in her heart.

She hugged her arms around her belly; the warmth of having his child comforted her. She'd go to Turni and find out for sure whether the man there was actually Miles. And if need be, when the war ended, she'd go to the United States and find him. And if he wasn't there, she'd keep looking.

For a few seconds, her mind wandered to Marcus, and the unbearable future planned with him. She wasn't going to let him ruin this moment. Yes, she had to figure out things with him, but not yet. For a few minutes, she wanted things to be about just her and this baby, and of course Miles.

As horrifying as it would be for people to know she was having a baby out of wedlock, and despite the shame it would bring upon herself, her throat still clogged with happy tears. Miles was the father of her child, and she'd never let anyone take that joy from her.

She walked through the long white corridor and wondered if her son or daughter would have sandy-colored hair.

****

"What is this?" Serene asked. Marcus stood in the middle of Cucina Moneto's main dining room as if he owned it.

"I found Franci here when I came. He was

working on the floor, but I told him we don't want strangers in our restaurant." He took a puff on a cigarette. "I'll take care of any work that needs to be done."

"Strangers?" Serene focused on the floor. Half of the bloodstain had been polished into a light pink, the other half left unfinished. "Why are you here?"

He grabbed onto her shoulders. "None of this restaurant business will be your concern any longer. Once we're married—"

Serene jerked herself away from him. "I started restoring my father's business, and I intend to continue. I still plan to reopen as soon as I can."

"Before we marry?" Marcus' jaw tightened. "What about the ones in Sicily and Naples?"

"The same with them. Sicily needs work, and Naples will take more money and time because of the bomb damage, but I'm sure my half of the dowry money will be more than plenty to get all three done."

"*Stupido*. You really think they will be profitable? He laughed sarcastically. "The restaurant's making no money for us now, is it?"

"It will soon. There's talk the war will end and things will be back soon to the way they were. You agreed to this—to the deal we struck. All the more reason to go on with our plans."

Marcus raised his brows and put his face close to hers. His thick breath was warm and musky against her mouth. "Deals are broken sometimes, *no?*"

Serene stared blankly into his good eye. Anger filled the base of her throat. He was more than right, and if she were in a better frame of mind emotionally, she would have told him so, right there, along with the fact that she had never felt even a spasm of love for him. She knew it as much as she knew her heart was beating.

"Why are you worried about the restaurants now? A few weeks ago, it was my problem. What about the factory? I thought it was going better?"

"My father wants machines fixed faster than we can do it." Marcus was yelling in his frustration. "There are no parts to be found. And the materials we do manage to get aren't enough. And he blames me for it!"

"Just tell him. Your father is an understanding man," Serene said. "Things will get back to the way they were."

"He put us in this predicament by agreeing to make guns in the first place. Now Mussolini's gone and what equipment we had left was destroyed in the blast. It will be a miracle if our plant ever sees another string of spaghetti."

Serene hesitated. "You know he didn't have a choice."

"You're naïve," he spat and flicked his cigarette, which landed on the only remnants of her father's blood. With the slow movement of his heel, he crushed the cigarette into the stone. "I don't want you working at Cucina Moneto."

Stabs of fury ran the length of her spine as she watched the ashes mingle with the dark pink stain. "You can't command me to stay away, like you own me."

"You heard what I said, Serene. There's no more discussion on it. I want you home. Let Veronica pack up the place and get it ready for a new owner. If I have to force my hand on you, I will."

"No, you won't," she said defiantly.

Marcus leapt toward her and slapped her cheek. "Do not defy me!"

Without a yelp or a tear, with no exclamation of pain, Serene bit back the sting and kept her eyes on him. "What I choose to do is my decision."

"When we're married, I make the decisions."

"Our deal was to split the dowry in half. I'm going to use mine to do this. If you don't like it, then don't marry me."

She had started to walk away when he grabbed her arm. "You heard what I said."

"I heard you." She glared at him. "But I wasn't listening."

"Of course you'll listen when the time is right."

"You're right about only one thing, Marcus. Your father. He must not trust your work, or he would use you more for the factory. And I'm also guessing you'll never get any *lire* from him. That's why you need *my* family's money. I never understood until this very moment. You need me."

Marcus opened his mouth, but any intended words were lost in a huff. Serene watched him stalk through the front door. Shaking, she burrowed her face in her hands and sat for nearly an hour before going to Franci's shop and convincing him that he was still loved and needed for the work. He promised to work on the floor if she promised to go to Santa Cecilia until he was finished. She laughed to herself when he suggested it. He didn't even known the full truth of what she had just experienced with Marcus. *Or about the baby.* But he was right, it seemed to be the only place to think.

Opening the front door to the church, she knew at that moment that Franci had been right. She felt it. She was there for a reason.

Heartache crowded her throat as she stared at the empty church, eyeing the pew in which Miles had sat next to her, rubbing her thigh so delicately. It seemed more like a lifetime had passed, rather than a few weeks. She closed her eyes for a second, to focus on her mission.

Honor to your family lives and breathes in your soul. Her father had recited that phrase as if it were the Bible.

Kneeling in the first pew, her hands clasped at her chin, her eyes rested on the effigy of Santa Cecilia. Lying on her side, just as she was found in the third century, Cecilia had three deep cuts in her neck and a cloth wound around her head, covering her face. Although tattered clothes barely covered her body, she radiated peace.

"Why?" Serene whispered out, wondering how she had gotten to this place in her life.

As she studied the ashen-colored sculpture, she remembered that despite Cecilia's vow to give her virginity to God, her family married her to a Roman nobleman. Even though her fate was determined, she still fought to teach the Christian faith, against the pagan belief. For this, she was tortured with hot vapors and eventually beheaded.

Serene's eyes filled, not so much for the torture the woman had endured but more for the glory Cecelia must have experienced when she realized her true purpose on this earth. Even though the saint had known it would end her life at a young age, she'd followed her path and followed her heart.

Raising her eyes to the cathedral ceiling, Serene wondered how many marriages had taken place out of obligation rather than love.

And like every other Italian marriage blessed in the eyes of God, Serene's would be unbroken. Living another person's desires, she'd walk a path of life that wouldn't be her own.

From the moment her Papa told her of the arrangement for her to marry Marcus Sturini, she had known it. As long as the sun shone, she could never love Marcus. Maybe if she had talked to her Papa more, begged him to understand. She wanted to put it all in a box and close it forever.

Never had she complained or questioned her duty as the eldest, with Papa at the restaurants or taking care of things at home. Through the years, like a slow-growing sickness, honor to her family had been replaced by guilt. Guilt to be the mother her family had lost so soon. Guilt to be the person her father wanted her to be. Guilt to marry the man arranged, so her family could survive.

Now, depending on her as for water, her family would barely survive the few months of savings left in the bank.

Letting her head hang lower, she gazed at her belly, and all that it stood for. Miles had opened her eyes to happiness, and when she couldn't fight for it, he gave her the strength with this new little life.

With a shudder, it came to her. Now she could fight for all three of them.

****

Relishing the quiet of the kitchen, sipping a cup of warm milk, Serene was suddenly jolted from her chair by the pounding at the front door. No one made visits so late into the night, nearly midnight, and especially during wartime, unless... She ran toward the hallway, nearly colliding with Anna, who was still putting on her robe, her face white as cotton.

"Who is it?" Anna asked frantically.

The pounding continued, pushing fear right into Serene's temples. She bit her lip hard enough to draw blood. "Stay here. I'll try and see who it is, but don't let Harry and Margot downstairs." She tiptoed closer to the door and jumped when more pounding came. "Who is it?" she called out.

With pelting rain slamming against the wood door, she summoned a huge breath and opened it.

"Veronica?" She nearly crumpled in relief. Her friend's dress and coat were drenched and caked with mud. Rain dripped from the hair hanging in front of her face. "I thought you were—someone else."

"Do you know a man named Miles Coulson?"

Serene's clutched her arm, feeling the cold spray

of rain. "Who?" she yelled above the sound of the rain. "Come in. You're shivering." She took a few deep breaths to try and relieve the small pains in her lower abdomen and led Veronica to the parlor.

"Who is it?" Anna called from the hall.

"It's fine, Anna," Serene said with relief. "It's just Veronica. Can you please bring some towels?"

Anna returned quickly. "Miss Veronica, you'll catch your death being out in the rain."

"*Grazie.*" With shivering hands, Veronica laid one of the towels around her neck like a shawl and used the other to blot her face and then rub the excess water from her hair.

"Do you want to make some tea, Anna?" Serene asked gently, her heart beating fast. When the woman had left, she asked, "What happened, Roni?"

Feeling Veronica staring at her face, Serene put her hand to her cheek. "It was nothing."

"Did someone hit you?"

"Roni—tell me."

"Do you know Miles Coulson?" The question was simple, straightforward, but it nearly knocked out the little air left in Serene's lungs.

"I used...to know him." Serene's nails dug into the fabric of the parlor chair she grasped for support. "You saw him?"

"The other night. I thought he was crazy," Veronica whispered, "but when I thought about what he told me, and how he called you 'Serry,' and the way you reacted the other day, then I didn't know what to think—"

"Slow down. Start from the beginning."

"At Antonio's house," she said with exasperation. "Remember that man I told you about, their guest? The man who was beaten?" She didn't wait for confirmation. "I thought he was a madman, asking me all those questions about you. His name is Miles Coulson."

Shivering, Serene folded her arms together across her chest. "Are you sure?"

"He has the clearest blue eyes I've ever seen. And a scar above one eye. And he's American."

Serene let out a cry and put her hand over her mouth, letting her body sink into the chair.

"Are you afraid of him?"

Unable to hold back, Serene cried softly, shaking her head. "What did they do—to him?"

"Horrible things, but Evita took good care of him. He'll stay there until he is better enough to go back to the United States. Who is he, Serene? How do you know him?"

With a small sob, she fought to calm the throbbing in her head. "Someone I met a few times at the restaurant."

Raising her eyebrows, Veronica sat next to her. "He called you 'Serry.' I've only heard your Papa call you that. Then he followed me out in the rain and tried to beg information out of me about you. When I didn't tell him, he got upset, almost desperate. You've only met him a few times?"

With wet eyes, Serene caught her stare. "Why didn't you tell me sooner?"

Another knock came at the door just as Anna returned with a teapot and cups on a tray. Serene jumped from the chair and held her breath until Anna answered. She couldn't see who it was, but the sound of friendly mumblings put her at ease.

"Why, Roni?" she whispered. "Why didn't you tell me about Miles?"

"I thought it was bad, or he was bad. I didn't know what to think. Your hand is almost given away to Marcus. If this man knew you at all, he must have known that. All of Rome knows that. Why would he ask so many questions about you?"

Because he loves me as much as I love him. Serene scrambled to keep a thread of composure.

Rubbing the towel down the length of her hair, Veronica abruptly stopped. "He told me other things, too."

"What things?"

She dropped her arms. "Things about Marcus. Things that can't be true."

"You have to take me to him, Roni."

"To whom?" Marcus' voice boomed through the parlor, making Serene's body startle as if it was hit. "Who's making my soon-to-be wife cry like this?" he asked in Veronica's direction.

Like a triangle of secrets, the three stared at each other for the briefest of seconds, Serene grasping for a legitimate answer.

"Old Franci next door to Cucina Moneto is very sick," Veronica said, her eyes fixed on Serene. "Before he passes on, he asked to see old friends, including Serene."

The breath Serene was holding exhaled slowly from her lips.

"I saw Franci just today and he seemed fine." Marcus smirked. "You come in the middle of the night to tell her?"

"I was worried and couldn't sleep myself. I apologize it's so late."

"It's fine, Veronica," Serene said, wiping the tears away. Her voice cracked. "We can talk some more about it tomorrow. Maybe we can meet at Cucina Moneto. Come by in the morning if you want."

Veronica paused, as if hoping Serene would say something else. After another goodnight, Serene held the door open.

They embraced and Veronica tugged her hand. "Try and get some sleep."

"I'll see to it that she does," Marcus said. "Now, good night." After he shut the door, he muttered, "That girl is a nuisance. She needs to find a bum to marry her."

Serene's heart beat wildly. Her thoughts of Miles were frantic and scattered. He was still in Italy. She started replaying the day the driver had picked him up. If it had happened the way Veronica explained, it must have been done by someone else. Or maybe after the driver had dropped Miles near Anzio…

She realized Marcus was staring at her. "Why are you here?" she asked, not caring whether he believed Veronica's blatant lie.

"The way we left things this afternoon," Marcus was saying. "I've thought things over some more and wanted to come and say good night."

"This has nothing to do with the fact that you slapped me?"

"That was a mistake."

Things about Marcus that can't be true. Veronica's words haunted her as she struggled to listen to him. "It's late and I'd rather not talk about this now."

She backed away before he could grab her.

"You will talk about this when I say."

"Not tonight." A hard coldness came from deep inside her bones. "We've had enough disruption for the night. Please let yourself out."

Before he had a chance to argue, she ran up the stairs and braced herself against the wall where he couldn't see. As she felt a stray tear land on her cheek, she saw Margot sitting on the floor. "What happened?"

When they heard the door slam, Serene slowly sat down next to Margot, her body weary. She felt too emotionally battered to tell her sister anything. And declaring that Miles might possibly still be in Italy would stir up more anxiety, while her own heart was already beating too fast, too much for the baby.

The concern in Margot's face prodded her to say more.

"He doesn't want me to work in the restaurant." She smoothed down a rough patch of curls above Margot's ear. "That's all it is."

Margot squeezed her sister's hand. "You've been holding onto Marcus like a martyr. Papa wouldn't have wanted you to have this kind of life. Things were different when he made that arrangement. You weren't his daughter by blood, but he arranged for your life the best way he knew. It was a different time then."

"How can you know that?"

"I've always understood things more than you ever cared to realize, probably because I'm younger, and you've always seen me as a child." She stopped and took a deep breath, "But you have a chance to change things. You're not married to him. It doesn't mean you're hurting anyone. And the money? We'll get by. No matter what we've faced as a family, we've done it."

"We all make our own choices."

"You'll die if you choose Marcus. Do you hear me Serene? Did you see the look in his eye when you told him to go home? I saw it from up here. I didn't miss the red mark on your cheek when you came home from the restaurant, but I kept it to myself. He has the strength to really hurt you. Is that what you want?"

"When did you get so smart?"

Margot grinned. "I always was. You just didn't see it."

Serene pressed her hands together, fingertips joined. For the very first time in a long time, something made sense. Now it was her turn to act on it.

Chapter Twenty-One

Serene couldn't close her eyes, let alone sleep. It had been hours since Marcus had stormed out. Restless, she moved around the bed. Sat up. Turned. Rolled over. And in those hours she let her mind drift from Marcus to Miles. From darkness to sweetness. She stared at the small crack in the corner of the ceiling, lit by the early morning light. She sat upright and used her feet to push the blanket to the bottom of the bed.

She couldn't shake the thought. She had to do it before she lost the nerve. And it was too early to go by the restaurant to meet Veronica. The bus didn't start for a few hours, either.

After pedaling her bike the one-mile journey, Serene found herself pounding on the Sturini's front door. She knew she shouldn't have taken the bike, since bikes had been banned on all Rome's streets, but with the short distance and it not yet dawn, the rebellion felt glorious.

Jack Sturini, dressed in checkered pajamas, opened the door with a bewildered expression. Genna stood at the top of the steps, her arms crossed, her hair and nightclothes meticulous.

"Where is he?" Serene asked, whirling by Jack into the main foyer, her robe flying behind her. Her hair hung loose and knotted, skimming the top of her shoulders. Her bare feet peeped out from under the bottom of her robe.

"My God, Serene, what is it? What happened to your face?"

"I came to see Marcus."

"Marcus?" Jack asked. "He's not here."

Serene searched the room. The rumors of him being with other women surfaced in her head like a slow-moving storm. None of that mattered any more. "Where else could he be?"

"Did he hit you?" Jack asked.

"This is nonsense," Genna said matter-of-factly. "Come, sit and have tea. He'll be home soon."

"I'd just like to know where he is."

Genna sighed. "Whatever my son does is his choice, and I'm sure he had a reason. I didn't teach my son to hurt a woman, but sometimes things need to be done. I'm sure your Papa would have said the same thing."

"Genna, please," Jack scolded.

"She's out in the cold, looking like that? She's the woman that's going to marry our son. Go home, Serene."

Serene put both palms on her stomach and took a deep breath in. Feeling anything for Genna except repulsion would take a lot of coaxing. The woman had not a warm bone in her body.

"He hasn't been here, my dear," Jack said. "Maybe he went to the factory to put in some extra work? That's an unusual thing for my son, but sometimes he does surprise me."

"Have things gotten that bad?"

Jack shook his head. "The damage to the factory requires much more than we anticipated. Marcus doesn't see all of it, I'm afraid, and tries to take shortcuts, and blames me for most of the troubles. I can't use him for the big projects, and unfortunately he resents me for it. He loves you and doesn't want to admit his shortcomings, and it's probably why he upsets so easily."

Serene digested the logical explanation, but the thinness of it rattled her. Remembering her purpose, she locked her eyes on Jack's. "I have to find him."

"I'm sure he'll come back if you give him some time. Sometimes a man needs to get the fight out of him. God knows I love him, but he's got a hot temper, just like his mother."

Genna cast him an annoyed glance and then scooped out a cigarette from the gold case on the table, waiting for Jack to light it before she took a puff and let the smoke billow from her nose. "The truth is that you can't make a man want more than he does. He'll probably warm to the idea, but it's your duty to support him and give him the kind of life he's used to. Don't make him angry enough to do something like this. It's really not his nature. When you're married, you'll learn that quickly."

"For God's sake!" Jack said, "The poor girl needs help with something. Marcus hurt her."

"He's my son, and I can say as much as I choose."

"No, Uncle Jack, she's right," Serena said. "There isn't a woman in this world who knows how to really take care of Marcus Sturini the way Genna can." Serene didn't find pleasure in being disrespectful, but rather, she found a small part of her own pride and let it be heard.

"What would your Papa have said?" Genna snapped and marched up the stairs.

"It's her way," Jack apologized.

"I know. I can see where that part of Marcus comes from."

"He's a stubborn man, I'll admit that." Jack ran a hand over the side of her face, his eyes tired. "Things will be fine, Serene."

Serene hesitated and then clung to him, not wanting to divulge her true intentions until she talked with Marcus. Holding him, she imagined what it would be like if it were her father holding her that tight. "I hope so," she murmured into his shirt.

Even though Jack had argued that she shouldn't be riding a bike, she left before he could persuade her to leave it and walk.

Welcoming the cool air racing through her hair, Serene took her feet from the pedals and let the bike glide all the way down the narrow street. At the bottom, she coasted around the corner to the main street. At six in the morning, a few vendors already bustled in the main piazza, preparing to negotiate with customers for miniscule amounts of chicken and fruit.

She absorbed the fresh air on her face and her neck, deciding the next step. Then she pedaled faster, watching the shimmering olive groves pass to her right.

Despite the ravages of war, in a few hours the midmorning streets would be stirring with the familiar sounds of life moving, changing. She had to change with it. Another life now depended on it. She had to find Marcus and make things right before she went any further with her life.

****

With a rapid pulse, Serene walked her bicycle up the villa's drive and leaned it against the front railing. Warmth touched Serene's eyes when she saw Veronica already sitting on the steps outside their villa. Dressed in a simple, belted dress, she was again a normal girl rather than the fiery redhead at her door the previous night.

"You're here."

Standing to greet her, Veronica took her hands in her own. "I couldn't let you down, Serene. This man must mean a lot to you. I understood that last night."

"I want to see him."

With a grin, Veronica glanced at Serene's bare toes. "Is that why you're outside in your bedclothes before the sun has had a chance to rise?"

Serene pulled her robe tighter to her body. "I tried to see Marcus. I need to tell him something first," she blurted, not afraid anymore.

"Then what are you waiting for? Get yourself dressed, sweetie. I'll take you wherever you want to go."

By the time Serene dressed, the morning busses had started their regular runs.

Both girls were quiet on the bus, and Serene wondered if Veronica understood that Serene was about to put aside her father's legacy in pursuit of her own.

With a sigh, she sat back and wondered how the day would end. Just the thought of Miles being in the same vicinity made her heart quicken. She'd have to do this first and then—then life could begin. In the short ride, they watched swarms of people in the piazza, where the bus was unable to reach the main street. When Serene saw someone waving a sign that Rome was finally free, she jumped from her seat, almost colliding with Veronica. "Is the war over?" she asked the driver.

"The Allies are here, in Rome. It'll be the end soon, God willing."

With a soft shudder in her belly, Serene left the bus and worked her way through the people and up the steps to the factory.

"Do you want me to come with you?" Veronica asked, trailing behind.

Serene shook her head. This was something she'd have to do herself. "Wait for me. It will only take a minute."

When the factory door shut, it muffled the noise from outside. Glancing upward, she noticed part of the roof had already been replaced. With a hand on the side of her stomach to stop the twinge, Serene approached the small desk. Behind it sat a dark-haired woman in her mid-twenties or so, with black-rimmed glasses. The regular secretary was nowhere in sight. When Serene passed behind her to open the double doors to the main factory, the woman stood and smiled tritely while trying to block her entry into factory. "How may I help you?"

"I need to see Marcus Sturini."

"He's in a meeting right now."

"If you'll excuse me, I'll check for myself."

The woman's nervousness confirmed that indeed Marcus was in the factory. "Mr. Sturini will not be happy about this."

"When he finds out you wouldn't let me see him?" Serene challenged, moving the woman's arm out of the way. "We are to be married, you know."

Her heart pounded as she made her way down the hallway into the main plant. The ceiling had been fixed and the walls appeared much darker and drearier than she remembered. A lot of progress had been made in replacing some of the walls. Workers glanced at her as she passed; some tipped their hats, but others didn't take their eyes from the equipment. She kept a grim smile pasted on her face and headed straight for Marcus' office. It was empty. The room off to the side was closed, but she knew Marcus only used that for storage. She checked to see if anyone was approaching, taking a second to catch her breath.

The pain in her stomach had worsened, but she tried to ignore it as she stuck her head out of the office to ask a few of the workers if they knew where Marcus was. Finding out nothing, she returned to the office and eyed the chair she had sat in those months ago when she gave Marcus the ultimatum. She knew now that it was a deal he had no intention of keeping once they were married.

Unable to sit still, she wandered the length of the office, peering at the workers through the glass windows.

The sound of a woman moaning startled her. She tried the knob to the adjacent room, and it easily opened. The light from the main office flooded the small storage room.

"Oh!" Serene gasped, slamming a hand over her mouth at the sight of the two people intertwined on a bed-sized cushion thrown on the floor, a bed sheet bunched at the bottom. Transfixed, horrified, she couldn't take her eyes from them. *Marcus and his secretary?*

At Serene's exclamation, Marcus jumped up, exposing Ava beneath him, her legs spread apart. "What?" Marcus quickly wrapped his lower half in the bed sheet. "What are you doing here, Serene?"

Ava did a cat stretch, completely naked, as if relishing the territory she had gained.

"I'm—I'm calling off our wedding. I came to tell you that."

"Because I'm with another woman?"

"No," Serene stated flatly, not letting her gaze rest on the woman. "Because I don't trust you. You never intended to let me use that money for the restaurant. You wanted to use it to build your own empire to get away from your father. I believed in the commitment our families made to each other, but I changed my mind."

"You don't have another deal to propose?" he drawled.

"Hardly. What is even better, I saw the truth in my father's purpose. He wanted me to be happy. That's all, just happy, and the reason he left the money to us is so that you would take care of me. But the only fault my father had was that he wasn't a fortuneteller. He couldn't predict the pig you would turn out to be. And that knowledge is better than any kind of dowry."

"Who put all this *immondizia* in your head?"

"You can't control me any longer, Marcus. Even

with all the dreams I had of rebuilding my father's place, you mean nothing to me. I should be thanking you for opening my eyes to who you really are. I've made my own choices all along, and now I'm making another one. Our marriage contract is broken."

"You can't let me go that easily, Serene. You need me. Remember? You have no money without me."

Serene stepped closer to him and whispered in his ear, "Because of the lady I am, I won't tell you the secret I've been holding, but you can figure it out for yourself when I give the child I'm carrying another man's name."

Speechless for a second, Marcus met her gaze straight on, and she watched it change from surprise to a vengeful triumph. "Poor man deserved what he got. It's sad he won't be around to enjoy his child."

Serene froze in midstep. "You know of what happened to him?"

"With the connections I have, the plan was spun like silk. And even your doctor friend didn't detect a thing, believing he was helping an ex-criminal. That driver was like dough in my hands."

Serene opened her mouth to ask why or how, but no sound came out. No words or a scream, or even a cry. She bent over, dizziness starting at the top of her head and running down her limbs. Marcus smiled at her, a mean, vile smile that added to the knife-like pain whipping through her center.

He tipped up her chin. "You think I didn't sense it, the attraction between the two of you? And to an American? It had to be stopped."

"How could you...?" It was all she could choke out.

"He deserved what he got," Marcus hissed to her, laughing, his voice hushing even the equipment and workers that surrounded them.

Warmth trickled down Serene's inner thigh and

she held a hand to her lower abdomen, praying. No! With a scream from deep inside her heart, she braced herself against the wall and prayed. Please don't let my baby die.

Drops of red splattered quietly on the grey cement floor. "I... need help," she moaned, feeling her breath lessen. "Please get me help."

****

Miles wandered through the hysteria that was Rome, squeezing between groups of people and soldiers. Nunzio had brought him as far as he could before returning to Turni. The allies had finally made it into the city and crowds of Italians were cheering and singing and walking freely for the first time since the beginning of the war.

Using a wooden cane, Miles kept on, trying to find someone who could tell him where to find Serene's villa, but with the mass of people and noise, and his lack of coherent Italian, it was frustrating. The expression that all roads lead to Rome may have been correct, but he couldn't find the one that led out of Rome to Serene's villa. The pain in his leg now reminded him of how grateful he was to still have a leg.

Veering from the hoards of people, he headed down an alley. Searching through all the streets of Rome would be like juggling the entire state of Minnesota in an hour, he thought.

Without realizing it, he had gone full circle and landed in front of a restaurant, Cucina Moneto. He knew the name, as much as he knew the hair on his head, but why didn't he recognize it? Curious, his heart pumping faster, he circled the building to the back, and there he knew it immediately. He eyed the bushes in which he and Clay had hidden. He could even smell the smoke of that night when her father had let them in. All of it came back as clearly as the bricks of the building in front of him.

Dropping his cane, he hopped up to the stoop and put his face to the door glass, only to find the inside dark.

"You." The man's voice sounded close, and Miles turned. "The American." Franci's eyes widened. "I know you."

"You helped save my life," Miles replied slowly, turning to face the man. Frank? Francis? He didn't remember him from that night, but Serene had told how he'd helped her despite the fear of death. Then again at the church. He had warned Serene about bringing Miles to the church for fear of the Germans.

"Yes, yes," Franci said. "Why are you not—celebrating?" His English was rusty, but Miles was getting it.

"I need to find someone first."

Franci. That was his name. Miles shook his head, "It's a shame she never re-opened it."

"Serene must do it now. The war has ended."

At the mention of her name, Miles did everything he could not to bombard the guy with questions. "I'm trying to find Serene."

"Come back in the morning."

"I can't wait," he blurted. Miles was pushing the man's good nature, but if it meant getting her back, he didn't care. "I just want to talk to her."

"She is giving her hand to Marcus."

"I know. Ever been in love, sir?"

He raised his eyebrows. "Love?"

"*Passione.*"

Franci smiled, "Ahh." He folded his arms. "Serene is a good girl."

"Can you tell me where to find her? Where is her home?"

Franci seemed to contemplate him. "Marcus will hurt her. He is not a good man."

"What?" At that moment, more than ever, he wished he had learned the language better, or at least had tried harder to learn it. "Did he hurt her?"

With a scowl, Franci stepped closer. "He is a bad, bad man."

"That's why I have to find her."

For whatever reason, Miles didn't want to begin to understand, Franci left and returned several minutes later. On a piece of paper, he had drawn a map to Serene's villa, complete with farmland and even a cow. He tried not to laugh as he took the paper from Franci. "*Grazie.*"

"You *capite?*"

"Understand?" Miles nodded, trying to translate the drawing.

Once again Franci motioned Miles to wait. When he returned, he wheeled a metal bicycle with enough nicks and dings to have been through several wars. At least the rickety frame had both tires. "You find her with this."

Miles shook Franci's hand and, holding the map in one hand and the cane parallel to the handle bars, he started off on the bike. Not too much pain in his bum leg, he reasoned, so he continued.

Franci's analysis of Marcus hit him in the gut hard enough to realize that he had to find her today.

Chapter Twenty-Two

"Everto, come in," Margot said, pulling open the front door to the villa. His face was the color of grey wool. "What's wrong?"

"Is Serene at home?" He started to say something else, then clamped his mouth shut and removed his hat.

"She should be back soon. Do you want to wait in the parlor? I'll have Anna bring you some tea."

He followed her in but didn't sit. Instead, he paced the room a few times slowly, back and forth, until she caught his arm. "Everto, what is it? You're more nervous than an expectant mama."

His forehead glimmered with the beginnings of perspiration. "I'll wait for Serene."

"You're worrying me, Everto. Is it something she should know now? If it is, I'll go find her. She went to see Marcus, and then... I don't know."

"You know a lot of money is at stake until Serene marries?"

"I know all about the dowry and the problems Papa left," she said quickly. "Serene told me everything."

"My job is to make her aware of any changes in the dowry money. I told your father I would look out for all of you..."

"Have there been changes?"

With a worried glance, he sat down. "Marcus Sturini came to my office this morning and withdrew the money."

"But they aren't...married." Dread filled Margot's stomach as she watched Everto's eyes get bigger. "Not for another few weeks."

"He came with signed paperwork." Everto spewed the information quickly, as he took a paper from his front pocket. With a heavy breath, he handed it to her. "This is the document they signed. It says they're married."

Reviewing the paper, Margot opened her mouth to gasp, but no sound came out. "This isn't Serene's signature. That is her name, but she didn't sign this." She reasoned every way she knew how and couldn't come up with a logical explanation. Her heart pounded with fear. "All of Papa's money is gone?"

Everto sat on the chaise directly across from her. "He told the bank it was for the two of them, starting a new business. I knew something wasn't right, but he had the paper. A new restaurant somewhere, not part of Cucina Moneto."

Margot stared into Everto's hopeful eyes, barely visible behind his thick lenses. "She wanted Papa's restaurants more than anything. She wouldn't have let that money be used for something else."

Everto removed his glasses with an unsteady hand. "Since the paper was signed, the bank was obligated to do it right away. In no more than twenty minutes, he left my office and got to the bank."

She breathed in, trying to push her anger away, protecting her baby from the monstrous feelings. "He can just take the money?"

Any answer he gave was lost when the front door flew open and Veronica ran into the parlor, her eyes full of tears. "Margot! Come quickly. Get Samuel! Serene is in trouble."

****

Miles stopped the bike. It hurt like hell to pedal, but at least his knee was still fully intact. Despite the crowds still mingling and laughing and cheering in the streets, it was as if time stood still when he saw the factory. The name on the front made his stomach twitch. *Sturini.*

Marcus Sturini's factory.

Ironic, he laughed to himself. It was practically in the backyard of the restaurant, and he hadn't even known it. Standing with the bike up on the first step, he scanned the crowd, a mass of flags waving and families hugging. The price of freedom had been paid, for the time being, and despite everything, life had a way of taking care of its own. Watching the people's faces, he knew now how true that was.

His gaze caught on Marcus, standing on the top step. Beside Marcus, hanging on his arm, was a girl in a tight purple dress, and from his other hand hung a large burlap potato sack. Dressed in black, he resembled the devil himself.

Miles dropped the bike and took his cane from across the handlebars. "Hello, Marcus." He moved closer and watched the guy absorb the shock.

"Look who's back, Ava," Marcus slurred. "God works in mysterious ways, no?"

Ava moved behind Marcus. "You're supposed to be—"

"Dead?" Miles offered, expertly using his cane to reach the top step. Nose to nose, the two men sized each other up briefly before Miles dropped the cane and punched Marcus in the stomach and then the face.

Hunched over, Marcus held his stomach. "You can have the bitch and her baby."

For a moment, Miles froze. *Baby?* "You're lucky I still have both my legs, or I would kill you right here. Where is she?"

"Find her yourself. She's not my problem anymore." He swiped the back of his hand across his mouth. "I got what I needed."

Using his cane, Miles limped quickly through the factory's double doors, ignoring the woman in front of them, and charged straight back, searching, down the center row, toward the office along the back wall. As he stopped to figure out his next move, he saw a blue scarf. When he picked it up, the softness rubbed against his fingertips, and slowly, he brought it to his face. God, it smelled like her. The smeared blood on the floor made his gut clench with fear.

He stuffed the scarf into his pocket and searched out Marcus again, where he leaned against the outside of the factory, nursing his face. "Tell me where she is, or I'll kill you right here."

"She's sick—" Ava started, but Marcus slapped her across the cheek.

Dropping the cane, Miles took him by the throat with both hands and rammed him against the wall, feeling his fingers throb with hatred. "You don't hit girls," he said through clenched teeth and punched him again in the stomach. Honest to God, he wanted so badly to kill the man with his own bare hands. With a final shove, he got him out of the way. "And you don't deserve Serene."

With a full body motion, Marcus swung the burlap sack at him, but Miles stopped it with his forearm, and with the abrupt impact the old sack broke apart, spraying money into the air. In a flurry of cheering and yelling, people raked their hands in the air, grasping for the bills and stuffing what they could into their pockets.

"No—" Marcus bellowed, slumping to the ground.

Miles grabbed him by the shirt. "Tell me where the hell she is!"

****

With a clenched jaw, Serene turned her face into the pillow. It smelled of soap. The pain in her abdomen had subsided, but waves of sorrow wedged deep in her throat. "I won't let you go, little one," she sobbed into the stiff fabric, holding onto her stomach. "I'll fight for you."

Of the five or so metal beds lining the hospital's main room, she lay in the last one near the double doors leading to the hall. A circular metal overhead light hung above the bed.

At the sight of Doctor Capelleti, Serene cried harder. "My baby—can you save my baby?"

"Let me finish, Serene," he said gently, the lines on his face told of the hundreds of babies he'd brought into the world. "Take a deep breath in and let it out slowly."

In the quietness of the tiny hospital, the doctor pressed the stethoscope gently on different spots across Serene's torso. Finally, plucking the instrument from his ears, he stretched the blanket back up to Serene's waist. "My dear, everything sounds strong."

"What about the bleeding?"

"I've seen it before in normal, healthy pregnancies. Could be a little chafing in your female parts." He patted her hand. "We have to wait and pray."

"Is it true that my mother died from having too many babies? I remember my father saying that. Did her body just give out?"

"Your mother had a different case of sickness, I'm afraid, a cancer that damaged her womb. As far as I can tell, and I've been around a long time, you have a healthy womb. The best you can do now is to get some rest. I'll check back in a little while."

Serene stared at the white ceiling, taking in long breaths. She closed her eyes and tried to drift to sleep, imagining herself in a sunny field, holding the baby in her arms. How beautiful he or she was. Hair the color of wheat. And bright brown eyes, the shade of cocoa.

"Serene?" The small voice called to her before

she heard the small footsteps. Dressed in his school uniform, Harry looked much more grown up than his eight years. "Are you sick?"

"Harry." As she hugged him tight, she saw Margot and then Anna coming through the door. Veronica trailed after. "I'm feeling much better."

"What did the doctor say?" Margot took her sister's hand in her own. "What is wrong?"

With a cry, Veronica knelt beside the bed. "I came into the factory, and I found you on the floor—I was so scared."

"I'm fine, Roni," Serene said, taking in a rush of air. "It's a baby."

"*Bambino*?" Veronica asked.

Margot slowly sat on the edge of the bed. "*Bambino*?"

With a smile, Serene nodded, all of her qualms gone.

Harry gripped Serene around the neck, his eyes wide with fear. "Are you going to leave us, like Mama did?"

"God took Mama because he needed her. I don't think he needs me yet."

"Is the baby healthy?" Anna asked.

With a shuddered breath, Serene regained her courage. "The doctor says I'm going to be fine. I guess I got too tired."

"You look so calm—and happy," Margot cried.

"This baby is a blessing. All of our lives will change, but I'm willing to try to be a good mother and show this baby the goodness in the world."

"Do what's in your heart and that *bambino's* heart." Anna smiled, the crevices at the corner of her eyes deepening, as if she understood for the first time.

Margot patted her own stomach. "Who would have thought that you and I would have babies at the same time?"

"Did you marry Marcus?" The innocence of Harry's question speared into the reality of the situation, the reality she hadn't been able to face yet.

"No—"

His next logical question would have been to ask why she was having a baby if she wasn't married. Anna must have sensed it, too.

"Come, come, Harry." She motioned to him. "Serene needs to rest."

Harry let go, his large brown eyes watery and hopeful. The image brought a flashback of the morning of her mother's death. How little and oblivious he was then, hardly more than a baby himself. And how much of a mother she had become to him through the years. She waved and conjured up the best smile she could. For him and for herself.

"I told him, Margot. I ended it with Marcus." Serene turned sober eyes on her sister. "He was so angry with me. And I told him that Miles is the baby's father."

"Is that how this happened?" Margot's face reddened with anger. "Did Marcus hurt you?"

"He is an awful man," Veronica commented. "When he knew you were in pain, he walked out of the factory with that woman—"

"And he took the money, Serene. He took it. All of it."

"What do you mean?"

"Everto came to the house with a paper that someone signed for you. Marcus lied to get the money."

"None of that matters now," Serene said, her voice cracking. "Things will be the way they're supposed to be. I have to find Miles. Can you take me to him, Roni?"

"I'm right here."

"Miles," she breathed, unable to control the shiver that warmed every ounce of her skin. Dressed in farmer's clothes, he had grown a full beard, and his creamy-colored hair brushed his shoulders.

Miles dropped the cane; the bang of it on the floor echoed against the walls as Serene nestled into his arms, unable to stop her tears against his chest. The sight of him standing in front of her had hit her with the emotional weight of a full-blown hurricane.

She touched his face.

His eyes.

His hair.

All of it seemed like a dream.

Soaking each other in, it was as if the world had stopped for that moment and let them freely breathe the same air. Somewhere in the distance, Serene heard Margot's voice saying goodbye and taking the others with her, leaving them alone.

Letting in all the newness of him, she didn't bother to wipe the warm tears spilling onto her cheeks.

"I got in a little fight," he murmured against her hair, sliding his hand down her back.

Serene touched the small cut above his forehead and then the jagged cut along the side of his neck. "Marcus did that to you, didn't he?"

"Shh." He put his fingers to her moist lips. "I don't want to talk about him."

Serene nodded, smiling between her tears. She kissed one of his eyes and then the next. She tried to stop touching him and focus on what had happened to him, but she couldn't keep her hands and lips away. Just hearing his voice put her heart back together. "I'm so sorry this happened to you. I wondered for so long why I didn't hear from you. I thought for sure—you forgot about us—about me."

"Did you have that little trust in me?"

Feeling the softness of his lips on her forehead made her breath stop. "No, I just thought, the way you left, and with Marcus there, you would never want to have anything to do with me again."

"You couldn't be more wrong. You're the reason I came back. Before the car got very far—before they attacked me, I tried to get back and tell you." Leaning closer, he took her face in both of his hands. "I want you." Dry and unmoving, his eyes searched hers. "That's why I left you. I wanted you too much, and I knew that threatened the life you had planned."

Serene caressed the scar across his eyebrow, her lips moist. "I hated you for leaving," she cried freely. Her wet face begged him for an answer, an answer she could understand, no matter that his words were the sweetest music, music she had waited so long to hear.

He took her head against his chest once more and sheltered her with his arms.

"I was a stupid coward. Someone wanted me dead. And if they had succeeded, I would have died a coward without ever telling you that I loved you. I love you so much it tears my gut apart. And letting you go was the worst mistake I ever made. When I left that morning for Anzio, that was when I realized how wrong it was that we were apart. I knew I'd be sorry for the rest of my life that I walked away from you."

"We both made decisions we regret."

"Your father gave his life for me that day in the restaurant. How could I jeopardize the life he had planned for you?"

Her face twisted up to face him. "I could have walked away from it, too," she said quietly. "I wasn't strong enough."

"Not strong enough? Both of your parents died and you were left to take care of your family. What choice did you have? You took your responsibility and did what you could. I respected that so much, I wouldn't let myself be responsible for another choice

261

you had to make."

She explained about the dowry money, and the stipulation with Marcus. "I wouldn't have been able to take care of my family without it, or to rebuild the restaurants. My father planned my entire life for me to marry Marcus. It's what Papa and Mama wanted so badly."

"They wanted you to be happy, that's all."

Serene cried harder. "I know that, now."

"Why didn't you just tell me about the money? I've got some stuff stashed at home. Anything you need I would give you. Anything I have in my life is yours. You must know that."

Pulling from him a little, she wiped one of her eyes. "I didn't think that for a little while—after Margot found Josie's letter."

After a second, Miles seemed to understand. "I got it when I was out in the field and didn't have a chance to open it until after I'd been to your place for a while. But, by then, you were already glued solid in my heart. I wanted you like nothing else, but I knew you had some rough decisions to make."

Serene nodded fiercely. They gripped each other in the quiet hospital. His hand wandered down the tan material of her nightgown, and paused at her stomach. His face was both serious and hopeful. "Is it true?"

Staring directly into his eyes, she was determined not to make another cowardly decision she would regret. "You are his father."

"I am?" He rubbed his hand on her abdomen gently, leaving it there. "Is he going to be okay? I saw the blood in the factory..."

"You were there?"

"I've been everywhere, Serry. I've been trying to find you my entire life."

With trembling hands, she held onto his shoulders. "I knew I couldn't...I couldn't make it without you. I tried so hard to forget you, but I couldn't. From that first moment in my Papa's restaurant, I knew something about you was different."

"Nothing else matters except you and me. I love you more than life. You hear me?"

As he leaned closer, Serene closed her eyes and felt his breath on her forehead. His lips came down on hers, this time with a force that took the breath from deep in her throat.

"I want to stay here with you forever," he said against her mouth.

"What about your life in Minnesota? The farm? Your history is there."

"My life there would have no meaning without you."

She pulled away, her expression hopeful. "We could go live there with you—me and the baby."

"And you would leave the rest of your family? You've taught me the meaning of family. I couldn't take you from them. How would Harry grow up without you? Or Margot. You couldn't leave her, with the baby coming. I know that."

Feeling her lips quivering, Serene let a few seconds pass. "You'd sacrifice your farm and your life in your country for me?"

"I want it more than life itself. My only wish is that my father were alive to see me like this—to see what I've found in you. But the memories of him are inside me." He put her finger to his chest. "I can take that with me anywhere."

Touching his hair, she realized the sacrifice he was making. "He sounds like a wonderful man to have brought up a son like you."

Miles closed the space between them, kissing the top of her head. "He was."

"Can you take me there sometime? I want to see where you came from, see where you were born."

"How about after the baby comes, then we'll go back. I can close things up and show you and our son my roots. Until then, I know people in my town who can continue to take care of the place."

"Our son? You know that for sure?" She chuckled. "What if we have a girl?"

"Heck, I'd take one of each. And if we do have a girl, she'll have a great dollhouse to play in."

With a nod, she kissed him again, gingerly at first, then tightening her arms around his neck, never wanting to let him go. "Do you remember our night at the dollhouse?"

Miles laughed, a deep glorious whoop of a laugh, and Serene couldn't help but join him. "Does this mean we'll have more nights like that?"

Chapter Twenty-Three

After the final vows, Serene skirted the bottom of her gown and stepped down from the main altar at Santa Cecilia's church. Padre Angelo made the sign of the cross. Holding on tightly to Miles' hands, Serene turned to face her new husband. An overwhelming sensation of peace came over her.

It had only been a week since she had fought to keep their baby, but now it seemed like it had been in a previous life. They were together and their baby was safe. Their lives were complete. And from the look of softness in Miles' eyes, she imagined he had the same feeling.

As the Padre completed the blessing, all that they had gone through to reach this point dissipated into the church air. All the pain. All the heartache. All the sadness they had endured sailed away, as if something was sucking it all away and leaving only the goodness.

Miles lifted her cream-colored veil away from her face and brought his lips down to hers slowly, gently, as if sealing their happiness. She wrapped her arms around his neck, and gave herself back to him. Consumed by his scent and skin, she sank into his chest. One more kiss, then another—

Feeling the Padre's eyes staring, Serene tried to pry her lips away, but Miles held her tighter. "You better let me go," she whispered, laughing, "or you get nothing to eat after this."

"It's not food I want," he said into her ear.

Warmth came into her cheeks as she faced the congregation, exhilarated. Finally, they stood as husband and wife. No more wishing or hoping. She was his forever.

Arm in arm, walking down the last few steps of the altar onto the floor, they passed Harry, who was sitting in the front pew beaming.

"Are we having the party now?" he asked.

Anna shushed him as the congregation laughed.

Serene and Miles bid goodbye to everyone at the outer door of the church. It startled Serene when Jack Sturini emerged from the crowd. She looked past him, but found no one following him, no Genna.

"Congratulations, Serene, my dear."

She kissed him on the cheek, sensing a sadness about him. "It was good of you to come."

"My son's behavior is not a reflection of how I feel about you." His eyes brimmed with wetness. "You were always like a daughter to me."

"I know that, Uncle Jack. You were good to my family after my Papa died. I will always remember that."

Jack cleared his throat. "When I found out how my son treated you, I was sick in my heart. My friendship with your Papa was so strong—he'd be ashamed, too, of the way my son has behaved. *I'm* ashamed and I can only imagine the extent of the hurt he has caused."

She touched his shoulder. "Everything turned out the way it was supposed to be, and I know you had nothing to do with what happened."

"After Marcus confessed what he had done, I went to Everto. I knew he did your Papa's papers. I wanted to help, you see? He told me that you have to sell your restaurants in Sicily and Naples."

He paused, then took her hands in his, his face clouding with sorrow.

"What are you saying, Uncle Jack?"

"I've come to give you my blessing—and a wedding gift."

"You being here and your blessing are all I could ask for."

"I bought both restaurants, and now, as a wedding gift, I'm giving them both to you." Jack took two metal keys from his pocket and pressed them into her palm. "And if you need help with money for Cucina Moneto, you just tell me how much."

Serene hugged him, holding onto him like she would have her own father. Tears puddled in her eyes. His selfless gift was beyond anything she could have imagined. Despite the pain she'd endured with Marcus, this man gave back what his son took. "Oh—Uncle Jack. How can I—thank you?"

"I know how important those restaurants were to your Papa and to your family. You can thank me by being happy. Enjoy the love you've found. Your Papa would be proud of that."

Letting the tears flow from her eyes, she watched him walk away, then squeezed Miles' arm. He was still engaged in a half-English/half-Italian conversation with Anna, but at his questioning glance, she nodded that she was fine.

"I'll translate everything later," she whispered, holding onto him tightly.

Margot approached her, smiling. "I know how happy you must be."

"It seems surreal—the ceremony, and with all of you here."

"See what happens when you let others know what you want?"

With a smile, Serene pushed back a curl that sat above her sister's eyebrow. "You knew all along, didn't you, Margot? You knew how much I loved him."

"I'm your sister. Of course I did." Margot gestured to the conversation between Miles and Anna. "Since you think I'm so smart now, I would take a guess that Anna may be warming up to the idea that you married a man other than Marcus."

"I think so." Serene chuckled. "But I think we'll know for sure when we see what she makes for our morning meal tomorrow. You can always judge Anna's feelings by the kind of meals she cooks." On a whim, she added, "Now, if you would just say yes to Sam, we'd be eating fine all the time."

"I am—I mean, I told him yes already."

"Are we leaving for the party now?" Harry interrupted, running toward them.

"Yes," Serene said, absently, giving her attention back to Margot. The two followed the group outside the church. "You told Sam yes? When?"

"She surely did," Sam spouted, joining them. He put his arm around Margot. "Finally, I've won my girl over."

Serene stopped. "And you kept it secret, Margot? My theatrical sister didn't shout the news?"

"He just asked during your wedding ceremony." Margot playfully hit Sam's chest. "Let me get through your wedding first. One a day is plenty."

"Did I hear that right?" Miles asked, shaking Sam's hand. "You're getting hitched?"

"With your help, m'friend," he said in a low tone.

"Mine?"

"All we need here now is a white horse and we'd have a bloody fairy tale on our hands. That would inspire any girl, even Margot."

Miles laughed, "Good for you. Then I believe the stout's on me."

When they arrived at Cucina Moneto, Serene and Miles stood together at the entrance, before them the spot where life had ended and begun, where her father had perished and where Miles had entered her life and changed it forever.

She reached up to kiss him, feel his cheek against hers. She stroked her fingertips through his hair. "Are you ready to be a married man?"

"If I'm with you, I'm ready for anything."

In the distance, Serene heard Veronica's voice coming from the kitchen. "Are you two going to stand there, or are we going to eat?"

Holding his hand, Serene led Miles into the dining area. Shiny sconces lit the room in a soft glow. All the imperfections and damages to the walls and floor were undetectable. The smell of spices and *grappa* made the restaurant come alive, as if welcoming her back.

She soaked in the newness of the room, then caught Veronica's eye as her friend set a platter of lamb in the center of the table.

"Did you do all this?"

"With help from everyone here. Oh, and Franci, too. He made the floors sparkle."

Serene met her halfway to the kitchen, embracing her. "You have been a wonderful friend to me. Without you, I don't know if I would have found Miles again."

"Without me," she said, wiping a tear from Serene's cheek, "you wouldn't have anyone to help get this place started up again—if you decide to. I know about the money, but somehow I can help you figure out a way to get it. You can't let this place go."

"It's taken care of. All of it. All three restaurants are ours again."

Roni nearly dropped the spoon she was holding. "What—how?"

"Marcus' father."

"Do I dare ask how that happened? No, don't tell me now. You should enjoy this meal and that beautiful man you have waiting over there. But I just want to say that I'll help you in any way I can. Anything you need, you just ask me."

"Don't be silly, Roni," Serene chided. "Of course you'll be here with me."

Veronica took an exaggerated breath of relief, then said quickly, "Then could you find a job here for Antonio, too? With the war being over, we can spend some time together."

Serene couldn't stop a laugh from escaping. "I knew your time would come."

With a smack of her ruby-colored lips together, Veronica winked. "Of course—now go sit down so we can enjoy the meal."

When she joined the others, Serene twirled her mother's wedding ring against her finger, feeling it, touching it, wondering still if it were a dream but hoping she'd never wake up. Her attention caught on Margot and Sam talking quietly. When Samuel touched her sister's belly, Margot let out a giggle that caused even Anna to smile.

"Happy?" Miles asked, resting his hand on Serene's thigh.

"This is the way it was supposed to be."

Scanning the table, she realized that every single soul in the world that she loved was sitting at the table.

Except one.

"Be right back," she said, pushing out her chair. She paused for a second and kissed Miles' cheek. "Will you save my spot?"

"You can't leave now," Harry moaned. "I'm hungry, and we still have to do a toast."

"I'll be back in a minute." Serene tousled his hair. "Your stomach can wait for another minute, can't it?"

She found Franci in the back of his shop, sweeping the floor. "Didn't Veronica tell you we were having a meal? How come you're not over there with us?"

He put down the broom. "Ah, I'm just an old man. Have the meal with your family, and I'll come by later to help close up things."

"You *are* my family, Franci. Yes. You've had your business next to ours for years. And you were there for every single one of the milestones in our lives, good and bad. You were there when my father passed, and you were there when I needed someone to help me look after things. You even gave Miles a bike so he could find me."

"He told you that?" Franci's cheeks reddened. "It was my father's bike. Very, very old."

"Because of you, we took him with us that night when the soldiers shot him. You helped me when everyone else wanted him dead. I'll always be grateful for that. Won't you come celebrate with us?"

Serene thought she detected a small smile.

"For a bit, I suppose."

As they walked from his shop to the restaurant, Franci interrupted her thoughts. "I finished cleaning that spot on the floor. You know the one, *no?*"

She nodded. The remnants of her father's blood. The same spot that Marcus had stamped his cigarette into. "How can I ever thank you, Franci?"

"By reopening Cucina Moneto."

Serene entwined her arm with his. "I'm working on that one."

Epilogue

The taxicab passed St. Patrick's Cathedral and Serene asked the driver to stop. She handed Baby Anthony to Miles and stepped out of the cab. "I'll be right back."

She ran up the cement steps and pulled open the massive wood door. The presence of life and beauty, all that is good, took her breath away. As if welcoming her, a sculpture of the Virgin Mary sat above an array of candles. After a quick sign of the cross, Serene took a stick from the sand and put it into the flame of a lit candle.

"Papa. It's me," she whispered, waiting for the stick to ignite. "I wanted to tell you I'm here with Miles and your grandson. I know you would approve, because of the strength of my love for him. It took over everything I tried to do. I tried so hard, Papa, to live the life you had planned, but I couldn't stop the love I feel for him. I know you loved Mama in the same way, so I think you will understand." She held the flame in the air and lit an empty candlewick toward the front. "I love you and all you've done for me." She blew out the flame on the stick and pushed the stick back into the sand.

Wiping a tear away, she let her eyes soak in the stained glass of the windows. Each of the panes told their own silent story of heartache or selflessness. One day, she'd have her own story to tell her son.

Settled back in the cab, Serene took the baby back in her arms and touched Miles' face.

He put his arm around her shoulder and made a funny face at Anthony. The baby giggled in return, and Serene smoothed her hand over her son's hair, the color of wheat.

"Are you ready?" she asked.

Miles nodded.

Keeping his promise to his buddy Walt, he was on his way to give the Piersons their son's dog tags. With a nervous pang in his gut, he had thought of ways to tell them of his arrival back home in the United States, and about the promise he'd made to Walt. In the end, he thought it better that it be a surprise.

What he'd gathered from the Army information was that the Piersons lived in an apartment not more than a few miles away from St. Patrick's. Along the busy streets, people were taking down the war propaganda plastered on nearly every building, street sign, anything visible.

The cab lurched forward. "We're here. You're sure you want to come with me?" Miles asked.

"He was your friend. I want to be there, too."

Miles paid the driver and, squinting against the hot July sun, surveyed the three-story brick apartment complex. On the top floor, a single gold star decorated the middle window. Only one other window carried the badge of a lost soldier, but it was on the bottom level. He wiped the moisture from inside his collar and helped Serene into the building.

"Mrs. Pierson?"

A gray-haired woman peered through the crack of the door. Her gaze looked him up and down, hesitating at the cane. "May I help you?"

Miles took off his hat. "I'm Miles Coulson, ma'am, and this is my wife, Serene, and our son. I was a friend of your son Walter. May I please come in? I would like to talk with you about him."

Emma Pierson opened the door a little wider, putting a strain on the chain, the lines around her eyes glistening.

"Em, who is it?" A heavyset man sat close to the window, engrossed in a newspaper.

"Someone who says he knew Walter."

Joe Pierson, eying the slit in the door through thick glasses, dropped his paper onto the floor beside his chair, slipped his feet into a pair of slippers and shuffled to the door. He unhooked the door chain. "You say you knew our son?"

"Yes, sir. My name's Miles Coulson." He slipped Walter's dog tags from his trouser pocket. "I was there when... where your son died serving his country." He dangled the pewter chain in the air; it twisted on its own. "I wanted to give you these. He would have wanted you to have them, sir."

Touching the chain in midair, Emma slowed it enough to read the name. She staggered, then slumped to her knees. Serene sat the baby on the floor and went to her.

Joe bent down on one knee and wrapped his arms around her. "It's fine, Em," he whispered over and over. His voice cracked and crooned as he smoothed her ashen hair.

"Ma'am, I'm sorry. I didn't mean to upset you."

Emma caught her breath between small bursts of tears, her whitened knuckles gripped around the chain she held to her chest. "Did he die without pain?"

"He made our country proud."

Miles swallowed hard, watching the little woman kneeling on the floor in her apron. His stomach churned at the memory of Walt's death. He wanted to leave, take back his visit. But the promise he'd made to Walt forced him to stay and recite the speech he had practiced over and over on the train.

"Come, Em, let's go sit down." As he led his wife to the sofa, Joe Pierson said over his shoulder, "Come in, Mr. Coulson. Bring your family and have a seat. The missus will get you some tea in a moment."

"We can only stay for a few minutes. Our train leaves soon."

The Piersons sat on the small davenport at one side of the room and Miles sat opposite, in a wing chair. The room was decorated the same way he remembered from his grandmother's home. Even the beige crocheted cloth on the wooden table brought back memories. He stared up at Lincoln's chiseled face watching over the room from above the mantel.

"You had a good son, ma'am."

Emma sniffled into her handkerchief and gazed at him, her eyes red-rimmed and glassy.

"He was a good soldier, my Walter was."

"I know, ma'am. He died in honor. That's the kind of soldier he was. That very day he passed on, Walt had the whole troop laughing. We all missed him very much."

Emma's lips curled up a mere fraction, her voice soft, "Thank you for coming here and telling us this." Her voice cracked. "It helps to know how much others loved him, too."

After several minutes of quiet, Miles stood. "We should be going. I thought you might want the tags. Your son—he made all of us very proud."

Following Miles and Serene to the door, Joe stared Miles square in the eye, his frame nearly a foot shorter than Miles'. "Did those bastards cause him a lot of pain? The missus couldn't take something like that, but you tell me the truth. Did those sons-of-bitches torture my son?"

Miles watched the old man's chest rise and fall with heavy breaths. Could he tell him that the Jerry had dropped their son like a gutted carcass? He was happy that his own father never would have opportunity to ask something like that, but at the moment he would have given anything for one minute with him. Miles cleared his throat and smoothed his hair back before putting on his hat. It was like looking into his father's eyes once again. "He never knew what hit him. And he died in honor, sir. You would have been proud."

Joe shook his hand. "What you said—you've helped me and the missus get through this."

Returning to the cab, neither Miles nor Serene spoke for several blocks. Serene turned to him, squishing the baby between them, her voice low. "Your father would have been proud of *you*."

He stared into her green eyes and touched her face. He kissed her, pushing her against the back seat of the cab.

Serene gave back to him, opening her lips and soul to him, just as she had always wanted since they had first met. How good it felt to be with him freely. No more hiding or pretending.

"Where to?" the cabbie asked.

"Train station," Miles didn't take his eyes from hers. "We're heading for Minnesota."

"You folks have a long journey ahead. Those train rides can be brutal."

Miles smiled and put his arm around Serene, snuggling Anthony between them. "Nothing we can't handle."

They both watched the sun play peek-a-boo on Baby Anthony's face as they passed through the line of tall buildings. Touching her fingertips to Anthony's soft cheek, Serene knew their journey together would last a lifetime.

About the Author...

Some people have called Christine a bookworm. And were they ever right! Growing up in a small beach town in New Jersey, she wouldn't have been caught on her beach towel without a good book. Nothing on earth equated to stepping into the library each week, hearing the creaks of the wood floor, and knowing an unable-to-put-down story was waiting.

Through all of this, she caught the fire of creativity and discovered she had her own story to tell. Not just one, but many! While earning her degree in literature, and developing her career as a technical writer, Christine kept writing and learning the craft of putting together a good story.

Now, with a growing family, endless driving to soccer games, and a crayfish that needs to be fed every three days, she still manages to get her characters down on paper.

You can visit her at www.christineclemetson.com.

Thank you for purchasing
this Wild Rose Press publication.
For other wonderful stories of romance,
please visit our on-line bookstore at
www.thewildrosepress.com.

For questions or more information,
contact us at info@thewildrosepress.com.

The Wild Rose Press
www.TheWildRosePress.com

Other Vintage Roses you might enjoy...

SHE'S ME by Mimi Barbour: A spoilt model pricks her finger on a rose thorn and is transported back to 1963 and into a chubby librarian's body. As "roomies" they learn a lot from each other and each finds the man of her dreams!

TIME TO KEEP by Susan Cody: In an English castle, Star Prescott unexpectedly embarks on a life-changing journey. The man she meets is familiar, and Star realizes she shouldn't be in this place or this time, but it's too late. Is she out of time with Colin, or is there *Time to Keep*?

A TRAIN THROUGH TIME by Bess McBride: On a sleek modern train heading to Seattle, Ellie awakens in the midst of a Victorian-era re-enactment. The leader of the group, handsome, green-eyed Robert Chamberlain, finally convinces her the date is 1901...

BAD BETTIE by Layne Blacque: In 1948 Los Angeles, a handsome cop's world is turned upside down when his squad raids a nightclub and he rescues the sultry blues singer.

SHATTERED DREAMS by Margaret Tanner: Three World War I soldiers leave a shattering legacy as they pass through Lauren's life. Which is killed? Which one's child does she carry? Which one does she marry?

And coming soon...

HE'S HER by Mimi Barbour: Same rosebush, different victims!

DON'T CALL ME DARLIN' by Fleeta Cunningham: In Texas, 1957, Carole the librarian faces censorship. Will the County Judge she's dating protect or accuse her?

SOURDOUGH RED by Pinkie Paranya: At the end of the Klondike gold rush, Jen and her younger brother search for her twin, lost and threatened in Alaskan wilderness.

LaVergne, TN USA
06 October 2009
160059LV00005B/26/P